She was just a little bit i̶ ̶ ̶ ̶ ̶ ̶ ̶ ̶ ̶ ̶ ̶, she had to admit it. But so what? She'd read somewhere that it happened to lots of women in her situation. Settled in a long, stable marriage. Middle age beckoning. The empty nest syndrome and all that stuff. And then – wham! A schoolgirl crush, all over again.

It was trivial, temporary and would soon pass. Like measles. She'd be laughing about it by the time Christmas was upon them. Might even be confessing it all to David. She really didn't know why she had been letting it bother her so much . . .

Also by Jennifer Curry

Counting the Ways

About the author

Brought up in a Sunderland mining village, Jennifer Curry has been a full-time mother, teacher, freelance writer and broadcaster. She is best known as a poet and anthologist for children, and has also written novels for children and plays for both the theatre and Radio 4. Her anthology *The Last Rabbit* won the Earthworm Award in 1992, and she is chair of the judges' panel for the Roald Dahl Foundation Poetry Competition. The mother of two grown-up sons, she now lives with her second husband in a historic water mill in Norfolk.

Peacocks' Acre

Jennifer Curry

CORONET BOOKS
Hodder and Stoughton

First published in Great Britain in 1997 by
Hodder and Stoughton
A division of Hodder Headline PLC
First published in paperback in 1998 by Hodder and Stoughton
A Coronet Paperback

10 9 8 7 6 5 4 3 2 1

A CIP catalogue record for this title
is available from the British Library

ISBN 0 340 68021 0

Printed and bound in Great Britain by
Clays Ltd, St Ives plc

Hodder and Stoughton
A division of Hodder Headline PLC
338 Euston Road
London NW1 3BH

For Tym, who is part of every page

ACKNOWLEDGEMENTS

I would like to thank:
* my good friends, Bill and Daphne Broad, with whom I happily explored boats and harbours and sailing language and lore;
* my new and friendly acquaintances, Stanley and Patricia Hayhurst, who, with typical northern generosity of spirit, directed me through glorious countryside to rediscover the valleys, rivers and reservoirs of my native Northumbria;
* my uncle, the late Walter Iley, for the inspiration of his book *Corbridge, Border Village*;
* Maureen Wilkinson, for permission to use the poem 'The Amnesiac's Dream' from her book *The Blindman Goes From A To B*, published by Peterloo Poets, 1990.

JC

PROLOGUE. SEPTEMBER, 1997

Sarah sat, stiff and upright at the table, tapping its formica top with her wedding ring. She was nervous. Her stomach was tying itself into knots. She watched as her husband paid for their coffee at the cash till, then lifted his head, looking for her. She waved her hand and her heart leapt as he saw where she was, and smiled. She still loved him as much as that. One slight smile and her pulse began to race. It was like a miracle. But she knew that he was feeling the strain too. His face had a stretched look about it, the eyes shadowed.

He reached her side and set down the tray carefully, lifting off the cups, sharing out the packets of sugar, the little pots of 'non-dairy creamer', the flimsy stirrers. Then he scrambled awkwardly into the narrow, fixed seat, folding himself up in the confined space.

'Damned service stations!' he growled. 'Why can't they make their restaurants a bit more comfortable?'

'It's their policy,' she told him. 'Feed 'em, water 'em, fleece 'em – and then get rid of 'em as quickly as possible. Don't want the punters hanging around feeling comfortable, do we?'

He grinned and they sat in silence, watching the hot water sink down through the conical filters into their cups as if it were the most fascinating process imaginable.

At last she plucked up courage to broach the subject that was on both their minds. 'Not long now, darling. How are you feeling?'

'I'm fine, lovey.' He smiled. 'Just fine.'

'But seeing her again, after all this time . . .'

'Four years!' He nodded. 'Strange that the break was so . . . complete.'

'She wanted it that way.'

'Yes.'

'Do you think she'll look much different?'

'I don't know. I always imagine her exactly the same.' He pursed his lips. 'Like when someone dies. They always remain exactly the same age in your mind, don't they?'

She reached for his hand. 'Try not to think about that, please,' she beseeched him.

'Don't worry, Sarah. I'm not going to brood on nasty thoughts of death and disaster and all that stuff. Not today.'

'She wanted us both to come, didn't she?' she continued. 'Made a point of inviting us specially.'

'Yes. And it really is her big, big day. The grand unveiling ceremony. All the big-wigs will be there. From all over the country, apparently. You wouldn't think she'd have asked us if she had any idea that it might be tricky. The three of us meeting up again.'

'No. So you must stop feeling anxious.'

'Right.' He took a deep breath. 'You, too. Promise?'

'Promise.'

They began to sip their coffee slowly, glancing around them at the other motorway travellers. The rep. at the next table in his smart dark suit and immaculate white shirt. The noisy, laughing family behind them, all dressed up for their car journey in track suits and trainers. The harassed woman desperately pleading with her two children to eat up their over-priced hamburgers. 'Please try! It's such a waste,' Sarah heard her complain, and she grinned. How many years since she'd looked like that, struggling with Merry and William, wondering why other people's children always seemed so much more amenable than her own. Well, they were still like that, her two, still ignoring her advice and doing their own thing – and in a way she was pleased. She was proud of them. Yes, proud of both of them, no matter what David said.

Her train of thought was interrupted by her husband's voice. 'What about you, lovey? Are you O.K? We're going to be very near Deredale. And we are bound to bump into people . . . old friends. Belle and Reggie and the others.'

'I know.'

'Any regrets?'

'Of course not.'

'Please tell me. It must all be coming back. Tell me if there's anything.'

She met his eyes serenely, steadfastly held his gaze. 'I have no regrets about Deredale, darling. Believe me. I had my happiest moments there – and my most terrible. But I have no desire to go back. None at all. "The past is a foreign country." '

'Who said that?'

'I forget. Eliot perhaps?' She shrugged. 'I don't know. But it's true, isn't it?'

'It is for me.'

'The only thing I do . . . well . . . dream about, sometimes, is . . .' He sat patiently, waiting, watching her face. She gave a brisk little nod, smiling. 'Peacocks' Acre,' she said. 'The first time I saw Peacocks' Acre. 1990. The first warm day of spring. I dream about that.'

I
MARCH, 1990

'It seems
I am a crazy bank of films
with different plots, but playing all at once;
a shadow play, a child's construction kit
made up with some improbable mistakes.'

CHAPTER ONE

Peacocks' Acre. It was the name that had made it sing out from the pile of estate agents' details that littered the breakfast table. Sarah had imagined jewel-coloured tail feathers, gorgeously displayed, as their owners strutted across emerald lawns. The truth, of course, was more prosaic. 'Peacock', she discovered, was the surname of the village family that had originally owned the land on which the house was built. And the proud acre had shrunk significantly through the centuries.

'Can we *really* live as far out as this?' she'd asked David, as their car crossed the Tyne Bridge and kept doggedly on, its nose pointing inland, towards the west. 'I thought we'd have to settle for a suburb. Somewhere green and pleasant, like Jesmond.'

'Jesmond is pricey! And distance isn't everything. Deredale is very accessible. A good fast road almost all the way to the school. And a regular train service into the centre too.'

'It's a commuter village, then?' Sarah couldn't keep the disappointment out of her voice.

'Much more than that. It's an ancient settlement. Pre-Roman. Oozing with history.'

'Look!' she shouted, pointing to a road sign. 'Deredale, three miles. We're almost there. Isn't it strange that all the time I was at Durham I never got up here? Never further north than Newcastle!'

'You were working too hard. *And* rushing down to watch me play football all the time!'

'What's the village like, David? *Exactly*?'

He frowned. 'I really can't remember *exactly*. Just that I

liked it. When I came up for the interview I didn't have much time to stop and stare. The road up the valley runs right through the middle. You come to a hump-backed bridge over the river, then old stone houses with gardens in front of them. A broad main street which opens out on to a square at the top end. There's a good-looking pub there and some quite decent little shops. But don't expect too much,' he warned her. 'It's probably quite the wrong house for us. It's been standing empty for ages. And it's so much cheaper than any of the other houses in the village – that's not a good sign.'

'We couldn't afford it otherwise.'

'We can't afford to buy a tip, either!'

'No. But I have a feeling,' she said, laying her hand on his as it rested on the steering wheel. 'I think this is going to be a very special place, David.'

They'd found Peacocks' Acre without difficulty. It stood at a cross-roads at the end of the main street, slightly raised, in a commanding position. A substantial merchant's house dating back to the eighteenth century, grey, square and dignified.

Sarah scrambled out of the car and David came and stood by her side and held her hand as they gazed up at it together. The front door, reached by a flight of three stone steps, was precisely in the centre, with a large window at either side and three others marching across the upper storey. The roof was low-pitched, with a broad chimney-stack right in the middle, just like a child's drawing. Between the house and the pavement lay a narrow strip of garden, overrun with weeds but vivid with purple aubrietia and some clumps of early daffodils that were pushing up through piles of dead leaves. A sturdy old rose tree spread its branches across the stone facade, rough and shaggy with age. For a while neither of them spoke.

Then – 'What do you think?' David asked.

Sarah shook her head. 'I think it's lovely, of course. Don't you?'

'It certainly used to be.' He narrowed his eyes, picking out the details. 'But look at that bottom window frame to the right of the door. Full of rot. And I can see one or two tiles missing, so the damp will have got in. And . . .'

'That can all be put right.'

'At a price.'

She was silent, already beginning to feel a numbing wave of disappointment well up inside her. A car slowed down behind their Astra, giving way to another approaching from the opposite direction, and David turned his head and watched.

'And it really is bang on the road,' he said. 'Traffic past the front door all day long.'

'I don't think that's a problem,' she argued defensively. 'It's hardly likely to be a *lot* of traffic, is it, in a small place like this?' Her eyes skimmed through the details she clutched in her hand. 'Besides, the garden's tucked away at the back. A *walled* garden, David. We'd probably live there, wouldn't we? At the back of the house, I mean. It faces west, gets all the afternoon sun . . .'

Miserably, she realised that already, before she'd even walked up the steps to the front door, she was looking upon it as theirs, imagining their lives unfolding within these thick walls. This, she knew instinctively, was where she wanted to be. But David was staring at it with his face wreathed in clouds of doubt and suspicion.

'Hello! Mr Page? Ralph Elliott. From Elliott & Black. We've spoken on the phone.' Sarah twisted round and looked at the small, portly man who was hurrying along the street, stretching out his hand to David, bobbing and ducking his bald head in greeting. 'Sorry if I'm late.'

'Not at all. We've just arrived,' smiled David. 'This is my wife, Sarah.'

'Good, good. How do you do? Right, then. First, I'll show you round Peacocks' Acre – *Not* the full acre, of course. Must make that clear straight away or you'll be threatening me with the Trades Description Act. Tcch! Tcch! And then, if this doesn't quite fit the bill, I suggest we go back to the

9

office – we're just along the road in Hexham – and see what else we can show you. All right?'

'Fine. Thank you,' David agreed. 'We really do want to make a decision quickly. We're just here for the weekend, and it's a long haul from Norwich.'

'Quite. So it's back to school on Monday, eh? I think you told me you were a teacher? Fine profession, teaching! Tcch! Tcch!' That laugh again. It was like a little dog sneezing.

Sarah decided that she didn't care for Mr Elliott. He was going to spoil it, casting his nasty piggy eyes all around this beautiful house. She wished she and David could look at it on their own. She glanced furtively at the keys in his hand, longing to snatch them away, but David was nodding and smiling at him as if they'd known each other all their lives.

'I'm sure we'll be able to fix you up,' Mr Elliott was insisting. 'You say you're making progress with your own sale?'

David nodded. 'We've been very lucky. The man who is taking over my job is coming back to this country from abroad, so he's anxious to buy our house as well. At a good price.'

'Excellent! Excellent! There are a lot of very good properties on the market just now. And it's a buyer's market, without a doubt. We have them all on video, you know. We find it saves everybody a lot of time.'

'Is Peacocks' Acre on video?' Sarah asked him suddenly.

'No. 'Fraid not. It's a lovely house and all that – don't get me wrong – but no furniture, you see. And . . . just a little bit of work needing to be done here and there. Doesn't really show up to advantage on the small screen. Tcch! Tcch!'

'It's been empty a long time, hasn't it?' David asked. 'Is there some structural problem?'

'Oh no! I certainly don't know of any such thing.'

'Dry rot? Rising damp?'

'No one has reported anything like that,' he said. 'But of course, you would be advised to go for the full survey.'

'Deathwatch beetle? Black Death?' added Sarah caustically,

and pulled a face when David shot her a warning look.

Mr Elliott was shocked at the very thought of such disasters. 'The old lady who owns it lived here for just about the whole of her married life, but she had to move into sheltered accommodation two years ago. Her family managed to get her into Meadowlands. Very exclusive sort of place, you know. But now, of course, they're having to sell the house to pay the fees!'

'Oh, poor old lady!' exclaimed Sarah. 'What a shame!'

Mr Elliott shrugged. 'She's eighty-three. Very frail. She'll never be able to come back here. And she's very well looked after where she is.'

'But it seems so sad. Her home! She must have loved the place.'

'I'm an estate agent,' Mr Elliott said. 'Old age. Death. Divorce. They're all sad. But together they provide me with about three-quarters of my house sales. Especially divorce. I'm afraid I can't afford to have feelings, Mrs Page. Not in my professional capacity, that is.'

Carefully he selected a key and slotted it into the lock. The heavy door swung smoothly open. He glanced back at them apologetically, wrinkling his nose at the musty smell, then stood aside to let Sarah pass.

She made her way from the large entrance hall, with its curving stairway, through an inner door and into a spacious drawing room, square and high-ceilinged. The bright, morning sun shone through the smeared windows and tiny specks of dust hung suspended in its light. Dead flies made a pattern of black lace on the window sill. Above, in one corner, the faded wallpaper was damp, as David had predicted, and it hung down in a forlorn curl, revealing flaking plaster behind. Sarah was blind to it all. In her mind's eye, curtains of gold chintz were draped at the windows, looping down to the ground, a glowing kilim lay on the pale, waxed floorboards, her own favourite pictures shone out against coffee-coloured walls . . . Suddenly she was aware that Mr Elliott was bustling about the place, professionally self-important.

'The open fireplace is rather a nice feature,' he said. 'Original, of course. The old fireplaces have been retained in all the rooms but there is, I'm glad to say, back-up central heating from the Rayburn in the kitchen. *These* are rather good, too. Let me show you.'

He unfolded the wooden shutters at either side of the window, then muttered and dabbed at his shoulders in distaste as a waterfall of antique spiders' webs floated down upon him. Avoiding David's eyes, Sarah managed to turn a giggle into a strangulated sneeze.

'The whole place needs stripping out and doing up, of course,' he continued, 'but this room is a very good size by today's standards. Now, here on the ground floor there are two other reception rooms plus a large kitchen with aforementioned Rayburn. Not fitted, I'm afraid, but with definite potential. *As* they say. Tcch! Tcch! Four bedrooms upstairs, big family bathroom, separate lavatory. No *en suite*. Where shall we start?'

It took them less than fifteen minutes to look round the house, stare at the old-fashioned bath standing tip-toe on its little claw feet, notice that the bedroom floors actually sloped downhill and the cupboards were nowhere near as big as the built-in variety that one got automatically in a quality modern home. Mr Elliott laughed apologetically at the porcelain sink in the kitchen but reassured them that in his opinion the walk-in pantry would convert into a very reasonable utility room. And as for the garden, well, it looked a bit of a shambles, he had to admit it, but at least the walls gave protection from their chilly Northumbrian winds.

David asked sensible questions, poked and examined, tapped woodwork and plaster with his penknife. Sarah wandered around in a trance, not saying a word. She felt numb. All she wanted was that Mr Elliott should stop sizing up this lovely, lost old house, calculating its market value with his cheque-book eyes, and leave it to its memories.

'Is there anything you would like to take a second look at?' he asked finally. 'Anything else you'd like to know?'

'No. Thank you. I think we've seen enough,' she said quietly.

David stared at her curiously, then turned to Mr Elliott. 'It would involve a lot of work. And a lot of money.'

'I'm afraid so.'

'It's a shame though. Because it's been a beautiful place in its time. Don't you think so, darling?'

Sarah gave him the briefest of nods, keeping her face turned away.

'Well then,' he continued, 'we'd better come along to your office, should we, Mr Elliott, and see what else you can offer us?'

They ate lunch in the bar of a grand-looking hotel tucked away behind Hexham Abbey. David watched Sarah silently as she toyed with her food.

'What's the *matter*, Sarah?' he asked at last, trying to keep the irritation out of his voice. 'Are you sulking?'

'No, I am not sulking,' she insisted. 'The soup is tinned. And the roll is stale. It's always the same in these "posh" places. So concerned about their image that they can't be bothered with good basic cooking. Just like houses really.'

'Look, it's not fair taking it out on me because we haven't found the right place. It's just going to take us longer than we hoped, that's all . . . oh, Sarah, don't start to *cry*. That's not going to help.'

'It's all so impossible, though, isn't it? We'll *never* find somewhere we both like. We're just not on the same wavelength.'

'Of course we are.' He could hardly believe what he was hearing. 'What are you talking about?'

'*You* thought they were all wonderful, didn't you? Those ghastly videos. You just lapped it all up. The executive villa with its barbecue terrace and security lighting. The prize-winning barn conversion featured in *Country Living*. You sat there gaping as if you were a five-year-old in Disneyland.'

'I had to show *some* sort of good manners. You treated

poor Ralph like the chap in the B.O. ads. He was just trying to do his job, for heaven's sake.'

'Ralph! Ralph! So we're on Christian name terms now, are we? Oh Ralph, please excuse my little wife. The poor darling finds it so difficult to make up her mind – Well, I *have* made up my mind, David. I hated all of them. *All* of them. So there it is. I'm sorry.'

Without a word, David pushed back his chair, got up and walked away. Sarah covered her eyes with her hands. Then she straightened her back and opened the elegant Elliott & Black folder that lay on the table in front of her. She spread out the house particulars they'd been given and began to scrutinise them one by one, trying to be calm. She must be sensible, rational and objective, she told herself, and try to cultivate all those other grown-up aptitudes that she didn't quite seem to have mastered yet. It really wasn't fair on poor David.

She'd just got to the 'edge-of-village, architect-designed house with double garage and outdoor swimming pool' when a large brandy appeared on the table, and David sat down beside her and took her hand firmly in his own. 'Now,' he said, 'drink that, darling, and tell me exactly what's biting you.'

'You won't be angry? Promise.'

'Cross my heart and hope to die,' he grinned.

She took a gulp from her glass and felt the fiery liquid tingle at the back of her throat. 'Please, could we go back to Deredale and look at the first place again? Peacocks' Acre.'

'But, Sarah . . .'

'*Please*. Without your friend Ralph. I'm sure he'll trust us with the key if we ask nicely.'

'But Sarah . . .'

'I know it's probably quite out of the question, David. I know. Woodworm and damp and rotten timbers. All that stuff. But please . . . I just want to see it again. Just to . . . see it. That's all.'

*   *   *

It was three o'clock. There was a glow of gentle warmth in the afternoon sun and they basked like lizards, side by side on a stone bench just beside the kitchen door. The walls of the garden were ancient, stained ochre and lime-green by lichens, overgrown with mosses and tiny plants. In one corner a gnarled plum tree fanned out its purple-grey branches against the stones, its bright leaves just beginning to unfurl. Beneath it lay a vivid pool of blue hyacinths that scented the air with their heady fragrance.

Sarah spoke in a voice that was hardly more than a whisper. 'Don't you think this place is magic?'

David wasn't listening. He was staring intently at the wall opposite. Abruptly he jumped up and went across to it, and Sarah watched him as he examined it, gently tracing out something with his fingers. 'Good Lord!' he exclaimed. 'Come and look at this, Sarah.'

Dreamily, she wandered over to his side. 'What have you found?'

'This stone. Do you see? It's carved. It's . . . it's an Anglian cross, I think.'

She stared. 'But why? Why would anyone carve that on their garden wall?'

'If I'm right it dates back long before the garden wall was built,' he explained. 'Sixth century! Then carried over here from some old church, to build a new house. All those years ago. Living history!'

She smiled up at him, her face radiant. 'I've found some living history too.' From out of her pocket she pulled two little manilla envelopes and held them towards him. On one was written, in faded spidery handwriting, 'Hollyhock seeds – black'. On the other, 'Love-in-a-Mist'.

He turned them over curiously in his hands. 'Where did you find these?'

'They were on a shelf. In the larder.' She laughed, blushing at the nonsense of it all. 'The old lady must have left them there. For us, darling . . .'

CHAPTER TWO

David hurled himself down on to the bed. His hands were throbbing and sore. His back hurt. He was aching in every joint. He had known from the beginning that it would be hard work bringing Peacocks' Acre back to life, but he hadn't been prepared for unalloyed agony. They'd been in the new house for a whole week now and the hard labour had never ceased.

Weakly he raised his head as Sarah came rushing into their room, wrapped in a big yellow towel. Her hair sent little rivulets of water trickling down over her eyebrows, dripping off the end of her nose. He smiled and stretched out his hand as she hurried past. 'Come here,' he murmured soothingly.

She shrugged away from him, frowning. 'It's not easy, trying to have a shower without a shower curtain.'

'Then you should have had a bath.'

'The bath, as you full well know, is full of plaster. I haven't managed to clean it out yet, and it doesn't seem to be one of the jobs on your list.'

He pulled a face. 'Sorry, love. But we agreed we couldn't do the curtain till the tiles were fixed, didn't we? All these things take time.'

'Well, don't blame me if there's water everywhere – I just couldn't help it.' She perched gingerly on a packing case and bent her head, trying to see herself in the propped-up looking glass.

'Calm down,' he said. 'Why are you in such a state?'

'I am in a state because we're running out of time,' she reminded him. 'We're due next door in five minutes. Oh God! Five minutes!' She picked up her hair dryer and it buzzed around her dark, curly head like an angry wasp. 'At least this is working. That's something to be grateful for, I suppose.'

David groaned. 'Do we have to go? I'm whacked! We've been working all day. There's so much to *do*.'

'Of *course* we have to go. It's Belle's meet-the-new-neighbours party, isn't it? And we're the lucky neighbours.' She clicked off the dryer and looked at her husband through the dressing table mirror. 'We're going to *enjoy* it, darling. You know we are.'

'No we're not! We can't stand Belle.'

'We only *met* her a week ago.'

He nodded. 'Hate at first sight! And, if we can't stand *her*, chances are we won't go a bundle on her "chums" either. She did really call them "chums", didn't she?'

Sarah giggled, beginning to relax at last, and padded across to the wardrobe. 'Think positive, David. We might meet someone we really like.'

'I don't think it's . . .'

'Do stop grumbling and get a move on, *please*. Wear your new trousers, will you? They're the only decent ones I can find. The others must be in one of the boxes we haven't unpacked yet, and . . .'

'Mum!' A disgruntled face peered round the bedroom door, eyebrows knitted, lips set in a determined droop.

Pulling her slip over her head, Sarah turned and gazed at the girl who stood there looking the very picture of despair. She sighed. Even more despairing than usual, and that was saying something. She should have known they were asking for trouble, she supposed, when they first began to call her Merry. Merry as in short-for-Meredith, that is.

'What is it, sweetheart?' she asked her, trying to sound cheerful.

'Do I *have* to come to the party?' Merry asked. Her plump body sagged dejectedly.

David gave a hollow laugh and Sarah glared at him. 'Of course you do,' she said. 'It's for all of us. To meet the people who live here. It'll be fun.'

'No, it won't,' insisted Merry.

'I don't want to go either,' David told her amiably, 'but I'm trying to be brave.'

'Thank *you*, David!' Sarah muttered. 'I thought you were supposed to be getting ready.'

'But it's not *fair*,' Merry wailed. 'William doesn't have to go.'

Sarah looked at her as if she'd taken leave of her senses. 'How could William go? He's not even here, is he?'

'Quite!' Merry nodded, deciding she'd scored a minor victory. 'It's all right for William. William's still in Norwich. With Zack and Pam. But I'm not allowed to stay there, am I? Oh, no. I have to come to this God-awful place and go to this God-awful party, where I won't know anybody, not one living soul, just because you say so. It's not fair!'

'Merry!' David exclaimed. 'Don't talk like that!'

'And try not to be so silly,' Sarah added. 'You're just fifteen. How could you have stayed in Norwich? Pam wouldn't have had room for you, anyway.'

'What's more,' David added, 'Deredale is not a "God-awful" place. It's a very pleasant place, and we're going to be very happy here.'

'Says who?'

'Says me!' David was firm.

'I hate it. I hate it!' Merry exploded. 'And all the people in it. I liked Norwich. I didn't ask to come here, did I?'

With a quick flick of her fingers Sarah zipped up her navy-blue dress and turned to face her daughter. 'Merry, we are late already,' she said. 'I will give you five minutes. And then I want to see you cleaned up, properly dressed and ready to go. O.K?'

'And a smile would be nice, too,' David called after her as Merry stalked out of the room, crashing the door shut on their grim faces.

'But of *course* you must join the Golf Club. That's where you meet *everyone*. Absolutely *everyone*.'

Sarah gazed up into the florid face of the man who had been monopolising her for the last fifteen minutes while he had insisted on describing, in minute detail, every single delight that Deredale had to offer. Fifteen minutes. It had seemed more like fifteen *hours*, she thought wearily, trying to keep the interested smile pinned on her face. 'I'm afraid I don't play golf,' she said faintly.

'All the better!' He popped an olive into his mouth and chewed it with satisfaction. 'I can teach you. It will be my pleasure.'

'Thank you. That's very kind of you. But I imagine it's . . .' she racked her brain for an acceptable excuse '. . . very time-consuming, isn't it?'

The man stared at her, his jaws briefly stilled. 'What better way of spending your time?' Then he narrowed his pebble eyes suspiciously. 'I suppose you're a . . . a working wife, are you? Career woman, like all the rest of them?' He grabbed a sausage from a passing plate and snapped it off its cocktail stick with bared teeth.

Sarah blinked and shook her head placatingly. 'No, I'm not, actually. But . . .'

'There you are, then!' The broad, rosy cheeks creased up with delight. 'Tell you what, first lesson Monday. What do you say? Strike while the iron's hot.' His hand flicked out like the tongue of a chameleon and captured a passing plate. 'Fancy a *vol-au-vent*, do you? They're awfully good. Prawn and . . . and . . .' He ran the pink tip of his tongue round his lips while his eyes gazed thoughtfully at the dark blue ceiling. 'Prawn and *fromage frais*,' he announced in triumph.

Sarah looked around the crowded drawing room, frantic for escape. David was leaning against the elegant mantel-piece, glass in hand, deep in conversation with Belle. Belle, she noticed, was being the perfect hostess, gazing up at him, wide-eyed and enchanted. Sarah didn't exactly blame her. David was looking very handsome, his long, slender body relaxed and graceful, his light brown hair flopping down over his brow. But Belle wasn't just looking. She was listening, too, totally absorbed, as if every word he spoke were pure gold. And David . . . David seemed to be enjoying it. He was smiling, eloquent. Holding forth, in fact. So much for hate at first sight!

Sarah's eyes moved sideways and came to rest on Merry. She was by the window, fiddling with the edge of the heavy rose brocade curtain, staring miserably out on to the street. She looked so alone and lost that Sarah's heart contracted. She wondered if she should go and rescue her, but then thought better of it. Merry had to work out how to get on at these things. It wasn't much fun, but it *was* part of growing up, learning about life and people.

The red-faced man, whose name she had already forgotten, coughed abruptly, trying to regain her attention, anxious to clinch their appointment on the green. Perhaps, she thought, she should be brutally honest and tell him that, when it came to golf, she was of the good-walk-ruined school of opinion. But that might hurt his feelings and he *was* one of her new neighbours. Maybe she should just lie, tell him she suffered from something horribly debilitating, like arthritis. Her right knee gave a sudden twinge at the thought of it and she decided it would be imprudent to tempt providence by pretending. She opened her mouth to speak. It was on the tip of her tongue to capitulate. 'I'll think about it. Thank you,' she'd say. At least that would fob him off for a while.

But then, just over his shoulder, she noticed a strikingly tall, pale-haired woman gazing at her intently, her face alight, amused. As their eyes met, the woman smiled and came across to them.

'Now, Reggie,' she said, 'you have had more than your fair share of Mrs Page's time.' She grinned at Sarah, stretching out her hand. 'I'm Claire,' she told her. 'Claire Richley. Dolphin House – just round the corner in Bridge Lane. I bet he's been trying to enrol you for the Golf Club.'

'How did you know?' Sarah was astonished.

'It's his favourite chat-up line.'

'Claire!' Reggie protested. 'Unkind! I was just being neighbourly.'

'I know. But I must take her off to meet some of the others now. Excuse us, Reggie.' She patted his arm firmly, then led Sarah to the other side of the room. 'Sorry about that,' she said. 'He means well, but he can be a bit much. Especially when he's had one or two.'

Sarah laughed. She liked this woman, with her bright face, her shrewd, intelligent eyes. 'He's very persistent,' she told her. 'He almost had me signed up. And I *hate* the game.'

'All newcomers have to go through it,' Claire explained. 'It's a sort of initiation rite. Look, there's Bridget. Come and say hello.'

Sarah didn't have to ask her who Bridget was. Standing side by side with Claire she looked exactly as Claire must have done when *she* was a young girl. They were both much above the average height, about five feet ten, Sarah guessed, towering over the other women at the party, and some of the men too. And Bridget had Claire's green eyes, and the same extraordinary hair that sprang out around her head like a silvery gold dandelion clock.

'This is my daughter.' Claire was unable to keep the pride out of her voice. 'Bridget, this is Mrs Page. She's just moved in to Peacocks' Acre.'

'Lucky you. It's a lovely old house.'

'A lovely old tip at the moment, I'm afraid. And it's Sarah, please.' She returned Bridget's radiant smile. 'You must meet *my* daughter, Meredith. She's not much younger than you, I imagine.' Even as she spoke she was appalled to realise that, while she gazed at Bridget, she felt a glimmer of shame at the thought of Merry, with her pudgy, overweight body and scowling face.

'Is she here?' Bridget asked at once.

'Yes. But she's rather shy. And homesick. In fact, rather miserable altogether. Perhaps I should have let her stay in the house, but I thought . . .'

'Bridget will look after her,' Claire said decisively. 'Won't you, darling? Point her out to us, Sarah. Where is she?' She craned her long neck. 'Oh, I think I see her! It must be that pretty girl in the corner, longing to fly through the window and escape us all.'

'That's her,' nodded Sarah.

Straight away Bridget began to weave her way across the crowded room. Sarah watched anxiously as she stopped in front of Merry and bent down to speak to her. Merry raised her head, looking almost resentful at first, but then her face cleared, and within a moment or two she was nodding, smiling, answering Bridget's questions. Sarah felt a flood of relief.

'You shouldn't worry so much!' Claire said. 'The young ones find their feet much more quickly than we do as a rule.'

'Do you think so?'

'Of course. They're very adaptable.'

'But she's missing William. Her brother. We've had to leave him behind, you see, with friends in Norwich.'

'Yes. Your husband – David? – told me about William. I did manage just a *few* minutes' chat before Belle command-eered him! He's taking up an appointment at Craiglands, I gather.'

'Head of History. He's very thrilled about it. Well, we both are. But . . . this business of moving. Pulling your roots up. It's hard, isn't it? Losing all your friends . . .' Sarah was aware of a pulse of sadness deep inside her and for a moment she understood exactly how Merry was feeling.

Claire touched her shoulder sympathetically. 'You'll make new friends. Promise,' she said. And Sarah was grateful for her serene certainty.

'Sarah!' Belle's voice cut through their conversation like a steel blade. 'You *must* circulate, my dear. Mustn't she, Claire? *And* your glass is empty. Now – tell me, who *haven't* you met?' She took Sarah's elbow in a determined grip and began to steer her away.

Hurriedly, Claire rummaged in the pocket of her dress, pulled out a tiny square of brown card, and insisted Sarah take it. 'Come and see me,' she urged. 'Soon. Not at home. I spend most of my time down at the Barns.'

Sarah scrutinised the silver printing.

'Claire Richley,' she read. 'Sculptor. Unit 3 – The Barns. Deredale.'

CHAPTER THREE

Sarah stood silently at the open door of the studio and gazed at the back of the figure she could see working there, stooped and absorbed, at the far end of the building. At first she had the idea that it was a man. The height, the breadth of the shoulders, the navy overalls, the blue peaked cap . . . She must have come to the wrong place. But then a sudden shaft of sunlight pierced the clouds, fell through the Velux window and spilled down, illuminating the workbench with its piles of soft, wheat-coloured sawdust, its clutter of tools, bottles, cloths and blocks of wood. It was as if a spell had been broken. The sculptor straightened up, pulled off the cap to release thistledown hair – and Sarah realised with a surge of delight that it was Claire.

At that same instant Claire turned, saw her standing there and came hurrying towards her, both hands outstretched. 'Sarah! I had just decided I needed a cup of coffee and a break – and here you are! How lovely.'

She led the way across her studio to a sort of cubicle screened off from the work space. As they stepped inside Sarah saw a sink with a draining board, and a bench stacked with mugs, coffee, biscuits and bars of chocolate.

'Emergency rations!' Claire grinned, flicking on the electric kettle. 'Sometimes I forget to go home. Sometimes I even forget to *sleep* when I'm working on something really exciting. But I never forget to refuel.'

'Are you working on something exciting now?'

Claire shrugged. 'Mmm. Not really. It's a repeat – nothing new. Coffee first, then I'll show you round.'

Sarah looked thoughtfully at the rough block of wood fastened into the vice on Claire's workbench. 'I'm sorry, I can't quite make out what it is,' she confessed at length.

'It isn't anything yet,' Claire laughed. 'Just a rather nice chunk of yew that I've been attacking with my mallet and chisel. But it's coming.' She picked up a small clay model from a shelf and held it out to Sarah on the palm of her hand. 'This is what it will look like when it's finished.'

'Oh! May I see?'

Enchanted, Sarah took the maquette and examined it carefully. It was in the shape of two figures, one male, one female, closely entwined. The man was tall and stiff-backed, his head bent, his arms linked behind the woman's waist. She was small and curved, all movement and grace. Her head was turned up towards his and she clasped him round the neck. Both their faces were smooth and featureless, as if inviting the observer to paint in the appropriate expressions with the mind's eye. The strength and passion of the piece came from the way each pair of hands was locked together, so strongly and smoothly that the couple was indivisible.

'It's beautiful!' said Sarah. 'Has it a name?'

' "Lovers",' Claire told her. 'That's what I call it. I made one like this for my god-daughter when she got married. Then her mother wanted one for a silver wedding gift. And now Treasures – that's our local gallery – they've asked for one.'

'The pretty green-and-gold place on the corner of the High Street? I've been promising myself a browse in there.'

'They're good, I think. They sell a lot of my stuff for me, so I couldn't let them down. I don't like repeating myself as a rule but this one seems special. And, of course, no two are ever quite the same. All made from different sorts of wood, to start with.'

Sarah followed Claire round her studio looking at the other pieces she had made – a mother and child, completed and ready for sale, a pair of doves waiting for their final finishing and polishing, a fox's head, begun and abandoned until inspiration returned. Then, perched on a high stool, her coffee cup replenished, she flicked through the red leather portfolio which held a photographic record of her work.

'You work to commission, then?'

'Sometimes,' Claire nodded. 'If I think the buyer is on my wavelength.'

'Are you very expensive?'

Claire laughed. 'How long is a piece of string? If someone really wants something, and I really want them to have it, we usually come to . . . an accommodation. Young ones sometimes pay me on the never-never! Why do you ask?'

'I was just thinking what a lovely idea it was . . . perhaps a special present for David sometime. Or William's eighteenth, next year.'

'If ever you want to think about it seriously, we'll have a chat.' Claire smiled at her. 'Now – tell me about *you*, for heaven's sake. We've been talking about me ever since you walked through the door. Have you got yourselves settled in now? And how are you enjoying Peacocks' Acre?'

'I fell in love with it the moment I saw it. I never imagined that we'd be able to afford such a lovely old place. We've been very lucky.'

Claire was watching her carefully. 'But?' she prompted. 'I can see there's something not quite right.'

'Oh, it's nothing really. Just . . . well, the traffic does get on my nerves a bit.'

'Ah!'

'We first came to look at it in early spring. It seemed quiet then. David did warn me that it was on a busy road but I refused to believe him. But now that the holiday season is on us . . . it *is* noisy. I think it's quite dangerous, too. I saw a car actually mount the pavement the other day to get out of the way of one of those horrible juggernauts.'

'You should hear Laurie on the subject,' Claire said. 'He has a positive thing about traffic. In fact, I warn you, if he hears you talking like this he'll have you enlisted in his road safety campaign before . . .'

'Laurie?' Sarah was puzzled. 'Did I meet him at Belle's party?'

'No. Laurie's never here in August. August is Laurie's month for Being Away. Every year without fail.'

'But who is he? Does he live in the village?'

'I'm sorry. I keep forgetting you're new here. Laurie's my husband. Laurence Richley.'

'Your husband!'

Claire was slightly taken aback by Sarah's obvious astonishment. 'Didn't you think I had a husband?'

'No. Well . . . yes. I'm sorry. I'd somehow got the idea that you were . . . divorced. I don't know why . . .'

Claire laughed aloud. 'Don't apologise, Sarah. It was an easy mistake to make. Laurence spends an awful lot of time away. Partly work – he's a solicitor in Newcastle. Senior partner. But mostly the Pilgrim Project. It's a sort of youth sail training scheme he's involved in. What am I saying, "involved in"? He's absolutely manic about it. So, Bridget and I do spend a lot of time on our own, especially in the summer.'

'That's a shame.'

'No. That's O.K. When Laurie's here we have good times together. And when he's away we manage just *fine*.'

'Do you?' Sarah felt doubtful. She thought of how closely her life was wound up with David's, how he liked her to be there for him when he came home from school, to keep her weekends empty and free for family things.

'Laurie and I both have our own hinterland,' Claire explained. 'Do you know what I mean? That's the way we like it.'

'We all work out our own patterns I suppose.'

'That's true.' Claire looked at her quizzically, head on one side. 'Do you possess a bicycle?'

Sarah blinked. 'Yes. Somewhere. In the garage, I suppose. Why?'

'Part of our pattern – Bridget's and mine, I mean – is to get out and about and enjoy ourselves while Laurie's sailing. The

Tyne valley's a marvellous place for cycling. The North Tyne, too. Why don't you and Merry come with us sometimes?'

'But what about David?'

'David will be pleased for you. Won't he?'

CHAPTER FOUR

Relaxed and sleepy in the high summer heat, Sarah lay on her back, her hands clasped behind her head as she watched the larks plummeting through the sky. She felt a guilty pang about David. He would have enjoyed this, she thought. She'd left him at home, totally engrossed in his books and lesson plans. It wasn't like her to take off without him, but this weather, and Claire's promptings, were tempting her away from her role as a dutiful wife.

Today they'd left their bicycles behind them for a change, driven for a while, then parked the car and walked, climbing out of the valley and up, up into the bright shimmering hills. Cushioned on the sweet springy turf, she felt a sense of drowsy contentment flood through her. But the contentment was tinged with regret. The wonderful holiday – for it *had* been a holiday – was coming to an end. Day after day the sun had beamed down upon them from a cloudless sky, and whenever they could she and Merry had joined forces with Claire and Bridget and set out on their wonderful expeditions. Occasionally they'd taken the car and driven to the coast. And there had been train journeys and bus journeys, cycle rides and hikes miles long, each one a voyage of discovery and delight. But now, Sarah knew, they were running out of time and there would never be another summer quite like it. The weather, the newness of their friendship, the way Merry had suddenly begun to ... to take off and *fly* – all these were special to this year and this year alone. In less than a week the new term would start and Bridget and Merry would have to go to school. David was already going in to

Craiglands for an hour or two every day. William would have his one special weekend at home with them and then he would start life as a boarder in Norwich. The end of the holidays. 'Summer goes, summer goes, like the sand between my toes . . .' She felt the same keen pang of loss she had always felt as a child.

Claire had warned her that very soon she must return to her studio and get on with some serious work. Treasures was clamouring for new pieces. As for herself, well, Sarah had a list of jobs as well. She had promised David faithfully that she would concentrate on Peacocks' Acre just as soon as school began. She hadn't even sewn up the hems of their bedroom curtains yet. David made such a show of fussing and tut-tutting every time he drew them that she had begun to make a point of going up to bed first, just to save herself the nightly pantomime.

David, admittedly, was sulking a bit. 'Why do you have to keep going off with Claire?' he'd demanded.. 'I'd have thought there was more than enough to keep you occupied here.'

'Of course there is. But we haven't managed to have a holiday this year, with the move and everything . . .'

'I haven't either . . .'

'. . . and I thought it would be good for Merry to get to know Bridget. Help her settle down. Besides, we have a good time, the four of us . . .'

'You used to have a good time with me. We've always done things together.'

He'd looked so crestfallen that she'd hurried across to him instantly, dropped on her knees beside him, wrapped him in her arms. 'I know, love. Of course we do. But you've been so busy preparing your courses, all the paperwork and everything . . . I didn't think you could get away.'

'You didn't even ask me. *I'd* have liked to have seen some of those places too. Alnwick Castle . . .'

'Why didn't you say so before?' He shrugged, his face set. 'Well, let's do that, shall we?' she suggested. 'Have a day out together. Just you and me and Merry. Tomorrow, while the sun's still shining. We could go to Bamburgh, somewhere exciting like that. Claire says it's . . .'

'We can't tomorrow,' he said. 'I've ordered a sanding machine from the hire shop. For the dining room floor.'

'You're going to sand the dining room floor tomorrow!' she exploded. 'In the middle of August. In all this heat! Why?'

'Someone's got to do it,' he said, pouting like a child. 'It was you who wanted the house, Sarah, but you don't seem to want to do the work.'

The injustice of his taunt stung her to a fury. 'That's not fair!' she declared. 'I'm prepared to work my fingers to the bone, and often do. After all, I don't have the luxury of a career, do I?'

He stared at her. 'What's that got to do with anything?'

'I have no precious school, or office, or studio to go to. Usually I just stay at home and do things about the house. Lots of things! I'm a better painter and decorator than you are.'

'No you're not.'

She ignored him. 'But just for one glorious month I am going to take a bit of time off. O.K? Just a few days here and there. I am going to have some sort of a holiday, and I don't care what you say. Do you hear me, David?'

'I should imagine the whole street can hear you.'

'I'm sorry.' She lowered her voice. 'I didn't mean to bawl you out. Anyway – when the autumn comes and you and Merry are back at school, I promise you I will more than make up for it. So please, don't try to make me feel guilty. We're not living in the Dark Ages, you know. I am allowed a life of my own.'

Afterwards Sarah had felt miserable about the row. She hardly ever pitted her will against David's. She usually found herself agreeing with him about most things. She thought it was because they'd known each other since they were children. They'd gone to the same school. Proverbial childhood sweethearts. And she'd always let him take the lead. But this time she was determined to stand her ground. For Merry's sake, even more than her own. Now she knew she'd been right.

She felt a tickle on her arm and glanced down. A tiny ladybird was crawling along the crease of her elbow. She coaxed it on to her finger, laid it carefully on a tall flowering grass and watched, smiling, as it spread its wings and flew off. The sky was the intense blue of periwinkles. She hadn't believed Northumberland could have summers like this.

'Better take your woolly pullies,' her friend Pam had told her when she'd heard about the move. 'It's always five or six degrees colder up there, I'm warning you.' And Pam should know. She'd been married to a T.V. weatherman until he'd taken off with a bimbo from Make-up, leaving her to struggle along as best she could as a single mother. Sarah sighed. She did miss Pam *and* all her problems.

She heard a shriek of laughter from Merry and Bridget and turned her head to see what was going on. They were sitting cross-legged on the grass, facing each other, playing some extraordinary hand game. First they clapped each other's hands, then they clapped their own. Next they made fists, beating one upon the other. Then, with their fingers pointing, they traced little circles in the air. It went on and on. It was all very fast and hugely complicated and sooner or later one of them got mixed up, made a mistake and was 'out', which meant they both had to start the whole routine over again.

Sarah lay quietly, watching Merry, and could hardy believe that this was the same surly girl she and David had dragged up north with them just a few weeks ago. Her skin was tanned, glowing with health. She'd discarded the frumpish calf-length skirts she'd insisted on wearing in Norwich and her legs looked long, even shapely, in her cropped denim shorts. Bridget had shown her a new way to do her chestnut brown, shoulder-length hair. Now she lifted and separated the top layer and plaited it, weaving a single vivid ribbon through the glossy braid from top to bottom. With her heavy mane pulled back from her face, her high cheekbones were accentuated, the deep-set brown eyes looked larger, more widely-spaced. Sarah remembered Claire's words when she'd first seen Merry. 'The pretty girl in the corner,' she'd said, and Sarah had thought then that she was just being kind. The truth was that Claire saw things, and especially people, more clearly. Merry *was* pretty. The way she looked now it seemed possible that once her puppy fat had melted away she might even turn out to be a beauty. She had Bridget to thank for the transformation, Sarah decided. Bridget was a . . . a 'life-enhancer', like her mother. It was Bridget who had taught Merry to live up to her name, made her laugh and shine, given her the self-confidence that had never had a chance to develop when she lived in the shadow of her brother. Now Merry dared to feel pleased with herself and the way she was. And because of that, she pleased other people, too. It was a new experience for her and she was revelling in it.

Suddenly Merry gave a bellow of laughter and keeled over sideways, helpless with giggles. Grinning, Sarah turned her attention away from the girls and focused it on Claire who was sitting on a smooth rock a few feet away from her. She was using her bent knees as a desk, scribbling thoughtfully in a little blue notebook.

'What are you writing?' Sarah asked, curious.

'Getting my journal up to date,' Claire muttered, her eyes still on the page. 'My commonplace book.'

'What sort of things do you write in it?'

'Oh, this and that. Little sketches and ideas for work. Quotations. Snatches of conversations.'

'Really?'

'Yes. I love those. I'm a terrible eavesdropper. Descriptions too, of people and places. I've got your ladybird.' She held out the book and pointed to a little pencilled drawing with notes jotted beside it.

Sarah was intrigued. 'What are you writing now?'

'Nosy!'

'Sorry!'

'It's all right. It's not private.' Claire smiled. She cleared her throat and began to read. ' "The last day of a perfect August. Shiny blue, gold and green. On the rooftop of Northumberland. Hadrian's Wall a grey snake below us. The river a silver ribbon. Birdsong. Tiny brown butterflies in the seeding grasses. My friend by my side. My daughter laughing with Merry, who is *merry*!" De-dah, de-dah, de-dah, de-dah.' Then she laughed. 'This is the important bit. "Check with Mr Renton for prawns and salmon steaks." ' She raised her eyes and looked at Sarah. 'Laurie will be home any day now. I'm planning his celebration feast.'

CHAPTER FIVE

'Mmm. Nice! Love you.' Laurie dropped a kiss on the end of her nose and rolled away from her, patting her tummy in a friendly way. 'Good to be home, Claire.' Then, almost at once, he was asleep.

Claire lay on her back and stared up at the ceiling, her eyes following a small, black spider that was scurrying busily across it. Laurie had been away for a whole month, yet their love-making had been, at best, perfunctory. Pleasant enough, but brief, almost automatic. 'Nice' was just about the right word. Is this what happened to all marriages? she wondered. Was it the same for Sarah and her macho hunk of a husband? So used to each other that there were no surprises left, no requirement to thrill and excite? When she and Laurie had first met, back in the sixties, they used to make love all night sometimes, challenging each other to rise to some new, delightful possibility, exotic, erotic and wonderful.

They'd met at the wedding of her friend Maisie. What had become of Maisie now? Claire asked herself. They didn't even exchange Christmas cards any longer. But back then, in the summer of '62, Claire had been her 'best friend' and so, naturally, her chief bridesmaid. She'd felt absurd, hovering behind the bride at the altar steps. She towered over Maisie, looking even taller than she actually was in her long, narrow silk dress that was in a shade of green that she couldn't bear. And on her head she'd had to wear a circlet of little white flowers. She must look like an elongated daisy, she thought miserably. After the speeches were over she vanished away from the hotel dining room and found a quiet staircase,

37

tucked around at the back of the building. She sat down with relief, opened her bag – green silk to match her dress – pulled out a packet of cigarettes and lit one furtively. Then she closed her eyes, stretched her long neck and inhaled deeply. It was marvellous.

'What a good idea!'

Her eyes flew open and to her horror she saw one of the ushers hovering over her, a friend of the groom's whom she'd never met before.

'Mind if I join you?' he asked.

She shook her head mutely and he sat down on the stair below her.

'Don't suppose you could spare one of those?' He pointed at her cigarette.

'Of course. Sorry!' She handed him the packet.

A little spurt of flame shot up from her lighter, illuminating his face.

'That's better!' He coughed, frowned. 'I keep trying to give up, but these things always bring out the worst, don't they?'

'What things?'

She must have sounded surprised because he stared at her. '*These* blasted things. Weddings! Do *you* like them?'

'Oh!' She considered the matter carefully. 'No, not much.'

'Me neither. I suppose it might be better if it were your own.'

Her eyes narrowed. 'It might be worse.'

'You haven't had one, then? A wedding of your own, I mean?'

'Oh no! Definitely not,' she assured him emphatically.

'Me neither,' he repeated.

Then they both laughed out loud because of the absurdity of it all, and the champagne that was bubbling through their veins. He pulled off his tail coat and dumped it on the stairs.

'You don't mind, do you?' he asked her.

'Feel free.'

Taking her at her word, he undid the pearl buttons of his dove-grey waistcoat, pulled off his tie and stuffed it into his trouser pocket. 'I'm Laurie Richley,' he told her. 'Drinking friend of the groom.'

'Claire Dickson.' She smiled. 'Painting friend of the bride.'

They shook hands, grinning, then she lifted up her arms and unpinned her chaplet of lilies of the valley. As she shook her head, her silver-fair, fly-away hair shone out like a halo and he gazed at it in amazement.

'You have wonderful hair,' he said.

Her lips pursed in an amused little smile. 'Thank you.'

'Does everybody tell you that?'

She shrugged. 'I suppose it's the colour. Almost silver. People find it strange. At my age, I mean.'

'How old are you? If it's not a rude question.'

'Twenty-two.'

'Ah!' He shook his head solemnly. 'Twenty-two. That takes me back.'

'Why? How old are you, then?'

'Twenty-three last birthday.' He laughed.

Suddenly, unexpectedly, Maisie arrived, en route to the bedroom that had been put aside for her to change into her going away outfit. When she caught sight of them, giggling together on the back stairs like conspirators, she was out-raged. 'What are you two doing, lurking about out here?' she demanded. '*You're* supposed to be helping look after the guests, Laurie. And I always thought it was the bridesmaid's job to attend the bride.'

Claire and Laurie exchanged glances. Maisie did *not* seem to be having a good wedding.

'I'm sorry.' Claire sprang up, stubbed out her cigarette and groped for her head-dress which was lying desolately on the carpet, looking like a squashed cream cake.

Maisie screwed up her mouth disapprovingly. 'Claire! You looked so *sweet* in that.' She took her firmly by the hand and began to drag her up the stairs behind her. 'Come along now. I need you.'

Reluctantly Claire followed, but before she'd climbed more than two or three steps she heard Laurie's voice behind her.

'See you later, Claire. Don't do a Cinderella on me, will you?'

'I don't want to be a wet blanket,' Maisie said, as Claire helped her off with the snowy tulle layers of her dress, 'but I really would steer clear of that one if I were you.'

'Of Laurie? Why? Has he got the pox or something?'

'Don't be flippant. I'm just telling you for your own good. He's a . . . bit of a maverick. A solicitor in his father's firm. Always set on doing things *his* way. He doesn't care what he says to people – and some of them have been in the business since before he was even born.'

'Oh Maisie! That doesn't sound very terrible to me.'

'But the law is based on precedent. Protocol. You can't just go around trying to break all the rules the way he does.'

Claire shook her head. 'Everything needs to change a bit though, doesn't it? Otherwise we'd stagnate.'

Maisie sighed. 'Don't say I didn't warn you, that's all.'

'For heaven's sake, there's nothing to warn me *about*. We were just having a fag on the stairs, that's all.' She lifted a hanger from the wardrobe and pulled off a swathe of tissue paper. 'Come on, honey. Let's get you into your little pink outfit. *Very* chic.'

Neither she nor Laurie could have known then, Claire mused, when they were sitting on the stairs at poor Maisie's wedding – which she now remembered had ended in tears only five years later – that their own lives were destined to be interwoven for the rest of their days.

After the reception he'd driven her back to her bed-sit in a suburb of Newcastle and they'd drunk black coffee together half way through the night. He'd listened, as if he were really interested, when she'd told him that she was a sculptor, still at art college, and that her greatest desire in life was to pick up the gauntlet thrown down by Barbara Hepworth and take sculpture into new dimensions.

'She actually had twins, you know. And she was always in the shadow of Ben Nicholson. Her *husband*. And Henry Moore, too. But she forged on and made her own discoveries about form and space and light. Earned her own place. That's what I want to do.'

Then it had been her turn to listen. Laurie was a solicitor with a mission. He was determined to be the champion of the little man, the enemy of the fat cat. He was going to cut a swathe through red tape and legalese, he told her, his eyes alight. Simplification was the theme. Plain speaking. It was high time that the poor, the underprivileged, were able to use and understand the law with the same ease as the affluent middle classes, who always knew exactly how to get to grips with the system and bend it to their own ends just because education and money had given them power.

Claire was dazzled. Her own friends could talk the hind leg off a donkey and often sat up into the small hours, smoking grass and drinking, while ideas bounced off the walls like squash balls. But they spoke a different language, dipping into the great unfathomables. The nature of art. Individual freedom versus the requirements of the community. Even . . . the purpose of life, for heaven's sake. Laurie's clear-eyed, specific crusade to banish the impotence of the under-educated in an inequitable society made her fellow students' concerns seem like the babble of infants.

They spent the rest of the summer concentrating entirely on each other, rapt and absorbed. Within three weeks they had become lovers. Laurie's love-making was inspired, Claire thought, and tried not to wonder how many women he had known before he slept with her. One night he took her to a folk club in a basement somewhere along the Quayside. There was a new singer they hadn't heard before, a young girl with a raw, yearning voice and the white face of a street urchin. She had the power of a Piaf, the ability to conjure emotion out of thin air and offer it as a rare gift to her audience. She ended her set with a Northumbrian lament about loss and longing that left both of them moved and shaken to the point of tears.

When she had finished Laurie stood up. 'Let's go, lovey. That was too good to follow.'

He steered her through the crowded tables in the dimly lit space until they reached the exit, stepped out into the dark street and hurried her off towards his car. Soon he was driving, not in the direction of her room, but out through the city, taking the road towards the west.

'Where are we going?' she asked.

'To a place I know.'

'Where?'

'Very secret. Very special. You'll love it.'

For about half an hour they drove swiftly along a narrow country road that hurtled them over humped bridges, sent them plummeting down into deep dips then had them grinding up steep hills again to erupt over the crest in triumph. Claire looked wonderingly at Laurie's face, but he didn't say a word and she daren't trespass upon his mood. Then, abruptly, he swung the steering wheel and the car swerved to the right and began to rattle along a dirt track, deeply ridged and bumpy.

'Laurie!' Claire protested at last. 'I'm being shaken to death!'

'Hush! Hush!' he commanded. 'We're nearly there.'

Five minutes later he had parked the car, seized her hand, and was tugging her along a tiny footpath that sloped gently downwards. Brambles snatched at her ankles. She smelt the fragrance of pine boughs brushing against her body, heard a sheep cry from a low hill. At last she was aware that they had reached a sort of clearing where the land levelled out. Peering around her in the semi-opaque darkness of the August night, she realised suddenly that they were very close to water. She could hear it rippling not far from her feet. There was a harsh stutter from a coot, or moorhen, then a splashing sound.

'It's a lake!' she exclaimed.

'Not quite. A private reservoir. My father fishes here.' He pulled at her arm impatiently. 'Come on. This way.'

She followed, unsteady on the rough grass, and was then brought to an abrupt halt as he bent down in front of her and tugged at something on the ground. There was a steady swish through the water as he pulled in an old flat-bottomed boat. He stooped over it, the rope in one hand, and steadied the craft with the other. 'Hop in,' he said.

Wordless, she obeyed him. Almost at once he had jumped in behind her and heaved up the oars from the bottom. He gave a hefty push away from the sandy shore and began to row, swiftly and smoothly, towards the centre of the stretch of water. Then he lifted the oars and slid them neatly at either side of the boat, allowing the little craft to float free. He looked at her solemnly. He raised her hand to his lips and kissed it gently, inside her curled palm.

'Take your clothes off,' he told her.

Like a woman hypnotised, she undressed and watched while he did the same. When they were both naked, he made a nest of their clothes in the bottom of the boat. Gently, firmly, he drew her down beside him, making her squeeze, breathless, into the confining space. Then he wrapped his arms around her bare body. From midnight until daybreak they made love. Like Siamese twins, conjoined, they lay together, Laurie erect inside her, still as a statue, for more than an hour at a time. They were in a trance of intense, tantalising, sexual excitement that Claire felt, hoped, might never end. The night was hot and breathless but his body was as cool as berries. A young moon rode above them, occasionally veiling itself behind a thin film of cloud, yet strangely, she could see no stars. Beneath them, around them, the boat rocked as if it were their cradle. They heard the muffled sounds of the night, a tiny wind among the trees, a rustling of the long grass. And all the time he was within her, part of her, so close that it seemed they really were one flesh, his lips brushing against her face, hers sucking at his neck, his nipples. At last she could bear it no longer. She must have more. She clenched her muscles around him, contracting rhythmically, urging him on. And the boat swayed gently, and the water flowed around them and through them, and she felt as if they were part of it all, the water, the sky, the moon, the whole universe, and that they were being borne away together, bound for ever in this wild and endless rapture . . .

Claire would never forget that night. She knew it would return to her on her death bed. It was the nearest she had ever got to ecstasy. Now, nearly thirty years on, she turned her head and looked at Laurie, lying in bed beside her but twisted away from her. Where had it all gone, she wondered, all that passion? What had happened? Well – life had happened, she supposed. And, life's near-misses.

Laurie's one-man battle to change the status quo had not been a success. The rest of Newcastle's legal profession had looked askance at this brash young upstart who really believed it was possible, even desirable, to do things differently. In the end his father, and even his brother Mark, who adored him and was usually his most ardent champion, had begged him to toe the line and accept things as they were. Changes would happen in their own good time, they'd said. But the way forward was through evolution not revolution. He must learn to be patient, gentler, more tolerant.

'Play a bit of golf and take out your frustrations on the ball,' his father had advised him. 'I can't have you antagonising our colleagues, it's bad for the firm. And my heart.'

And now – she could hardly believe the way the years had slipped by – Laurie was nearly fifty. Bored out of his skull as often as not with all the humdrum paraphernalia of wills and settlements, deeds and divorce. The fire had gone out of him long ago as far as the law was concerned. All his old energy and enthusiasm he'd funnelled into sailing instead, mastering the skills of racing and navigation with his usual hunger and speed.

And *she* had had her problems, too, Claire thought sadly. She had hoped to make her mark in the art world. To create objects that would persuade people to look and think and ask questions and even, perhaps, to extend their horizons. Instead she made little pieces that were beautiful, even desirable, but *safe*. She had become – dreaded word! – commercial. Barbara Hepworth would not have approved.

She hadn't thrown in the towel so abjectly.

Claire took a deep breath. But all this, of course, was simply skirting round the edges of what had really happened to her and Laurie. She rubbed her hands over her tired eyes. Weary though she was, there was no way she was going to get to sleep. She slithered out of bed, picked up her dressing gown from the chair and crept downstairs. Mechanically she made herself some hot chocolate, then sat down, holding the mug between both hands, watching the swirl of bubbles on the surface. Her mind was racing, dragging her, reluctantly, back into the past.

She and Laurie had married in the spring of '66. Harold Wilson had just squeezed the Labour Party into power by a cat's whisker. Macmillan's wind of change was blowing through society like a typhoon. And, according to John Lennon, the Beatles were more popular than Jesus. Yeah! Yeah! Yeah! The world was an exciting place, they were in love and the very air they breathed tasted like wine. And then, in September, Claire had a miscarriage. The next year she miscarried again, twice. And the year after that it happened again. The doctor let it slip, thoughtlessly, that it was just possible that there was some congenital problem, that Claire might be physically incapable of carrying a child full term. Laurie shrugged it off. There were more important things in life, he said, than babies. They had each other, their work, their friends. You could have a rich, happy life without having a family, he told her. In fact, families could be disappointing. Difficult. Really hard work.

Claire knew he was bluffing. Laurie longed for a child, particularly, though he would not dream of admitting it, for a son. Another Richley to add to the firm's brass plate. '*Richley, Richley, Burgoyne and Richley. And* – please God – *Richley.*' She told her doctor she would like to have a second opinion about her case, and in due course she was admitted to hospital for extensive tests. After a few days she was informed that she could go home with a clean bill of health. Nothing could be found to explain the miscarriages. There was no apparent reason why she shouldn't have half a dozen healthy babies, even more if she wanted.

The consultant obstetrician had patted her hand kindly. 'Try to put all this behind you,' he'd said. 'Relax. Stop worrying. Make love and enjoy it.'

'Make love and enjoy it.' Easier said than done. Spooning the last of the chocolate from the bottom of her mug, Claire smiled ruefully, remembering the anxieties that had plagued both of them. Would *this* be the time she got pregnant? Was there anything they could do to improve their chances? And if it happened . . . oh, if it really did happen, would they manage to have a healthy baby?

After the hospital tests there were no more miscarriages. No more pregnancies either, for years and years. Thinking back to that long chilling period in their lives, Claire realised that it was then that Laurie had come up with the idea of the Pilgrim Project, diverting his need for a child of his own into other people's children, especially those who needed a bit of support, a sympathetic nudge in the right direction. And *she* had found her studio at the Barns and forced herself to make work that would sell, so that at least she could honestly call herself a professional sculptor. She had to be *something*, after all, since she'd been such a failure at motherhood.

Then, at last, the miracle had happened. For a while Claire hardly dared believe it. Hardly dared even think about it. But when she went to see her doctor, her heart beating so furiously that she was afraid she might faint in a heap on the waiting room floor, he confirmed that she was indeed pregnant. And that she must take no risks, go home, go to bed and stay there, or he would not accept responsibility. 'I know it'll be awfully boring, but there it is. Be a good girl, put your feet up and no moaning.'

In fact it hadn't been boring at all. Claire remembered her feet-up period as halcyon days. She read and drew. She listened to amazing talks and plays and stories on the radio and became hooked on *Woman's Hour* and *The Archers*. And she got into the habit of keeping a journal.

'I really could get used to all this,' she told Laurie one evening when he'd cooked her supper and came to sit on the bed beside her while they watched *Z Cars* on her little television set.

'No chance!' he'd said. 'Just a few weeks now and His Nibs will have made his entrance. He'll have you run off your feet.'

'Don't count on it being a boy,' she'd begged him anxiously.

But he was convinced. He had the strongest of all hunches, he told her. 'Dads have an instinct for such things.' He'd laughed. 'This one does, anyway.'

She went into labour one week before her due delivery date. She could not *believe* the pain. Nothing in her experience had prepared her for it. But she didn't care. All she could think, through the endless hours of panting and groaning and blowing, and shouting out loud sometimes to try to release the tension that was building inside her, was – 'Don't let me mess it up this time. Let it be all right. Please, *please*, let this child be well.'

Laurie was with her when at last the baby was born. He took it from the midwife and laid it tenderly, proudly, in Claire's arms. 'Meet your daughter,' he said. 'Well done, lovey. She's a beauty.'

Claire felt helpless, buffeted about on a sea of emotion, fathomless love, terrible vulnerability. But Bridget lay quietly, gazing up at her with eyes wide open, calm and clear, green as grass. It seemed as if she knew and understood everything, as if she was saying, 'It was me. It was *me*. I'm the one you've been waiting for. But it's all right now. I'm here.' And hardly knowing what she did, or why, Claire bent down her head over the tiny, upturned face of her baby, and wept.

CHAPTER SIX

'Make yourself at home, my dear.' Belle pointed to a chair.
'Coffee coming up in just a minute.'

Sarah sat down at the kitchen table and picked up the
Valley Bugle that was lying there. 'May I?'

'Of course,' Belle said. 'Don't you get our local rag?'

''Fraid not.'

'Oh, you should. All human life is there, as they say.'

Sarah smiled faintly and began to flick through the pages,
turning them over and smoothing them out flat beneath her
hands as she examined the headlines.

'11-year-old angler scoops Tyne Valley prize.'

And there was a photograph of young Kevin Sprotley,
gangling and bespectacled, beaming with pride as he held up
his silver cup.

Behind her, at the far end of the kitchen, Belle was clattering about, spooning coffee into her cafetière, holding up two
porcelain mugs for Sarah to admire. 'National Trust. Don't
you think they're sweet? I bought half a dozen last time I
went to Wallington. Have you been there yet? The herbaceous borders are stunning.'

'I haven't, I'm afraid.' Sarah shook her head apologetically.
Vaguely she looked down at the paper again but her mind
kept straying to her children instead. Today was Merry's first
day at her new school in Hexham. How was she coping?
Sarah wondered. Was she making friends with the girls in
her class? Did she like her teachers? But really she knew that
she had no need to worry. As Merry had hurried along the
street with Bridget, talking so much that she had only just

remembered to turn and wave before she disappeared round the corner, she had been brimming over with excitement. For the hundredth time, Sarah thanked her lucky stars that Merry had been lucky enough to find such a friend.

Suddenly a name she recognised leapt out at her. Meadowlands. What did she know about Meadowlands? Of course! It was the place Ralph Elliott had mentioned – where the old lady who used to live in Peacocks' Acre had moved. She read the first lines of the news item.

'Lady Serena Bennet opens new wing of Meadowlands Residential Home. "We must care for our senior citizens as carefully as we care for our children," she told our staff reporter.'

The allusion to children sent her mind scurrying back to the matter that had been troubling her. Strangely, unusually, it was William, not Merry, she was upset about. William had always been the perfect child. Gentle, clever and funny. Good at everything, schoolwork *and* games. He'd never given them the slightest tremor of concern.

And then David had got the job at Craiglands and the whole family had sat down and talked things through in a sensible, adult manner, and come to the conclusion that William should stay on at Norwich while the rest of them moved to Deredale. He had agreed that it was the best, the only possible thing to do. In fact, looking back, Sarah realised that it had been William's idea in the first place.

'If I'm really serious about going to Cambridge,' he'd said, in a matter of fact way that nearly broke her heart, 'it would be stupid for me to start a new school half way through the sixth form, wouldn't it? I'll just have to board, I suppose.'

But he'd changed. From the moment the decision was made. Even before they'd left their old house, while he was still with them, he seemed separate. Distant. Even then, when she knew he was sleeping in the next bedroom, Sarah had woken in the night sometimes, her cheeks wet with tears because she was missing him so much. And now that pain had turned into a dull, persistent ache.

All through the summer she'd been looking forward to having him with her just for this one last weekend before his term began. It was going to be her special treat before life went back to being grey and workaday again.

' "Regeneration is key to our future," claims Councillor Prewitt.'

But then, last night, William had rung to say he wouldn't be coming after all. Mr Gallagher, the man who owned the garden centre where he'd been working, wanted him to do one last job for him, was even offering to pay him double time.

'Darling,' she'd protested, determined not to whinge, 'we haven't seen you for over a *month*. Please come. Dad and I will give you double time, whatever that comes to. And pay your fare, of course.'

He'd laughed, but he'd been firm. 'It's not the money, Mum. He's counting on me and Zack to help him. A hundred young trees to plant! It's the least we can do. Anyway, you're coming down next week, aren't you?'

'Of course. I want to get you off to school properly. Make sure you've got all your stuff together for the new term.'

'Well, I'll see you *then*.'

'But I wanted to have you *here*, darling. This is our home now, and you've only spent one night under its roof. It doesn't seem right, you not being part of it.'

'Oh, Mum! Don't make a thing about it. I'll be there for half-term, won't I?'

And that had been that. Peering over the garden wall this morning, studying Sarah's woeful face, Belle had noticed at once that there was something wrong. 'Come on in for elevenses,' she'd insisted. 'We'll have a good old natter.'

When Belle carried the coffee across to the table Sarah began to fold up the *Bugle* but her eye was caught by a large square photograph dominating the centre of the page.

'PILGRIMS' PROGRESS. The *Matadora* leads the way home,' blared the headline above it. Four people gazed out at her from among the smudgy newsprint. Two of them looked like schoolboys. One was a young woman, smiling, her hand raised. But it was the other who mesmerised her, commanding her attention. The face was that of a middle-aged man and it was the most extraordinary she had ever seen. It was dominated by hooded eyes, half-closed beneath the line of the eyebrows. The nose was bony, beaked. The mouth was surprisingly small, the chin jutting. It was a face that would stand out in any crowd. And yet there was an arrogance about it, even, perhaps, a streak of cruelty. It was those narrowed eyes, straight-set and uncompromising, that made it so riveting. Sarah stared at the photograph again.

'Who is this?' she asked Belle. 'Do you know him?'

'Let me see. Which one?' She followed Sarah's pointing finger, then laughed. 'Don't you know? That's old Laurie. Laurence Richley, no less. Sailing home from his summer knees-up!'

'Claire's husband?' Sarah couldn't understand the apprehension that invaded her.

'Yes. You and Claire have got very thick, haven't you, while he's been away?'

'Mmm. She's been great. Bridget, too.'

'Now you'll meet her other half.'

'What's he like?' Sarah asked. 'Is he as nice as Claire?'

Thoughtfully, Belle put her head on one side. 'I certainly wouldn't call him "nice". He's a dry sort of a chap. Never afraid to tell people what he thinks, and he can be downright rude. He's one of the local nobs, of course. His family have just about *run* the village for ever, so it's probably in the blood to treat the rest of us like peasants. There have been Richleys living in Dolphin House ever since it was built. That must be about two hundred years.'

'Really?'

'I wonder how you two will get on? I should tell you . . .'

Sarah flashed a sudden smile and tossed the paper to one side as if she'd quite lost interest. 'Oh, I meant to ask you, Belle. I still haven't found a decent hairdresser. Which one do *you* go to?'

'Which hairdresser?'

Sarah's eyes flickered away from the surprise in Belle's face, but she couldn't help it. She didn't want to be told anything else about Laurence Richley. Not by Belle. Not by anyone. The very sight of that hawkish face had filled her with the most incomprehensible feeling of alarm. She was going to *hate* him, she thought. Her friend's husband and she couldn't stand the sight of him. But the strangest thing was, though she had never met him, though she could never even have seen his face until this minute, she felt that she had known him all her life.

CHAPTER SEVEN

David was sitting in his study at Craiglands staring moodily at his desk. They were only a week into the new term and already work was beginning to pile up. He glared at the papers in his in-tray. *And* he had his first lot of sixth-form essays to mark. 'Robespierre versus the Cult of Reason'. *Not* his favourite period. Or topic. Set by his predecessor as a holiday task, and performed with understandable dullness, no doubt. He glanced at his watch, stifling a yawn. Six o'clock already. Sarah would be wondering wherever he was. He stood up, fastening his tie, and lifted his jacket off the back of the chair.

'Hi, David!' Tom Jackson's amiable face beamed at him from the open door.

At once, David's spirits lifted. Tom was a bullock of a man, short, stocky, with broad shoulders and huge hands. Born to play rugby! He had a shock of hair the colour of a fox's brush and his beard curled vigorously around his chin and cheeks. He was the school's head of PE and ever since David had volunteered to take over the football teams so that he could concentrate on the game that was closest to his heart, he'd treated him like a blood brother.

'Fancy a swift half?' Tom asked.

'I thought you'd cleared off hours ago.'

'No. I've just been doing a work-out with some of my first team hopefuls. A couple of them are shaping up quite nicely.'

'I trust you're not thinking of poaching young Taylor,' David warned. 'He's one of my best long kickers.'

'What's it worth? Pint of Best?'

David grimaced. 'I should be getting home. I'm late.'

'Look, man, you're so late already that another half hour or so will hardly be noticed.'

'You may be right.'

'Give Sarah a ring. Tell her an important meeting has just come up. Games Organisation Committee.'

The beer tasted as good as Tom had promised. The Wig and Pistle was the staff's favourite watering hole, he explained, when they needed to wind down after a stressful school day. Which was *most* days. 'And as for their cheese and onion pasties. Food for the gods! Why don't I stand you one?'

'No!' David protested. 'Thanks. But Sarah will have supper ready.'

'Sarah will have supper ready?' Tom's face was a picture. 'Good grief! I didn't think women *did* things like that any more. There'll be a note from Wanda. *If* I'm lucky. "Pizza in deep freeze." But usually she ignores food. We just sort of . . . forage when we're hungry.'

David tried not to look smug. 'Sarah quite likes cooking.'

'Does she now? Has she found herself a job yet?'

'Sarah? No. She doesn't want a job.'

'What does she do, then?'

'What do you mean, "do"?' David laughed. 'She looks after us and the house. And the garden.'

'Sounds pretty boring to me.'

'She's very happy. Apart from missing William a bit. She's never gone out to work, you see. No qualifications.'

Tom snorted. 'Wanda only has two rotten GCSEs but she's always worked. Catch her staying at home all day!'

'That's different, though.' David took a deep swallow and emerged from his tankard with a foaming moustache. 'Sarah used to be a high-flier. Cleverer than me by a long chalk. But she . . . well, she had to give up before she could take her Finals.'

'She was ill, you mean?'

'Something like that. And then we got married and William

arrived and we decided that one of us had to stay at home. As things worked out, it had to be her.'

'Rightly so! A woman's place.'

David coloured slightly. 'I know it sounds old-fashioned these days, but neither of us approves of child-minders, or latch-key children. Unless it's a matter of necessity, of course. And as it happens, Sarah's really enjoyed all that. Being a mum.'

'Great.' Tom nodded and pointed to David's tankard. 'Do you want another one in there?'

'No, thanks. I'm driving.'

Tom grinned. '*I'm* walking.'

'My shout.' David lifted his hand towards the man behind the bar.

'How old is William now?' Tom asked casually.

'Eighteen next birthday! It's hard to believe . . .'

'Eighteen years!' Tom exploded. 'Don't you think it's time you gave the poor woman a break?'

David was startled. 'But there's still Merry to think about. She's just fifteen.'

Tom gave a sardonic laugh. 'Have you *seen* the fifteen-year-olds round here? Some of them could have you for breakfast. On toast.'

'But you're missing the point,' David insisted. 'Sarah *likes* being at home. She's got her freedom. She can go off and enjoy herself whenever she wants to.'

'That's all right, then. Good for Sarah.'

David could see that Tom was not convinced. For some reason it needled him. He felt he had to justify himself. 'It's true! Last month, when I was sweating over books and syllabuses and God knows what *and* trying to get the house half decent, *she* was popping off all over the place with Claire Richley.'

'Richley?'

'Yes. Mrs Richley. Dolphin House.'

Tom's brow cleared. 'I thought I knew the name. She must be married to Laurence Richley, the legal eagle?'

57

'That's the one. We haven't met him yet. You know him?'

'Yeah! Everybody does. Amazing guy. Runs the Pilgrim Project. He came to school last year to talk to the children about it.'

'What is it? The Project?'

'It's a brilliant outfit. He collects up kids from all walks of life, some "disadvantaged", as they say. Young offenders, absconders, school refusers. A few of them disabled, sometimes. Some perfectly fit and normal. Then he mixes them all up together and takes them sailing. I think he said they have three big sailing boats now. They buy them second-hand and refurbish them. In the summer they go off for a whole month at a time.'

'That must be a bit hairy.'

'I don't know. They're very professional. Have to be, of course. They've got a team of highly experienced officers. All the latest safety equipment. Fantastic discipline. But the children seem to love it. Richley reckons it teaches them all they need to know about coping with life. He's a fanatic. When he's not on board he's stamping about the country giving talks, showing videos, persuading people – ordinary people as well as big business and industry – to part with their dosh and give these kids a chance. He raises thousands.'

'He sounds like good news.'

A look of acute pain crossed Tom's face. 'He even had me writing out a cheque for a hundred quid. How could I do that? One hundred pounds, David. On *my* salary. The man must be a wizard.'

David smiled. 'I can't wait to meet him,' he said.

Sarah laid down her trowel, dragged her attention away from the ground elder which had infiltrated her iris bed and looked up at David. 'What did you say?' She could hardly believe her ears. 'You want us to have a dinner party?'

David grinned. He looked young and relaxed, almost boyish, his hair tousled and shining in the light. He was still in his pyjamas and blue plaid dressing gown but the mild

September sunshine had lured him out into the garden where Sarah had already been hard at work for more than an hour.

'I've had my breakfast,' he told her. 'I think I might have a long hot wallow in the bath.' He stretched luxuriously. 'I *love* Saturday mornings.' He bent down and tugged thoughtfully at a clump of achillea. 'Is this a weed?'

She gave his hand a playful slap. 'I think you'd better leave the weeding to me,' she suggested. 'The topic on the table was dinner parties, and your sudden interest in them.'

'You wouldn't mind, would you? I thought it was a good idea.'

'But you *hate* dinner parties. Whenever I suggested such a thing in Norwich you moaned. "Can't stand *dinner parties*," you used to say. As if I were suggesting a jolly trip to the dentist or something. "Can't stand *dentists*."'

'But things are different now, aren't they? There are people who have been kind to us. That I'd like to know better.'

'Who, for instance?'

'Tom, for instance. Tom Jackson and Wanda.'

Sarah gathered together the debris she'd removed from the border and put it carefully in her bucket. Then she got to her feet, wiping her hands on her apron. She looked anxiously into David's face. 'I haven't even met Tom.'

'That's what I mean.' His face was alight with enthusiasm. 'He's longing to meet you. He says you sound like . . . what was it?' He laughed, remembering. ' "A pearl of great price." ' He caught Tom's Geordie voice exactly. ' "Why, man, your Sarah sounds like a pearl of great price." His very words.'

Sarah was instantly suspicious. 'What have you been telling him?'

'Oh, nothing. Just general chat, you know. Then there's Claire Richley, of course. And her husband. He's home now, isn't he?'

'I believe so. But we don't know *him* either.' She screwed up her face. 'Do you really think this is such a good plan, darling? People we've never even met.'

'We never will meet them, will we? Unless we make an effort.'

Reluctantly she gave in. 'All right, then. Claire and Laurence Richley. Tom and Wanda Jackson. Have you thought of a date?'

'Hang on, we haven't finished yet.' He sat down on the bench and stretched his legs, enjoying being slow and lazy for a change. 'There's Belle too. We'll have to have her. She had a party for us, remember. So, Belle and . . .'

'Just Belle on her own,' Sarah said. 'She's a widow, didn't you know? Her husband died of a coronary ages ago. No children either. She's all alone in the world.'

'Belle and Reggie.'

'Reggie?'

'Reggie Bray.'

'What?' Sarah was appalled. 'Not that boring golfing man with the belly and the brick red face.'

David laughed. 'Reggie to a T.'

'You're not suggesting that he and Belle . . . I mean, Belle's smart . . . quite good-looking.'

'If you like stick insects.'

'And he . . . he's *awful*, David. I can't believe . . .'

'Reggie is Belle's *amour*, I'm telling you,' David assured her. 'Anyway, appearances can be deceptive. Underneath that unprepossessing exterior there might lurk a sensitive soul, aflame with poetry and passion.'

'And I might be the Queen of Sheba.' She sighed. 'O.K. then, David. If you insist. The Jacksons. The Richleys. Belle and her "amour". That will make eight of us.'

'And Merry. And Bridget.'

'They can have fish and chips in the kitchen. You check with Tom, will you, and I'll ring the others. It might be fun.' She pulled a face. 'I suppose.'

'Of course it will be fun.' He pulled her down on to the bench beside him and gave her a hug. 'And I'll help with the cooking. Promise.'

'Just one thing, though,' she warned him. 'I really don't

want to have to think about all this till I've been down to see William. Please. He's my top priority at the moment.'

CHAPTER EIGHT

Neatly, Sarah slid the car along beside the kerb outside number ten, Treacle Street, then switched off the engine with a sigh of relief. She thought, for perhaps the hundredth time, that Norwich was a *very* long way from Northumberland. In more ways than one. Already her life in this beautiful city that she knew so well, loved so much, was receding into memory. Peacocks' Acre, her new friends in Deredale, her neighbours – these were her real life now. She began to gather her things together, keys, overnight bag, the *Guardian*, and looked through the side window at Pam's house which sat drowsing in the late afternoon sunshine. It was a good little house, she decided. Pam had been lucky to find it after she and Jake split up. Red-brick, mid-terraced, well-built and solid. And its position, sandwiched between the inner-ring road and the outer one and just a stone's throw away from the Roman Catholic cathedral, meant that the city centre was easily accessible and so was the lovely countryside and pale, stretching coastline of north Norfolk. The best of both worlds. The only problem was that it had been built long before individual garages and drives were considered necessary, so parking was a perennial nightmare. Sarah glanced along the street smugly. She really had managed to nab the last space. It must be her lucky day.

Pam Peters answered the doorbell almost instantly, her round, pleasant face worried, her black hair a rumpled mess. 'God!' she said. 'You're here already! How awful!'

Sarah grinned, stepped through the doorway that gave straight on to the front room and kissed her friend's flushed cheek. 'What a welcome,' she said. 'Have you been practising?'

Pam shook her head in dismay. 'I had no idea of the time. I was going to be all ready. Flowers on the table, kettle boiling, all that stuff.'

'Where's William?' Sarah asked her, peering along into the kitchen, then up the stairs.

'He's not back yet. He and Zack went into town hours ago. Some new CD they wanted. But once they vanish off there's no knowing *when* they'll turn up. Sorry, Sarah, I did remind him. I think.'

'Never mind. I'm sure he won't be long.'

Pam picked up Sarah's bag. 'Come on up. I'll show you where you're sleeping, then I'll get us a drink. The boys are going to bunk up together so you can have the spare bedroom.'

Sarah unpacked her smart suit and shoes, laid her nightdress on the bed, had a quick wash, then joined Pam downstairs. Gratefully she took the brandy and ginger she was handed and sank down on to the sofa. 'Wonderful!' she said. 'I've been looking forward to this since round about Scotch Corner.'

Pam shooed away the marmalade cat that was trying to establish itself on Sarah's lap. 'Get down, Jake. Sarah doesn't love you the way I do.'

'What! You've called the cat after Jake?'

'He was a stray who wandered in.' Pam grinned maliciously. 'I really enjoyed taking him to the vet to have his balls snipped off.'

Sarah gave a shocked giggle. 'You get worse.'

'Don't worry. It's all talk. I still love the bastard, you know.'

'He doesn't deserve it.'

'No. Well . . . let's change the subject, shall we? You didn't think of coming by train?'

'You should see the boot of the car. I've brought him masses of stuff. Including the proverbial fruit cake. And I'll have to take him shopping tomorrow, too. Shoes and sports gear, all that stuff.'

'Tell me about it. They cost a fortune at this age, don't they?'

Sarah grimaced. 'Thank God for plastic! We're spending a bomb on the house.' Her eyes searched Pam's face. 'How is he feeling, Pam? About being left here, and having to board, I mean?'

'Fine, as far as I can tell.' Pam shrugged. 'You know Will. He smiles and is lovely, but he doesn't give much away. Not to me anyway. He might open up to Zack a bit more, I suppose.'

'They do get on well, don't they?' Sarah sipped her drink reflectively. 'Since their very first day at school.'

'Don't *remind* me. So embarrassing.'

'Yes. The pair of us snivelling into our hankies and Will and Zack, blithe as butterflies, toddling away with their teacher. Never even a backward glance.'

Pam nodded. 'Sarah, I'd love to keep him here, you know. But it's difficult, only having the one spare room.'

'I know. I wouldn't dream of it anyway. It wouldn't be fair on you, when visitors come . . .'

'Oh, blow visitors. No, it's Matty, really. She doesn't *often* come home – doesn't even think of it as home – but when she does I want her to feel her own room is there for her.'

Sarah sensed the sadness Pam was feeling. Her daughter Matty was nineteen now. She'd been sixteen when her parents divorced and she'd found it hard to forgive them. 'I suppose she's having to work pretty hard,' she suggested, trying to be a comfort.

'She is. She's just landed a job at the BBC. "Daddy" used his influence! But she always has time to visit *them*, you see. Jake and his precious Ellen.' Pam's face clenched with bitterness. 'Zack says Matty and Ellen get on really well together. They would, of course, wouldn't they? Being practically of an age!'

'So, tell me about Zack,' Sarah said, steering the conversation into safer waters. 'Merry sends him her love, by the way!'

'Just wait. You won't believe your eyes. Hair in a pony tail.

Single gold ear-ring. Designer stubble ... The works. You should see him and Will in the evenings, getting into their gear to go out clubbing.'

Sarah groaned. 'We must be getting old, when our own sons are such sexy hunks that you could *eat* them.'

Pamela gave a guffaw of laughter. 'Oh, Sarah, I do miss you. Why did David have to drag you off to Northumberland of all places? I need you *here*. To keep me sane. And cheerful.'

'Mm. It's terrible, isn't it, the way "the breadwinner" decides to change his job, and the whole family has to be uprooted. And then ... things are never the same again, are they? Not really. We all begin to turn into different people somehow. As if we've left a bit of ourselves behind in the place we used to be.'

Pam looked at her thoughtfully. 'Then you start to add on new bits, do you? In the next place?'

'Yes, in a way.'

'Sounds uncomfortable.'

'It is. Sometimes I feel really happy up there, you know. Peacocks' Acre is just wonderful. Grey and Georgian and perfect. I've brought some photographs to show you.'

'I'm longing to see what it looks like.'

'I'll fetch them down after supper. When Will's here. And – I've made one very good friend. Claire.'

'I'm pleased for you.' Pam tried to sound enthusiastic but her tone was wistful. 'Perhaps I'll get to meet her some time.'

'I hope so. She's been great. But sometimes it hurts so much, missing Will, and the old house, and you, and all the things we did ... I could curl up and die of it.'

Pam leaned over and patted Sarah's shoulder. 'It'll get better,' she told her gently. 'Give it time.' Then her voice changed, became bright and jokey. 'At least, since you went, I've managed to get some work done. No distractions. I've been ger-lued to that machine of mine, I kid you not. A model of self-discipline and determination.'

'Gosh! Doesn't sound like you at all!' Sarah turned to examine the far end of the living room, which served as Pam's office. A built-in desk-top ran from one wall to the other, and on it were ranged a computer, a printer and a sophisticated fax machine. Beneath there were drawers, and shelves stacked with files and boxes. A black swivel chair was pulled up, facing the screen. 'You're certainly looking very professional,' she said.

'I've up-dated my technology,' Pam told her proudly. 'I can offer a first rate secretarial package now.' She crossed the room and picked up a fat manilla folder, dog-eared and stained with coffee. 'I'm working on a novel. One hundred thousand words.'

'A hundred thousand!' Sarah was impressed.

'Most of them garbage,' Pam said. 'Poor cow can't write for toffee. A sex scene on every other page and it's my belief she's never even *done* it.'

'Pam!'

'It's true. I've tried one or two of the positions myself – strictly in the name of research, of course – and I reckon that unless you're double-jointed, or have had one or two sticky-out bits cut off, they are impossible.'

Sarah laughed out loud. 'Have you told her? The novelist, I mean?'

'Oh, no. I just take the money, honey, and hot-foot it to the bank.'

'Hi! Mum! When did you get here?'

Sarah's heart sang as she heard William's voice behind her. She swung round to look at him, then jumped to her feet and gave a breathless laugh as he hugged her almost hard enough to crack her ribs. He seemed huge, filling the small room with his energy. Sun-burned. Glowing with health. 'Will!' Her voice was shaky. 'You look marvellous. Really well.'

'I should do. Out of doors every day. And we've had a good summer down here.'

'So have we. Up there! But we've missed you so *much*. Merry's been desperate. We're longing to take you round the place. Show you off. Introduce you to Claire. And Bridget.'

'Half-term, Mum. It'll all happen then.'

'Hello, Sarah.' Zack hovered politely in the background. He was as dark as Will was fair, as small, slender and neat-boned as Will was broad and muscular. He seemed older, too, his eyes shrewd and amused, his face with a knowing look about it, as if, already, he saw through the polite veneer that people adopted in company and understood exactly what was going on under the surface. Sarah felt strangely uncomfortable. What had happened to Zack, she wondered, remembering the chubby little boy he used to be, laughing in the paddling pool, weeping over a burst birthday balloon. Where had this . . . wariness come from? He was only seventeen. Then he stepped forward to greet her, reached out to shake hands, thought better of it and kissed her awkwardly so that their noses bumped. And as he blushed and laughed, the cynicism she'd imagined slipped away from him and he was the same old Zack again, cheerful and cheeky, full of chat and swagger.

Sarah sat on William's narrow bed in the double study he'd been allocated and felt herself shaking with dismay. 'But we were promised you'd have a room to yourself,' she said. 'We were led to believe that all the rooms at the Grange were single studies.'

The Grange was a large Victorian villa, the garden of which bordered the school's playing fields. It belonged to an elderly couple, Mr and Mrs Clifford. Mr Clifford had once been Head of Classics but had long since retired from teaching. He and his wife were childless and their house had more rooms than they knew what to do with. Consequently it had seemed a good idea that they should allow the school to rent some of them, when they were needed, as a useful way of augmenting their pension. Despite the fact that the Grange was large and rambling, the students' bedrooms, all of them situated on the second floor, were surprisingly poky. 'Servants' quarters in the "good old days",' Sarah thought bitterly. 'Obviously the working classes didn't need sunshine and space the way their masters did.'

The Cliffords had furnished the rooms on a shoe string, picking up bargains at back street sales and auctions. Sarah looked grimly at Will's shoddy chest of drawers with its shiny yellow coat of varnish, the uncomfortable wooden chair, the unwieldy wardrobe that jutted across the edge of the windows, shutting out even more precious light. But it wasn't just the mean ugliness and discomfort of the room that was distressing her. It was the fact that an extra, unexpected, bed had been shoved in. William had had a room to himself all his life. And now, with exams hovering over him, he needed privacy and solitude more than ever.

'I really don't believe this,' she exploded. 'There must be some mistake.'

William hadn't said a word so far, not since Mrs Clifford had ushered them into the room with a grand gesture as if she were offering them a suite at the Savoy. Head on one side, eyes screwed up to decipher the handwriting, he was busily examining the label on the suitcase that had been dumped on the bed beneath the window. Suddenly he shouted, 'Charles Denvers! Mum, it's Denvers!'

'I don't think I know . . .'

'But he's horrible. He's a slob. A fat slob! I can't stand . . .' He closed his eyes in despair. 'God. I can't be cooped up in this hole with Charlie Denvers! I just can't!'

'I'm going to see Mr Trent,' Sarah said firmly. 'This is quite ridiculous.'

'What's the point?' Will frowned. His face was ashen, his eyes dull. 'Once they've decided, you can never budge them.'

Looking at him, Sarah felt desolate. The radiant boy of two days ago, so full of strength and vitality, had vanished. Will seemed to have shrunk. 'We'll see about that,' she said. 'I'll tell them we want something better. Even if we have to pay twice as much. It'll be worth every penny.'

'You promised us a single room,' she insisted, when at last she was admitted to Mr Trent's study, having been kept waiting in the corridor until he was 'available'. 'That's what we were shown when we came to see you in the spring. Will can't be expected to share.'

The deputy headmaster was not sympathetic. 'As you know, Mrs Page, the Grange is purely overflow accommodation. We have half a dozen rooms there at our disposal, that is all. Emergency boarding for boys whose parents suddenly have to move or go abroad or find themselves in . . . unexpected domestic difficulties. If it wasn't for the generosity of Mr and Mrs Clifford, allowing us to use their home, we could not have helped you out when you asked us to keep William. The fact is, we were doing you a favour.'

Sarah was outraged. 'A favour! You know very well that Will is just about the star pupil in your sixth form. When he goes to Cambridge it will reflect very well . . .'

'If. *If* he goes to Cambridge.' Mr Trent shook his bloodhound jowls at her. 'Let us not count our chickens, Mrs Page.'

'I know what my son is capable of,' Sarah told him with dignity. 'Even if you don't. Anyway, that's not what it's about. You promised us a single study.'

'I made no promises. I said we would see what we could do. In the event two RAF families have had to leave the country and Alan Jones's mother is ill and needs long-term hospitalisation. All these extra boys need to be accommodated. We have had to double them up. I'm afraid there are no single rooms, for William or anyone else.'

'But this is going to be his home. For a whole year.'

'I really think you are making too much of this.' Mr Trent smiled icily, pressing his lips together in a tight line. 'It is purely for sleeping, you know. He has the rest of the school as his home. Common room, library, cafeteria. It's not so very dreadful, now, is it?'

Sarah struggled, desperately aware that she was losing her battle. 'Could Will not at least share with someone else? He and Denvers don't hit it off together. It's a very small space for two boys who are not . . . not on the same wavelength, to put it mildly. I'm sorry if I seem to be making a fuss, but I want Will to be happy here.'

'Oh come now, Mrs Page!' Sarah writhed at the patronising tone of his voice. 'What do you think school is all about, mm? Rubbing along with other people, that's what. Learning a bit of give and take. Preparing to take one's place in society. That's real education, isn't it? Not just swotting for exams.'

She looked at him coldly. She hated his rigid, smug superiority. All she wanted was to tell him there and then that she was removing William from his rotten school and the Cliffords' rotten garret and taking him home with her to Peacocks' Acre, where he belonged. For a moment the possibility flitted through her mind as a real solution. William could go to Craiglands. David would be able to fix it. And he was so bright, he'd catch up with his exam work wherever he was, even if he had to take an extra year. She stared at Mr Trent, the words trembling on her lips. 'I am withdrawing my son from your establishment.' That's how she'd phrase it, very formal and dignified. But even as she opened her mouth to speak she imagined David's reaction. 'You've done *what*?' he'd say. 'You've always fussed too much over William, but this time you've gone too far.' That's what David would say, she'd heard it all before. She realised that Mr Trent was gazing at her, wondering why she was still there, taking up his time, keeping him from more important duties. She cleared her throat. 'So what you are telling me is that you categorically refuse to do anything at all?'

'As matters stand it is quite impossible. All the beds are allocated and we decided on who should share with whom quite deliberately. William is an amiable, well-behaved boy. We believe he may be a good influence on Denvers. Steady him down a bit.'

'Yes, but . . .'

'And who knows? Denvers is a jolly, extrovert sort of chap. He may have something to teach William. We can all learn from our fellows. Let matters be, Mrs Page, that is my advice to you. These things tend to sort themselves out, you know. And now, if you'll excuse me. I don't wish to appear rude but there are other parents waiting, I believe.'

As Sarah let herself into Will's room again, he raised his eyes quickly. Her heart sank. She could see from the look on his face that, despite what he'd said, he'd been hoping against hope that she'd manage to persuade Mr Trent to change things. She shook her head grimly and sat down on the bed beside him. 'I'm sorry. He insists that it's impossible.'

William turned away from her and stared moodily at the blank wall. 'O.K.' he muttered. 'It's all right. I'll cope.'

'William, I don't know...' To her horror, he suddenly covered his face with his hands and his shoulders convulsed. He was crying. This six-foot giant of a boy, overwhelmed by a storm of weeping. 'Darling!' She put her arm round him. 'Oh, please... Denvers might come back soon. You don't want him to see...'

His head jerked up and he glared at her, blinking fiercely. 'No, of course not. Must put a brave face on things, mustn't we?' He got up, walked across to the hideous cupboard and kicked it viciously. 'Just one year. Why couldn't Dad have waited one lousy year before he did this? It's not much to ask.'

'You know very well the job just came up. We didn't plan it.'

'Why not? What's wrong with a bit of planning? Why couldn't you have *planned* to stay in Norwich for one more year? Then I'd have been off to Cambridge and Merry would have just been beginning sixth form. It would have been perfect. One more year, that's all we needed.'

'It was a wonderful career opportunity for your father,' Sarah said. 'He couldn't turn his back on it.'

'Couldn't he!' William shook his head, looking dismally round the room. 'This is not fair, Mum. It really isn't.'

Driving back to Treacle Street without him, feeling helpless and defeated and more alone than she'd ever done in her whole life, William's words reverberated through her brain. It was what Merry said too, and they were right. It wasn't fair. What was David doing to them, to *all* of them, for the sake of his wonderful career? Beavering away towards an eventual headship. Deep within her she knew that their family life would never be the same again. That part of William was lost to her forever.

Pam was appalled when she opened the door to welcome her back. 'Whatever is it?' she asked, scrutinising Sarah's white face. 'What's happened, for God's sake?'

Sarah shook her head, hardly able to speak. 'He was in *tears*, Pam. I can't bear it. He's having to share, and it's an ugly, cramped little room, with no light . . .'

'They're making him share! Who with?'

'A boy called Charles Denvers. Will doesn't seem to . . .'

'Not Charlie Denvers! Oh Sarah! Zack's told me about him. He says he's an absolute shit. They all loathe him.'

The two women looked at each other in despair, then Pam said firmly, 'You'll have to insist on having Will moved.'

'I tried. Believe me. But you know Mr Trent. "Absolutely impossible, dear lady." He enjoyed putting me down, Pam. He really did. I bet it would have been different if David had come.'

'So what are you going to do?'

'What *can* I do? I did think I'd just call the whole thing off and take him home with me.'

'Why don't you?' Pam's face creased into a relieved smile. 'He *should* be with his family. He's always been a bit of a home bird, hasn't he? I don't think he's really ready to spread his wings yet.'

'I wish I dared. But David would go spare, wouldn't he? He's always accusing me of babying William. Spoiling him. He'd be furious.'

'Bugger David. He's just plain jealous of his lovely son, that's all.'

But Sarah's eyes were blank. 'Don't you see, if I forced the issue it would be impossible? If he thought I was taking Will's side against him, he'd make life . . . well, it wouldn't be happy families exactly.'

'O.K.' Pam's mouth snapped shut. 'Just give me five

minutes.' She hurried across to her work bench.

'What are you going to do?'

'I'm going to switch off my PC, switch on my answerphone and scribble a quick note to Zack. He's got his key. Then you are going to drive me back to the Grange and we're going to do a snatch and bring William back here. Bingo!'

'You can't do that. It's very kind of you but . . .'

'I can do that. And I will. He's going to come and stay with us. I know it's not the same as being at home but it's the next best thing.'

'Pam. We've been into all this. You need the room for Matty.'

Pam shook her head. 'Phooey to Matty. If she ever bothers herself to visit us, then Will can easily move in with Zack for a few days. But let's face it, I'm not really expecting to see much of her.'

'But when she *does* come, won't she feel that Will's put her nose out of joint?'

'So what?' Pam smiled wryly. 'They say blood's thicker than water but it's not true, you know. It'll give me a real kick to see Will happily settled under my roof. I mean it. Matty brings me nothing but bitterness.'

Sarah spread her hands helplessly. 'I don't know what to say.'

'Don't say anything, honeybunch.' Pam grinned. 'Save it for old Trent. I can't *wait* to see the bastard's face when you tell him exactly where he can put his precious "double study". And Denvers too.'

CHAPTER NINE

Sarah murmured her excuses, slipped off to the loo, sat down glumly on the lavatory seat and read her wall. All life was there. Lovely views. Reproductions of great art. Even the odd piece of poetry and prose. The Nun's Prayer. 'How Do I Love Thee?' Henry Scott Holland's 'Death Is Nothing At All'. Entertainment to fill the shining hour. Words jumped out at her – 'I'm just a teeny weeny bit pissed off', and a little cartoon man glared balefully, the noose ready around his neck.

'And I am too!' Sarah thought. 'We should never have had this wretched dinner party. I did tell David. It's a recipe for disaster. People we hardly know. People we don't even want to know! I wish they would just go home.' She looked at her watch desperately. 'Nine o'clock and we *still* haven't eaten.' She flushed the cistern, washed her hands, combed her hair, scrutinised her face with disapproval, then went back to try to get her guests organised. 'Right,' she said brightly. 'The lamb is almost ready, I think. We can make a start on our first course, anyway.'

Obediently they all got to their feet and followed her into the dining room. Sarah stood at the end of the table, waving her arms around as if she were a traffic policeman. 'Claire, would you like to sit here, next to David's place? Belle straight opposite, on his other side. Wanda, beside me, perhaps. Would that be a good idea?'

She gazed admiringly at Wanda. She was barely more than a girl, tiny, with pretty hands and feet. Her honey-coloured hair was piled up on the top of her head in a loose knot from which little tendrils escaped, floating down and framing her face. She was wearing a simple shift dress, cunningly tie-dyed in shades of sea-green and water-blue, and she had slender gold-strapped sandals on her bare feet. She was like a china doll, Sarah thought, vulnerable and delicate. She found herself wanting to look after her, to mother her. What she did *not* want was to feel completely inadequate because she couldn't even manage to get a meal on the table at a civilised hour. Wanda crossed the room to join her, and the women took their seats, smiling at each other, exclaiming, admiring everything.

Belle bent forward and touched the little posy of daisies and white rose-buds in their cut glass vase. 'So perfect I thought they must be artificial,' she murmured.

Laurie pulled a cigarette lighter from his pocket and waved it towards the tall ivory candles. 'Shall I?' he said, his eyes upon Sarah, asking for permission.

'Oh!' She felt herself blushing. Why should the wretched man make her *blush*, she wondered. Claire's husband was perfectly ordinary really, when you met him face to face. He wasn't as tall as David. His hair was much greyer, and there was less of it too. He didn't seem as striking as he had done in his photograph. Not as alarming either. Yet every time he looked at her with those strange, steel-grey, mocking eyes – which she still sensed, somehow, that she recognised – she began to blush. It was ridiculous. She hated feeling so gauche. She was, after all, a mature woman, almost middle-aged, not a tongue-tied teenager. 'David usually lights the candles,' she said, and realised at once how stupid it sounded. Slightly disconcerted, Laurie withdrew his hand and took a step backwards. 'But *do*, please,' Sarah urged him. 'That would be very kind of you.'

She looked around anxiously. David had vanished off into the kitchen, for some reason, just when she most needed him to help her get people seated. Chatting up the girls, no doubt. Pinching Merry's chips. The other men were still hovering round the table, wondering what was expected of them.

'Right!' said Tom heartily. 'I'll take this chair, shall I?' And he sat down between Wanda and Belle.

Belle tapped him on the arm. 'Not there. You can't sit beside your own wife.'

'Can't he?' Laurie gave a snort of laughter.

'Well, where can I sit then?' Confused, Tom struggled to his feet again and began to amble round the table.

'Just sit wherever you want,' insisted Sarah. 'All of you. Please. It really doesn't matter.'

And then she could have bitten her tongue off as Reggie poured himself into the chair next to hers and sat there in a glassy-eyed stupor. He was greatly the worse for wear, she realised, regretting the double whisky David had pressed upon him the minute he'd stepped over the threshold. Suddenly she was aware of yet another focus for concern at the other side of the table. Wanda had swung round in her chair and was looking Belle full in the face.

'Did I hear you right?' Her voice was light, high-pitched like a child's.

'What do you mean?' Belle looked alarmed.

'You said I was Tom's wife. For goodness sake, I'm not *married* to him.' She turned her attention to Tom. 'You haven't been telling them we're married, have you?' Her baby-blue eyes shone dangerously.

'Of course I haven't.'

'I'm sorry,' Belle began, 'I thought Sarah said . . .'

'Oh dear, my mistake,' Sarah apologised. She fixed her gaze on David as he came strolling in from the kitchen and casually took his usual place at the top of the table. 'The way David spoke about the pair of you, I just took it for granted, I suppose. I'm sorry, Wanda. It doesn't matter to me. I mean, I don't care whether you're married or not.'

'Don't you? Well, that's all right then!' said Wanda, with heavy sarcasm.

Laurie, who had finally settled himself in the seat vacated by Tom, looked at her with interest. 'So, what *is* Tom then?' he asked, obviously enjoying himself. 'It's one of the burning questions of the day, isn't it? What do you call him? Is he your Significant Other?' He glanced round the table, laughing, inviting suggestions.

'Your Other Half, perhaps?' David chipped in.

'Or your Luvveur,' said Belle, drawling out the word seductively, wagging her finger at Reggie as he gave her a drunken leer.

'I'll drink to that one,' Reggie said, downing half a glass of wine in one swallow.

'I'm just her partner,' Tom snapped, irritated by the lascivious note that had crept into the conversation.

Sarah could see that Wanda was angry, too. She gave a silent groan. And it was entirely her fault. They'd all had too much to drink before the meal. Red wine always made people aggressive, especially on an empty stomach. She still hadn't got the measure of the Rayburn, and this was the first time she'd attempted a large roast. She should have gone for something safer – a good hearty casserole, perhaps, but everyone said that was terribly old hat nowadays. Suddenly she realised that Wanda was talking to *her* now, leaning her elbows on the table and addressing her comments to her alone.

'What is it with you, Sarah?' Wanda asked, her little-girl voice belying the full frontal harshness of her attack. 'This is 1990, for God's sake. Why do you think that everybody should get spliced?'

'What? Me? I don't think I do.'

Tom groaned. 'Wanda. Please! Don't start.'

'Don't interfere, Tom.' She never took her eyes off Sarah's face. 'I just don't understand it. You're still quite young. I mean, you don't exactly look like a dinosaur.' She gave a breathless little laugh. 'And you're bright, aren't you? Educated. Yet all you are is "a married woman". Tom's told me. It's people like you who put back the cause a hundred years.'

'A bloody feminist!' croaked Reggie, his eyes rolling, his face as red as a turkey-cock. 'I knew she was. I can smell 'em.'

'Reggie!' Belle said in a warning voice.

'Bloody man-hating feminist. Can't stand 'em. What she needs is a good seeing to. I'd do it myself if . . .'

'*Reggie!*' Before Sarah could work out what was going on Belle was out of her seat and moving. She stalked round the table on her stiletto heels, levered Reggie from his seat and began to propel him out of the room. 'Ignore us,' she said over her shoulder, and they heard her calling into the kitchen. 'Bridget. Merry. Give me a hand will you? I'm just taking Reg next door.'

For a moment the table was as quiet as the grave. Tom stared furiously across the table at Wanda, who crumbled her bread roll and moodily examined the Elizabeth Blackadder watercolour on the wall.

'Do you like it?' Claire asked her. 'I think it's beautiful.'

All of them gazed at the picture. Purple irises, in a transparent glass vase, set against a window. Sarah had used an unexpected legacy to buy it. It was her most treasured possession.

Wanda shrugged. She seemed doubtful. 'Do you know about art?' she asked Claire.

Laurie laughed. 'She should do. Her whole *life* is art.'

Claire shook her head at him, then tried to answer Wanda's question. 'I do think she paints flowers magnificently. Captures the essence of them. I suppose it's because she's a gardener as well as an artist.'

Sarah nodded, her eyes alight. 'Yes. She understands irises, doesn't she? As if she can imagine them from the inside, almost.'

Wanda ignored her, concentrating on Claire. 'Do you paint, then?'

'I'm a sculptor.'

'Are you any good?'

'Just about the best in Northumberland,' Laurie said.

Wanda dimpled at him prettily. 'But that's not saying much, is it? Best in Northumberland.' She gave an artless laugh.

Laurie's eyes narrowed, the lids drooped dangerously. Watching him, Sarah trembled. 'What do you do, Wanda?' he purred. 'What is your life's work?'

'Me? I'm a demonstrator.'

'Demonstrating what?'

'All sorts of things.' She shrugged her slender shoulders. 'Icecream-makers. Carpet-shampooers. I'm promoting a brilliant new microwave just now, at Bainbridges, and . . .'

'Really!' said Laurie. 'How very interesting.' The tone of his voice made it perfectly clear that he could think of nothing less interesting in the entire world. He turned from her and smiled at Sarah. 'Let me help you clear away the avocados,' he suggested. 'They were delicious, by the way. Especially like this, with your own vinaigrette.'

In the kitchen, David, driven out by the sparring match, had already begun to carve the shoulder of lamb. The girls had returned from next door and taken themselves off to Merry's room. Sarah refused Laurie's offers of help and shooed him back into the dining room. Then she transferred vegetables from the steamer into heated dishes, and dotted them with herb butter.

Distracted from his own task by the way she was banging down pans and clattering spoons, David lifted his head and smiled at her reassuringly. 'Don't worry, darling. They're having a great time.'

'No they're not. How could they, with Wanda savaging them at every turn? Why didn't you warn me that she was a bitch? A Rottweiler?'

'She's not. She loves a good argument. Lots of people do, you know. She's enjoying herself.'

'Boadicea masquerading as Marilyn Monroe! She's appalling.'

'Don't be silly. You're just a bit worked up. You haven't been yourself since you got back from Norwich. All that driving . . .'

'I am myself. They're all being horrible, apart from Claire. Laurie's been deliberately needling Wanda, right from the beginning.'

David laughed. 'I think he fancies her.'

'Now you're just being ridiculous.' She felt extraordinarily angry. She marched away, carrying carrots, courgettes, peas, and placed them all on the hot tray beside the gravy and potatoes. Then she turned round and gazed at her guests with a radiant smile. 'David's just bringing in the joint,' she told them. 'I'm sorry we've kept you waiting, but it looks absolutely delicious.'

An hour later they had munched their way through the meat course, followed by *petits pots de chocolat*, fresh peaches and an excellent Stilton, and the time had come to collapse comfortably in the drawing room with their coffee. 'A feast!' Tom had declared it. 'A veritable feast. I wish my Wanda could cook.' Belle, having put Reggie to bed on her sofa, had managed to effect a smooth return to the party with nothing but a muttered 'Sorry about that' to disturb the tenor of the conversation, which had now veered to the less dangerous waters of sailing and the RSC's visit to the Theatre Royal at Newcastle.

As midnight struck, Laurie looked at the clock and sat up. 'Time to make a move, I think.'

'Don't go yet,' said David. 'Another half hour won't hurt. I have a very fine Calvados you must try.'

The liqueur tasted like nectar in Sarah's mouth. She felt it trickle down her throat, strong and smooth, reminding her of their visit to Normandy last year when Will had just done so brilliantly in his exams. She smiled at the sunny memories that flooded back, then felt brief tears prick behind her eyes. She stretched, relaxed, began to think that the evening hadn't been a total fiasco after all. That perhaps these people *were* her friends. Wanda was talking to David, her face animated, her hands as busy as butterflies. She must have felt Sarah's gaze upon her because suddenly she looked across at her and smiled like an angel, her head tilted, questioning.

'Why do you disapprove of marriage, Wanda?' Sarah asked her.

'Sarah!' David sighed. 'Not again, please.'

'I just want to know, that's all.'

Wanda gave her question for question. 'Why have you got such a hang-up about it?'

'I always thought it was a good way to live,' Sarah said. 'I'd just like to know what *you* think.'

'I've never fancied the idea of one man giving me to another,' said Wanda.

Laurie nodded. 'But that doesn't happen in a civil ceremony.'

'No.' Wanda thought for a moment. 'I just don't think the whole ritual is necessary, that's all. What is it – this famous marriage contract? Just a bit of paper you can tear up after a year or two if you don't fancy it.'

'It's more than that,' Claire said. 'A commitment. A declared attempt to make it last.'

'But you can have that without filling in forms,' Wanda urged. 'Tom and I know that we love each other. Don't we, Tom? We'll try to stay together. Isn't that enough?'

'Maybe it is.' Sarah rolled the idea around in her head, trying it out, testing it. 'But what about the children? Isn't it better for them if their parents are married? Don't they feel more secure?'

'You have so many preconceptions, you see,' Wanda lisped. 'Why should marriage make people feel more secure? Have you seen the latest divorce statistics?'

Tom grunted. 'Almost one in three, I think. That must be horrible for the kids. We see it at school. It really knocks them back.'

Zack's face floated into Sarah's mind. Careful, watchful, a little suspicious. He'd never been like that before Jake walked out. And Matty too, keeping her distance, breaking Pam's heart.

'I don't know,' she said. 'You may be right. I always thought that children did better if their parents were married, for at least part of their lives.'

'I haven't decided yet whether I want a family.' Wanda pursed her lips. 'We have a great time in bed, don't we, Tom?'

She gave a suggestive laugh. 'He's very inventive, you know, my Tom. Athletic, you might say.' Tom squirmed in his seat, trying to avoid David's amused glance, but Wanda was oblivious. 'And, you see, kids could spoil that, couldn't they? Too many... disturbed nights. Too tired to perform properly...'

A small silence greeted her words. Sarah coughed, and took a large mouthful of Calvados.

'What a choice to have to make,' Belle said drily. 'Lucky old you!'

Wanda surged on in her innocent voice. 'If you really want to know what I think, Sarah, I imagine that children just need two parents who are nice to each other and who both love *them*. I shouldn't think they care about a silly old marriage certificate.'

Belle nodded, leaping to her feet, tucking her handbag under her arm. 'I'm off,' she said, kissing Sarah, reaching to hug David who had stood up to see her to the door. 'Please forgive poor Reggie. He'll be abject tomorrow.' She smiled at Wanda. 'I wish you well, my dear. But you'll never get anywhere with these two. Sarah and David have been happily married for ... how many years is it?'

'Nearly eighteen!' beamed David, putting his arm round Sarah's shoulders.

Laurie pushed himself up out of the armchair then reached out his right hand to tug Claire to her feet. 'Poof!' he said. 'Mere newly-weds. This is our silver wedding year. What about *that*?'

'Good grief!' exclaimed Wanda. 'You deserve long-service medals. All of you.'

Claire resisted the silken barb. 'You're sure it's O.K. for Bridget to stay over?' she asked Sarah.

'Of course. With luck they'll be all tucked up and fast asleep by now.'

Laurie raised his eyebrows. 'Fat chance. Just getting their second wind, more likely.' Then he looked serious. 'We haven't managed to talk about traffic, Sarah. Too many other exciting topics on the agenda.'

'Traffic?' David asked. 'What about traffic?'

'I'm hoping to enlist your wife on to my road safety committee.'

'Good idea!' David was delighted. 'She needs something to get her teeth into.'

'I'm sure she's just the person we've been looking for. See you soon then. Thanks for the splendid evening.'

The front door opened and they all spilled out on to the dark street, laughing, calling out their goodnights, exclaiming against the chill of the September night. Laurie's voice floated back as he hurried away. 'I'll be in touch, Sarah. Don't forget. I'm counting on you.'

CHAPTER TEN

My dear Will,

How *is* life with you? You sounded a bit *remote* on the phone
last time you rang, and I can't help worrying. I hope you are
feeling happier now that you have escaped the threat of the
dreaded Denvers. Things are very quiet here. Dad and Merry
have both left for school by eight in the morning and don't get
home until four-thirty at the earliest, so I have lots of time on
my hands. And my friend, Claire, is working very hard just
now so I don't like to distract her. I'm busy with the house, of
course. I want it to be transformed by the time you see it again
– it looked such a mess the day we moved in, didn't it? All that
rain, and mud everywhere.

So – what's been happening up here? We've had our first
dinner party! Dad's idea, would you believe? It seems quite
funny in retrospect, I suppose, but while it was happening it
was the dinner party from hell! We all got rather drunk, and
argued the whole evening about the rights and wrongs of
marriage, and love, and parenting . . . all that stuff. I kept
thinking about you, and Zack, and wondering what the pair of
you would have said if you'd been here.

We all miss you. Write soon, please. A nice long letter would
be an absolute treat.

All love,
Mum

She walked to the post office to buy stamps. Autumn was
settling down round the village like a comfortable old coat.
Cottage chimneys had begun to send up spirals of fragrant
blue smoke. The colour of the distant hills changed daily,

almost imperceptibly, from haze-blue to earth-brown. David had ordered a load of logs and checked the level of the oil tank. Sarah spent her time gardening, and walking, and reading and felt that her own life was slowing down, too, adapting itself to the rhythms of the countryside. She felt placid, almost sluggish, as if she were preparing for hibernation. She still hadn't decided what to do with her long solitary hours. In Norwich she'd always been busy with her 'good causes'. David had been very keen on those.

'You see,' he'd told her, 'you're in a specially privileged position, darling. You have a lot to offer, and you don't need to be paid for it. I can earn enough to keep the family and you can put something back into society, from *both* of us. It's perfect.'

David, she thought, had always been an idealist, ever since he was a schoolboy. It was one of the things that she'd loved about him, and she'd been happy to go along with his master plan. She'd really enjoyed her days in the Oxfam shop, her letter-writing for Amnesty. But now, something held her back. She felt as if her life had reached a cross-roads. She wanted it to be different.

She wrote to Will twice a week, long, chatty letters that painted in detail the daily life of Deredale, little snippets that caught her eye in the *Bugle*, which she had begun to read avidly, photographs of Merry and David, the garden, the village. She wanted him to feel part of *everything*. Every morning she watched for the postman hopefully, longing for an envelope with Will's writing on it. When they came his letters were usually disappointing, brief and to the point. But his reply to her dinner party letter was quite electrifying.

Dear All,
No need to worry. Everything is O.K. The work is going quite well, but is sometimes a bit boring. 97% for French translation last week. Trent deigned to say I was 'acquitting myself reasonably well', pompous old fart. I'm getting on all right here. Pam

is a hoot. She says she doesn't know whether she's supposed to be a surrogate mum or a professional landlady, because you insist on paying her! In the end, of course, she's neither. Last week she completely forgot about supper and the only thing in the freezer was a giant packet of garden peas, so she sent Zack out to get some fish and chips to have *with* them. Then he went and bought us each a carton of *mushy* peas instead! Sometimes it's a laugh a minute. It's not like the old days though, when we were all at home together.

Love to everybody. Roll on half term.
Will.

P.S. Zack has been 'excluded from school'! What a joke! The staff didn't think much of his pony tail.

Wide-eyed, Sarah read it through again. Zack excluded from school! She couldn't believe it. She flew to the phone and dialled Pam's number.

'What's all this about Zack?' she asked her. 'You must be worried sick.'

Pam's throaty laugh came gurgling down the line. 'Oh that! All over now. It was just a little blip, really.'

'But what happened?'

'Stupid teachers! "We can not allow long hair in the classroom." As if it damaged the brain cells or something.'

'He's cut off his pony tail?'

'He certainly has.' Pam gave a snort of amusement. 'Now he's had a suede head, or whatever it's called. He's got the staff over a barrel. They said it mustn't be too long but there's no rule about it being too short. And the *Daily Press* has been having a field day. Before and after photographs, the lot. ZACK THE REBEL WINS THE DAY. I'll send you a copy, shall I? He went out and bought half a dozen.'

'Aren't you worried, though? It must have put a bit of a strain on pupil-teacher relationships.'

'Mm. Zack thinks they're a load of pillocks, and they're probably watching his every move. But we're on the last lap, Sarah. Come June and it'll all be over. Things will loosen up when they're at university, won't they?'

'I imagine so. Thanks again for looking after Will, Pam. You have no idea what a relief it is.'

'We love having him here. Both of us. By the way, did he tell you he's invited Zack up to your place for the half-term? I hope it's O.K.'

Sarah's heart sank. She didn't want anyone for the half-term except Will. They had so much catching up to do. She'd imagined lovely long walks and bicycle rides, just the family, complete and together again. Sitting on his bed and talking for hours in the mornings when she took him a cup of tea. Taking him to all the special places she'd found in the valley. Showing him off to Claire. No, she thought miserably. It really wasn't O.K. at all. Then she realised that Pam was still talking.

'It'll certainly be a load off my mind because I have a huge thesis to complete. All horrible tables and graphs and foot-notes. Horrendous. I'll really need a bit of peace and quiet to concentrate.'

'Of course, Pam. It'll be lovely,' Sarah assured her. 'It'll be great for Will to have a friend with him. After all, as far as he's concerned, they're all strangers round here.'

That night, David came home from the Eagle, bursting with enthusiasm. 'What do you think!' he exclaimed. 'I've been playing chess. With Laurie. It happens in the pub every Friday night apparently.'

'Just as well I didn't come, then.' Sarah smiled. Chess was a game she'd never got to grips with, despite David's attempts to initiate her. The trouble was, she didn't seem to have any competitive spirit. Besides which, she was convinced that games that demanded brain power were a contradiction in terms. 'As you know, I always preferred tiddlywinks.'

'Yes. I worry about you,' he said. 'But Laurie's a great bloke. We must see more of him and Claire. Get something organised, for the four of us.' She didn't answer, bending her head over the book she was reading. 'By the way, he sent you a message. There's a meeting of his committee at Dolphin House next Wednesday. Seven-thirty. I promised you'd be there.'

'Did you?' She lifted her head. 'I don't think I will. I'm not very keen.'

'Why ever not? You've been wondering what to do with yourself. This would be something really useful.'

'I'm just not terribly interested, that's all. I'll ring him up and apologise.'

But David refused to let it drop. 'Darling! You're always moaning about the traffic past the door. Saying that it spoils the house, and how dangerous it is. You're right, too. Did you know that Laurie's brother was run over on this very road when he was a little boy? That's why he's so obsessive about it. All these years and it's just got worse and worse, he says, and nobody *does* anything.'

'Laurie's little brother? Killed, you mean?'

'No. But seriously hurt. Permanently disabled. They're very close, it seems. Mark – that's his brother's name – he's a solicitor too. Laurie's partner.'

'Claire's never mentioned him. Anyway, David, I'm sure Laurie's got quite enough people to help without me.'

'But that's just where you're wrong. They're planning a huge campaign. They need as much help as they can get. Demonstrations. Letters to MPs and the media. Leafleting. Posters. Wholesale canvassing, you know. And they've really done their homework. They've drawn up all sorts of alternative traffic plans. A one-way system through the village. A ban on heavy vehicles. Traffic calming measures. There's even a vague hint of pressing for a possible by-pass . . . That would be marvellous.'

'Well, if you find it so interesting perhaps *you* should be on the committee,' she suggested tentatively.

'Don't be silly, Sarah. I have to work for my living. *Our* living. Don't I?'

She bridled. 'I'm sorry, but I'm *not* going to do it.'

'But why? I just don't understand you.'

She shook her head, laid her book on the arm of her chair, stood up and yawned. 'I think it's my bedtime,' she said, making her way slowly towards the door.

How *could* she explain? How could she tell her husband that his friend – who also happened to be the husband of *her* friend – came to her bed, in her dreams, and made love to her? The whole thing was ridiculous. She didn't even fancy Laurie. She'd never really fancied anyone except David. And then she'd been sixteen, seventeen perhaps . . . younger than Will. And yet, every night, Laurie visited her. Always in a different guise. Once he'd been Lawrence of Arabia and carried her away on a huge and mighty stallion. Once Lancelot, and she'd been his doomed Guinevere. Then there'd been Heathcliff and Catherine. Mellors and Lady Chatterley. Even JFK had paraded through her dreams, but whether she'd played the role of Jackie O. or Marilyn Monroe she couldn't remember.

And the places they'd been to! They'd come together gently on an emerald green forest floor, encircled in a rainbow. Beneath a waterfall, its thunder muffling the sounds of their ecstasy. And once in an express continental train as it rushed, whistling, through a long, dark tunnel.

So many different fantasies, but always those disturbing grey eyes had smiled at her, and always they'd made love. After the love, after the climax, she'd wake, tossing about in bed, unbearably excited, embarrassed by the moistness between her legs. Then, almost at once, she'd long to sleep again so that she could dream once more.

At first she'd felt guilty, lying by her husband's side, dreaming of making love to another man. But gradually the guilt had worn off. She enjoyed her dreams. They were fun. Sometimes, next day, she'd laugh out loud, remembering the things they'd done, the *Kama Sutra* gymnastics, the sheer, exultant, breathless imagination of it all. And there was an unexpected bonus. Her dreamtime activities had given extra zest to her relationship with David. After eighteen years and more they'd begun to seem rather too much like comfortable friends. Passion was at a premium. But now all that was changing.

'What's this?' he'd ask, grinning at her sleepily as she leaned over him in the middle of the night, running the tip of her tongue round the rim of his ear, slithering her hand down over his taut belly and waking him into desire. 'It must be this bracing Northumberland air! It's turning you into a proper little sex-pot.'

'Are you complaining?'

'I'm not complaining!'

So she'd stopped worrying about the fact that Laurence Richley had metamorphosed into her phantom lover. She was no Jungian. She couldn't understand her dreams, she couldn't prevent them, and they didn't seem to be doing anyone any harm. But of one thing she was quite sure. She didn't want to spend any more time in Laurie's solid, real-time presence than was absolutely necessary. She knew she could hardly bring herself to meet his eyes.

'I'm sorry, David,' she repeated, as she slowly climbed the stairs, calling down to him over her shoulder. 'I've absolutely made up my mind. Laurie's going to have to manage without me.'

CHAPTER ELEVEN

Sarah dipped her brush into the pot of paint and stroked it gently along the window sill. She wanted Will's room to be full of colour and light. She surveyed the apricot walls, the pale amber carpet, with satisfaction. He would love it, she knew. She bent to her work with redoubled concentration. The summer sun had stopped shining. Now that she had the house to herself again she had got back into the old swing of things, active and well-organised, the way she liked to be.

When the telephone rang she thought at first she'd ignore it, but it went on and on so insistently that at last she didn't dare.

'Sarah?' Laurie's voice was uncertain. 'I was just beginning to think you were out. Are you busy?'

Ludicrously, she felt herself blushing. 'I'm decorating,' she told him. 'My hands – oh dear, and the phone now – are a stunning shade of radiant coral. What can I do for you?'

'This is a bad time, then. It's just that Claire . . . perhaps I'm just making a fuss . . .'

'Claire? What is it, Laurie?'

'She seems to have picked up a bug. She's feeling absolutely rotten and I've had to tuck her up in bed and leave her. I was just wondering . . .'

'Don't worry. I'll go round straight away.'

'Thanks.' He sounded relieved. 'That would be very kind. There's a key under the watering can inside the back porch.'

Sarah knocked gently on Claire's bedroom door.

'Who is it?' Claire's voice was startled.

'Just me.' Sarah bustled into the bedroom, her arms full of bronze chrysanthemums. 'I've come to minister.'

Claire smiled wanly from her crumpled bed. 'How did you know?'

'Laurie rang.'

'Idiot!' Claire protested. 'I'm fine.'

But Sarah could see that her eyes were streaming and her skin was white, beaded with sweat. 'You don't look fine to me. You look poorly. I'll go downstairs and make you a drink and put these in water.'

'They're lovely. Thank you.'

'I'll just be a minute.'

Half an hour later, propped up against fresh pillows, with Sarah's hot lemon and aspirin brew soothing her throat and banishing her headache, Claire was beginning to look better and brighter. 'I think it's just a fluey thing, you know,' she told Sarah. 'And at least it's given us a chance to see each other again.'

Sarah nodded, aware that, almost unconsciously, she'd been avoiding Claire since she'd started dreaming about Laurie. 'I've hardly seen you since our ghastly dinner party.'

'It wasn't ghastly. Usually people just talk about the weather and their holidays.'

'I could have murdered Wanda.'

'Why? Laurie loves it when people get on their high horse like that. He thought she was hilarious.'

'But the things she said. She was so rude. To everybody. Except David, of course. She just flirted with David.'

Claire laughed. 'You can't be jealous. Not of an airhead like Wanda.'

'But she was so aggressive.'

'No.' Claire spluttered and groped for her handkerchief. 'Assertive. That's the word. I bet you anything, she's been on one of these assertiveness training courses. They all come out like that. "Look at me, aren't I wonderful?" '

'Well she's certainly *not*. Not in my book, anyway.'

Sarah stood up and walked across to the window. The

garden stretched away below her, its broad lawn scattered
with leaves now, michaelmas daisies glowing pink and mauve
in the herbaceous borders. Beneath the old walnut tree there
was a stone sculpture of a child, standing on tiptoe, head
thrown back, arms raised. 'Is the girl Bridget?' she asked.

'Yes. I did it just after her tenth birthday. Laurie was
showing her how to fly the kite we'd given her and she was
hopping up and down, trying to catch it even though it was
miles high. It seemed so much *her*, always reaching out for
something beyond.'

Sarah turned and saw Claire's face, radiant with memory.
For a brief moment she looked well again. 'How can Wanda
say she doesn't know whether she wants children?' she asked
her. 'Perhaps I *am* a dinosaur. I always expected to marry
David and have a family.' She frowned. 'The trouble is, that's
all I've done, you know. Nothing else.'

'Isn't that enough?'

Sarah shook her head fiercely. 'How old is Wanda? Twenty-
two? Twenty-three? I suppose I am *almost* old enough to be
her mother . . .'

'I certainly am!' Claire groaned.

'But she seems light years away from me. Another planet!
So – what's been going on out there since I had William? I
don't even seem to have noticed.'

'We all make our own choices.'

'Not really. David and I "had to get married", you know.
As we used to say in the Dark Ages.' She laughed. 'I can just
imagine what Wanda would make of that. But that's the way
it was. For us, anyway. I was going into publishing. I might
have been Carmen Callil by now. Then I got pregnant and
just . . . gave it all up and let David get on with *his* career
instead.'

'Do you regret it?' Claire asked, studying her face.

Sarah shrugged. 'I don't know. I hardly thought about it
until now. But now I find myself thinking about it all the
time.'

And the *other* thing she was thinking, though she kept it to herself because it would have seemed disloyal to discuss it with Claire, was . . . perhaps that was what David had wanted all along. For her to take second place.

In the August just after her twentieth birthday, Sarah and David went on holiday together. They pottered on their bikes around East Anglia, criss-crossing the area from Ipswich to King's Lynn, staying in Youth Hostels wherever they could or in cheap little B&Bs. Sarah felt absurdly, stupendously happy. They'd started planning it all the Christmas before, creeping away from suffocating family parties to pore over their collection of maps and books, working out estimates of miles to be covered daily, discussing alternative routes and detours and sights not to be missed. David was writing a paper on 'The Mediaeval Manor and the Sheep Trade' as part of his degree work, so their itinerary had to be planned to the last detail. Poring over pictures of lost villages and massive churches, stately halls and gardens and huge buttermilk beaches, Sarah had found it difficult to believe that it would ever really happen, that the long haul of her second year would come to an end and she'd have three months of glorious freedom to be with David again.

She was reading English at Durham University, working with obsessive determination. Her father had gained a starred First at Cambridge, had had a glossy career in the Civil Service, and expected her to do at least as well. She was his only child. 'A chip off the old block!' he used to tell his friends. 'She'll never be satisfied with less than the best.' And her mother would smile and nod her head with serene conviction.

Hundreds of miles away, David was studying History in London. He took his work seriously, but played football for the university with a passion that bordered on mania. 'It's important. It'll help me to get a good job when I start teaching,' he told Sarah, when she complained about the game eating into the few weekends they managed to be together.

Soon she'd resigned herself to long hours huddled at the edge of chilly football pitches, cheering herself hoarse with the rest of the team girlfriends as they sipped foul coffee out of chipped enamel mugs. But to have him all to herself again for the long lovely weeks of summer, with no work, no lectures or essays, and above all, no *football* . . . Sarah could think of nothing more wonderful.

By the time they reached Blythburgh, she could no longer remember the difference between a trochee and an iambus, the solutions to the Anglo-Saxon Riddles or how exactly her tutor could *prove conclusively* that Christopher Marlowe had written *Titus Andronicus*. By the time she got to North Elmham, she couldn't remember whether it was T. E. or D. H. Lawrence who spelt his surname with a W rather than a U, or whether they both did, or neither of them. And by the time she saw the sea, she couldn't care less. She was brown and strong, the blisters on her hands had healed, her calf muscles had stopped hurting. And she was fathoms deep in love.

Some days they left their bikes for a while, padlocked together in a church porch or the back yard of a pub, and went on foot instead.

'I've gone native!' Sarah exclaimed joyfully as they walked through the scented pine trees that fringed the spectacular sweep of Holkham Bay. 'I want to catch fish and cook them on the beach, dance naked on the sand and make mad, passionate love among the crashing waves.'

'Really!' David laughed, raising his eyebrows. 'Why don't we, then? Sounds all right to me.' No sooner had the words left his mouth than there was an enormous, ear-shattering crash of thunder. He roared with laughter. 'That's your father. Sounding out his wrath.'

She began to giggle helplessly, drunk with her own joy, twirling round and round until she was dizzy. David held out his arms to her. 'Oh, Sarah, come here. You're *incredible*.'

She stumbled and he grabbed hold of her, kissing her wildly, and as the first drops of rain began to plummet down from the livid sky, he pulled her with him on to the ground. The earth was hard beneath them, the pine needles prickly against their bare legs. They could hear the rain pattering above them but the canopy of branches was so thick that they remained perfectly dry. For a moment they clutched each other, their eyes turned upwards towards the darkness of the trees, their ears assaulted by the rumbling of thunder.

Sarah was entranced. 'Don't you *love* storms? They make me tremble inside.'

'Sarah!' His voice was urgent, his face tense. 'Let's make love here. Here, in the rain. It would be marvellous.'

She was frightened. 'No! Someone might come. We're not far from the path.'

'No one will come. They've all gone for shelter. Come on! Don't you want to?'

'Of course. But is it safe? I mean . . . have you got anything with you?'

'No.' He groaned. 'But I'll be careful. Promise. I won't . . .'

He fumbled inside her shorts, dragging at her pants, and weakly, at first, she pushed his hands away. But then it was too late because he was inside her, moving faster and faster. Her body opened out to him and she felt as if it were charged with electricity. She was quite unable to deny her own desire or fend him off with sensible words or precautions. At last he sank on top of her, letting his head droop beside hers.

She lay quite still, her heart pounding. 'You went all the way, didn't you?' she asked him at last. 'I can feel it.'

'I'm sorry. It happened too fast. I couldn't stop.'

'But you should have. You promised.'

He was silent. Clumsily he tried to cover her up, pulling her clothes about to make her look more decent.

'What am I going to do?' A cold clutch of fear grabbed at her. 'Tell me what I'm going to *do*?' she repeated, her voice rising.

'Sssh.' Gently he put his arm round her. 'Don't worry. It'll be all right. Just the once. And it was so quick. Just once is not much of a risk. Most people go for months, years even, before they get pregnant.'

She began to cry then, her mouth wide open, her eyes staring.

He dragged out his handkerchief and dabbed at her tears, smiling down at her as if she were a child. 'What a worrier you are. I'm telling you, it'll be all right. Everybody takes the odd chance.'

By the time the new term was due to begin, Sarah had just missed her second period, and she felt, though it might have been her imagination, that her breasts were a bit swollen. But there had not been as much as a glimmer of morning sickness. She tried to tell herself that it was all a false alarm, that the very fact of being so scared was making her irregular. Furtively she searched the medical section of the city library and found a book that reassured her that all sorts of factors other than pregnancy could disrupt the menstrual cycle – nervous stress, fatigue, diet, infection. There was even such a thing as a phantom pregnancy! She travelled up to Durham on the day before the academic year began, trying to convince herself that once the term had got under way everything would settle down again and her body would return to normal.

A week later she made an appointment to see the college doctor. He was elderly and bald, with watery blue eyes and a wart, prominent on his chin.

'I don't seem to be very well,' she told him. 'I'm having problems with my periods. I think I must have been working too hard or something. And I've had a bit of a tummy upset.'

'I see.' He rubbed the wart reflectively. 'I think we'd better examine you, all the same. Just hop up on the bed.' When he had finished he washed his hands with scrupulous care. His face was grave. 'When exactly was your last period?'

The blood drained away from her face. She was able to tell him the date exactly, without a second thought. She had looked it up in her diary a hundred times, hoping against hope that somehow she had got it wrong.

'And since then you have had unprotected sex?'

She nodded, dumb and frozen.

Again his fingers strayed to the wart. He sighed, scribbled on a bit of paper. 'By my reckoning, Miss Challis, your baby is due on about the twenty-eighth of May. I'm sorry. You're not going to be in great shape for your Finals.'

After supper, when she knew he'd be in his room studying, she telephoned David. She felt icy calm, completely in control of the situation. She was sorry, he'd have to miss his Saturday match, she told him. They must both go home to Norwich for the weekend, and break the news to their parents together. Then they would work out what they were going to do.

CHAPTER TWELVE

Proudly the little phalanx of musicians marched through the Gardens beneath the Castle, drums beating, pipes skirling, kilts swinging and polished black boots keeping perfect time as they moved steadily along beneath the massive face of Castle Rock. People stopped feeding the birds, reading their papers, hurrying along with their baskets and plastic carrier bags and gazed around them in surprise. Bands didn't usually march about the place in November, especially not here, through the Gardens. During the Festival, of course, it was quite a different matter. Nothing surprised them then – belly dancers on Calton Hill, hot air balloons descending over Salisbury Crags, white-faced clowns running through Jenners. But now it was almost winter and most of the tourists had gone home, thank goodness.

A gardener straightened his back, stuck his spade into a denuded rose bed, then mopped his brow with his handkerchief. He looked at the band and nodded sagely. 'Practice march!' he told a spry old lady. She was bending over trying to calm her Bedlington terrier who was jumping up and down on the end of his lead, yapping excitedly. 'They're off to tour Australia and New Zealand next week.'

'Be quiet, darling!' the old lady said to her dog. 'It's just a silly old practice march. They're off to the colonies soon.'

Sarah, sitting on a bench close by, heard Claire chuckle as she reached into her pocket for her notebook, and watched, smiling, as, with one or two deft lines, she captured the likeness of both the Bedlington and his autocratic owner. The eyes of the woman and the dog were identical, perfectly round and clear, like shiny brown buttons. Sarah was enjoying her day immensely.

At first she hadn't wanted to come. 'A complete day in Edinburgh,' David had said. 'Next Saturday. Just the four of us. We'll have an early breakfast and leave about six-thirty. Stop for supper on the way home. That way there'll be time to explore the whole city. Laurie knows it well.'

At once she had searched for excuses. 'But what about Merry?'

'That's all arranged,' he'd told her. 'Merry is going to team up with Bridget and a cousin of hers. Alison, I think.' His brow furrowed as he tried to remember. 'Yes, that's right! Alison. She's Mark's daughter apparently. Eighteen, and very grown up and sensible. They'll all stay at Dolphin House, get a take-away for supper and a couple of videos.'

'Are you sure?'

'Quite sure. Laurie says last time they went away Belle kept an eye on them – from a distance, you know. Rang up, and then dropped in during the evening for half an hour or so. Don't worry. Merry will be fine.'

'I really don't know, David.'

He'd looked at her with exasperation. 'Claire and Laurie are really nice people, darling. They want to be friends. I can't think why you're going on like this. You're turning into a proper little kill-joy.' She was silent, her eyes lowered. 'What is eating you? I know you were disappointed at half-term,' he continued, searching for an explanation. 'The way Will just vanished off with Zack all the time. But he's a young man now, Sarah. You can't expect him to want to hang around with Mum and Dad all the time.'

'I know that.'

'Anyway, there's no need to take it out on *me*. It wasn't my doing. It was what he wanted. We're going to have to get used to living our lives without him soon, aren't we? So why don't we go off for a day with the Richleys and enjoy ourselves?'

Now, thrilling to the heart-stirring sound of the bagpipes,

Sarah looked at David sitting quietly at one side of her, and Claire and Laurie, laughing over the sketch, at the other, and grinned. David had been right, as usual. She'd been afraid of Laurie. There was some sort of magnetism, or chemistry, that scared the life out of her. But here they all were, perched in a row like four sparrows on a barrow, and everything was fine.

'Right. Where to now?' asked Laurie, as the band strode away into the distance, leaving a feeling of anticlimax hanging over the Gardens like a grey mist. 'Any requests?'

No one spoke. They'd already puffed their way up all two hundred and eight-seven steps of the Scott Monument, browsed briefly in Princes Street, admired Charlotte Square, looked in at one or two little art galleries and had an early lunch in Rose Street in a wonderful old pub which was reputed to stock fifty different malt whiskies. Sarah felt she'd had more than a day's worth already.

'Time for the Old Town,' said Claire. 'Quick whizz around the Castle, then down to the Museum of Childhood. How about that?'

That was perfect, as far as Sarah was concerned. The Royal Mile intrigued and delighted her, with its quaint old wynds and courtyards and mediaeval houses. It was only later, when David had suggested that they should forget about the museum and have a stroll round Salisbury Crags, that she began to discover how tired she was. Trekking off at a tangent behind Holyrood House, they rapidly found themselves on a rugged hillside that seemed extraordinarily wild and untamed considering that it was only a stone's throw from the city. They struck out along a well-trodden, grassy path that led steeply upwards and then gradually petered out until it was nothing more than an uneven track.

'Come on!' David was delighted with it all. 'The view from that ridge must be sensational, right across the city to the Firth of Forth, if the light holds. But we haven't got much time.'

'No.' Claire looked up anxiously. 'It does get dark quite early, remember. Especially up here.'

'We can do it though, if we hurry.' He darted ahead. His hours spent running the length of a football pitch were standing him in good stead, Sarah thought. He looked as if he could run right to the top and back again without the slightest effort.

And it was just as he had said. After about quarter of an hour of stiff, uphill walking, they reached a vantage point where the view was superb. Edinburgh spread itself at their feet in all its ancient glory. Even as they watched though, lights began to go on here and there, one after another, pinpricks of gold shining out against the darkening sky.

'Better not hang around,' Laurie said. 'We've come quite a long way. It'll be no joke if we get stranded up here in the dark.'

David laughed. 'But we're quite safe. It's all so near.'

'I think we should move.' Laurie's voice was flinty. For the first time Sarah could imagine him on board one of his Pilgrim boats, keeping his crew up to the mark.

'O.K. O.K. You're the boss.' At once David began to lope away downhill, swift and sure-footed.

Claire followed him, her long legs striding in his wake, and with a brief glance back over his shoulder to make sure that Sarah was with them, Laurie fell in easily behind his wife. Sarah was at the end of the line as they made their way down the hillside in single file. With every footstep she found it more and more difficult to keep up. She hadn't known they'd be doing this sort of walking so she'd worn quite the wrong sort of shoes, little suede slip-ons that were wonderfully comfortable for city streets but kept threatening to slip *off* on the rough path. And she was so small, compared with the other three, that her short legs just could not cover the ground at their speed, no matter how hard she tried. She was almost running now, desperate to keep up, afraid of falling farther and farther behind in the gathering dusk, and her breathing was harsh and laboured.

'I'm just not fit,' she thought to herself. 'I must get more exercise.'

And then she caught her foot on a rock that jutted up under the surface of the track, lost her balance and went lurching forward, her arms flailing, sobbing and gasping for breath, convinced that she was going to tumble head first on to the ground and make a complete fool of herself. In the nick of time she managed to check the full thrust of her fall but sank to her knees, her heart pounding, hot tears starting to her eyes.

At once, alarmed, Laurie turned round to see what had happened. 'Are you all right, Sarah?' He peered at her through the gloom, then he stretched out towards her. 'Here,' he said in a low voice. 'Take my hand.'

And as their fingers touched Sarah felt as if she had had an electric shock. *That* boring old cliché! She couldn't believe it. But it was true. It had really happened. Like the charge of static that sometimes jumped at her from the handle of a shop door. She flinched, then searched Laurie's face to see if he had noticed.

He looked serene, untroubled. 'We're almost there now,' he said, pointing ahead. 'You see, the path gets much better soon. We'll slacken our pace, shall we? No need to kill ourselves.'

Afterwards, sitting with Claire, drowsy and warm in the back of the car, Sarah looked at the outline of Laurie's head as he drove them home through the black, starry night. It occurred to her that she had been behaving like a child. She *was* just a little bit infatuated with him, she had to admit it. But so what? She'd read somewhere that it happened to lots of women in her situation. Settled in a long, stable marriage. Middle age beckoning. The empty nest syndrome and all that stuff. And then – wham! A schoolgirl crush, all over again. It was trivial, temporary and would soon pass. Like measles. She'd be laughing about it by the time Christmas was upon them. Might even be confessing it all to David. She really didn't know why she had been letting it bother her so much.

CHAPTER THIRTEEN

Monday morning. It was cold and grey with a thin, chilling wind. Saturday's mild sunshine had vanished completely. Already the day in Edinburgh seemed like a far-off dream. Sarah sat glumly at the breakfast table. She was scraping butter on her rather burnt toast and listening to the unrelieved gloom of the news headlines on Radio Four when she heard the rattle of the letterbox.

'I'll get it,' said David. 'Time I made a move anyway.' He gulped down the last of his coffee and scrambled to his feet.

She heard him in the hall, shouting up the stairs to Merry. 'Have you seen the *time*, sweetheart?' Almost at once he was back, dropping an unopened envelope beside her plate. 'From Mum and Dad.' He shuffled through the rest of the post. 'Nothing much here. Bills mostly. And Visa!' He sighed. 'Dump them on my desk, will you, darling? I'll go through them when I get home.'

She followed him to the door, kissed him gently, then stood and waved until the car reached the bend in the road. 'Merry!' she called, on her way back to the kitchen. 'If you don't get a move on you'll miss the bus.'

It wasn't until she had the house to herself and was wandering upstairs to strip the beds and gather up the laundry for the washing machine, that she realised she hadn't read the letter from Jim and Muriel. She'd keep it for her coffee break, she decided. A little treat to look forward to. When, eventually, she pulled out the close-written pages and scanned the first few lines, she gave a little gasp of delight.

My Dears, she read,
Jim and I have just been talking about Christmas (it's getting
horribly near!) and – this is just an idea so please yell *instantly*
if you think it's a bad one – we wondered if we could come,
with Chris, and spend it with you and see your wonderful new
house etc. etc. Of course you might have made other plans, or
this might be very inconvenient . . .

Inconvenient! Sarah could think of nothing in the world that
would give her greater pleasure. It wasn't usual to be devoted
to your in-laws, she knew, but as far as she was concerned,
they were among her top favourite people. She'd known them
for well over twenty years, ever since David had taken her
home one Saturday when they were both still at school. She'd
been bracing herself for the sort of formality that her own
parents valued, careful introductions, polite conversation.

'There's nothing wrong with good manners,' her mother
used to say if ever Sarah begged her to be more relaxed.
'Manners maketh man!'

It never ceased to irritate her, that stupid little mantra that
was trotted out with monotonous regularity. 'Manners
maketh man.' But Jim and Muriel Page, she discovered, were
the exact opposite of her own mother and father. From the
moment she'd walked into their house they'd treated her like
a friend. An equal. As if she belonged, somehow. And that's
the way they'd always made her feel, loved and valued.

'No one stands on ceremony in this place,' Jim had said,
leading her into the cheerful chaos of the kitchen to help him
sort out a scratch lunch of soup and bread and cheese. 'Come
one, come all, and everybody welcome.' He'd rummaged
with gusto among the tins in the cupboard. 'Now, what do
you fancy? Asparagus or Bacon and Lentil?'

It was Jim and Muriel, Sarah thought, who had made her
life possible when she was first expecting Will. In fact, they
had probably been responsible, quite literally, for making
Will's own life possible because there were one or two people,
her own father among them, who had hinted, obliquely

perhaps, that maybe this foolish and inconvenient pregnancy could be . . . dealt with.

'You are *what*?' her father had demanded, staring at her with such icy contempt that she'd felt paralysed. 'And *when* can we expect this "happy event"?'

'The end of May,' she'd muttered.

'May! You stupid little *fool*.' He was beside himself with rage.

David, standing close by, felt her tremble. He'd made a brave attempt at a smile. 'It's not *that* bad, Mr Challis. I mean, we always intended to get married. It'll just be a bit earlier than we planned.'

'Married!' George had roared. 'Do you think I care a fig about *that*, you idiot! What about her exams? Her career?'

Sarah looked at her mother, longing for some support, some understanding and kindness. But Ann was gazing out of the window, studying the sparrows on the lawn with desperate concentration. 'Perhaps I could take my degree the year after,' she suggested timidly. 'When David's doing his Education diploma. He could come up to Durham. Get a flat.'

George snorted. 'Airy-fairy nonsense! Who'll look after the child? Where's the money coming from for that? And three mouths to feed. How will you study with a baby bawling and keeping you awake? The idea's preposterous. Do try to use the few wits you've got left, girl.'

She began to cry quietly. 'What am I going to do, then?'

'Do? It's no use coming here and asking me what to do. You should have thought of that before you got yourself into this condition.'

Her mother took out a tiny lace handkerchief and blew her nose. She remained standing by the window, turned half away from them, her eyes still fixed on the little birds which were being seen off by a bully-boy blackbird.

'You shouldn't shout at Sarah,' David said bravely. 'It was my fault. I persuaded her. But I didn't mean this to happen.'

'I'm not interested in you,' George snarled. 'It's my

daughter we're talking about. Sarah was going to do great things. Till *you* came along.'

'She still will.'

'Don't be so ridiculous.' And then his tone changed. 'Not unless there's some way of undoing the harm that's been done.' He looked speculatively at Sarah and she reached for David's hand and felt his firm, steady grip. Side by side they stood and faced up to her father, their expressions blank, pretending that they didn't understand the terrible implication of his words. At length he shook his head. 'I give up. It's your life.'

Sarah swallowed. 'I was really trying to ask for your advice. Where shall I live? Before it's born?'

Suddenly Ann swung round and looked at her husband. 'Yes. We've got to think about that,' she said. 'And there are other things that need to be ironed out.'

George ignored her. He sat down heavily in his armchair and picked up his newspaper. 'You'll go on living in college, of course. Where else? Getting on with your work. And who knows – I suppose there's an outside chance that you might be able to take your exams. The birth might be late or something. There's many a slip . . . even in the best-planned of pregnancies.'

As he opened his *Times*, giving vent to his feelings with a great deal of noisy rustling and page-turning, Ann looked bleakly at David and Sarah. 'I suppose I'd better put the kettle on. Would you care for a cup of tea?'

'Not for us,' said David brusquely. 'Thank you, Mrs Challis, but we're going to see *my* parents now.'

Hand in hand they walked the mile of city streets that separated their homes, silent and numb, feeling as if they were moving through a nightmare. As David led Sarah into the sitting room, Jim and Muriel could see at once that something was seriously wrong. David's face was grim and set. Sarah looked sickly white, as if she might faint at any moment.

Alarmed, Muriel jumped up from her chair and hurried

across to them, taking the girl's arm. 'Whatever is the matter?' she cried. 'Bad news, is it?'

'You might say that.' David did not bother to mince his words. 'I'm afraid Sarah is pregnant.'

'Pregnant?' Briefly, Muriel's face registered surprise and then dismay. Then, almost immediately, it lit up with joy. 'A baby! David, never say that's bad news. Babies are marvellous news.' She turned to Jim who was laughing, his arms wide open to embrace them both.

'Well, well, well!' he said. 'Well, well, well, well, well. This calls for a celebration. Where are the glasses, I wonder. When's it going to be, then?' He began to rattle about in the drinks cabinet. 'You're going to be a grandma, Muriel. What about that, my beauty?' Then he wrapped Sarah in a huge, enveloping hug. 'Just tell us what we can do to help, my dear,' he said quietly. 'Anything at all.'

Looking at her coffee growing cold in its mug, Sarah thought of them now, her parents and David's, and how time had dealt with them all. Jim and Muriel had thrown themselves heart and soul into arranging a Christmas Eve wedding. George and Ann had turned up at the church, handed over a cheque for five thousand pounds in a manilla envelope on which her father had written 'to help see you and the child through the next year or so'. But they had categorically refused her entreaties to go along to the reception, and from that day had bowed out of her life. Sarah could count on the fingers of one hand how often she had seen them since the wedding. By the time William was born they had left Norwich and moved to the Suffolk coast, to Aldeburgh, where they retreated into a life of chilly gentility, of bridge and classical music, the crossword every morning, a Swan Hellenic cruise every other summer. They kept themselves to themselves and, apart from sending an annual Christmas card, containing a twenty pound note but no message, they showed not one iota of interest in her, or David, or even the children. Occasionally she had toyed with the idea of telling her father how brilliantly well Will was doing at school, how he was almost certainly going to fulfil all the ambitions he had once cherished for *her*, and be a grandson to boast about. But she had kept her silence. The hurt went too deep to heal. Sarah still had the letter he'd sent her a few days after she'd broken the news that she was expecting a baby. She remembered collecting it from her pigeon hole in college, ripping it open, hoping against hope for there to be some words of comfort, reconciliation.

'You were our shining star,' he'd written. 'Now you are our shame.'

She shook herself, trying to get rid of the memory that still ached inside her. Well, all that was over now, she thought. She'd lost her own parents, but she had David's instead, and they were worth more than diamonds.

Her train of thought was shattered by the shrilling of the telephone. Claire's voice sang down the line. 'Hi! I was just ringing to say wasn't that a great day out on Saturday. Hope we didn't wear you out completely, trailing you around the hills like that.'

'One of life's experiences!' Sarah said. 'Remind me to take my walking boots next time.'

'So – what are you up to this morning? Anything exciting?'

'Thinking about Christmas, actually.'

'My God!'

Sarah giggled. 'David's Mum and Dad are coming up.'

'Where from?'

'From Burnham Market. Do you know it?'

'Only by reputation. Pretty little cottages round a big village green.'

'That's right. They used to live in Norwich and I stayed with them for a few months when Will was born. They're lovely people.'

'You must bring them over. I'll see if I can rustle up the odd mince pie.'

'They'd like that. They're bringing Chris, David's young brother. David's *very* young brother. He was a sort of after-thought, I think. He's only twenty-five.'

'Right. We might need more than the odd mince pie to keep Chris happy.'

'He's very easy-going. He's usually perfectly content to mooch around with Will and Merry.'

'We'll introduce him to Bridget and Alison then. They'll all keep each other amused. Sarah, are we really talking about Christmas *already*? I don't feel as if I'm done with summer yet.'

'Frightening, isn't it? But it's only about six weeks.'

'I'd better get down to the Barn and do some work. Treasures will start clamouring at any moment. Thanks for jogging me.'

Christmas remained on Sarah's mind for the rest of the day. As she shoved the clothes into the dryer, wandered along the High Street to buy bread and fruit, searched the freezer for something for supper, she thought about Christmas. And by the time David arrived home, bursting through the door with his arms full of books and files, bending his neck to kiss her, telling her he was famished *and* knackered, she had her plans laid. 'Darling,' she said, 'I have found my new project. We're going to have a *marvellous* party, on Christmas Eve. I've been planning it all day. Jim and Muriel are coming, and Chris – that's what the letter was about – and I'm going to invite all the people we know, and a few more probably. It's going to be a house-warming *and* a celebration for Christmas *and* for our wedding anniversary. Eighteen years, David! All three rolled into one. I'm going to make Peacocks' Acre look like something out of a fairy story, and we'll have dancing and games and music and *sensational* food and drink, and it's going to be quite, quite *wonderful*.'

CHAPTER FOURTEEN

The Peacocks' Acre Christmas party was a triumph, everyone agreed. Sarah had thrown all her energy into making it exactly right. She'd started freezer-cooking in November, stashing away pies, pastries and pâtés, savoury dips, spreads and sauces, tubs of fruit puree, exotic iced puddings. Whenever she went shopping she'd buy a little luxury for her food cupboard, tins of smoked oysters, lumpfish caviare, crystallised fruits.

At the beginning of December she began planning the decorations. She wanted the house to look magical. First she chose a colour scheme, deciding that everything would be silver, green and gold, the colours of the countryside in winter. Merry and Bridget helped her by combing Deredale Woods for fallen branches snapped off by autumn winds. These were carried home in triumph, brushed down, and painted silver. Then David hoisted them up to hang in a canopy from hooks he carefully screwed into the joists of the high ceilings. Gradually, day by day, Sarah fastened a few glass baubles to the branches, taking her time about it, enjoying the effect she was creating. She began with green and silver ones, and then, when she saw how lovely they looked, she added blues, reds, ambers, even purples, to the spectrum of colour. The fragile balls spun and twirled in the slightest draught, sending little fish-scales of reflected light flicking around the walls. She was enchanted. It was like living inside a kaleidoscope.

The next job was to order a Christmas tree from the garden centre. She found a perfect specimen that stood twelve feet high and decided that they would put it outside, close to the front door, to show the whole world that this was a family that was celebrating in style.

Finally, on the last free Saturday before either Will or her visitors arrived, Sarah and David and Merry scurried about in the garden and collected a barrow-load of ivy, holly, silver-headed honesty, flame-coloured Chinese lanterns. Just as they were carrying it all indoors Laurie arrived on their doorstep, grinning, holding something behind his back.

'A little contribution!' he announced, and swung round his arm to show that he was carrying a deep wicker basket crammed full of mistletoe.

'You brilliant man!' Sarah congratulated him. 'Mistletoe costs more than gold in the market.'

'I know,' he said. 'But I have my personal supply. I always keep some by me for Christmas emergencies!'

David laughed. 'What are you lot up to today?'

'Nothing much, I don't think.' Laurie looked vague. 'Mooching about. You know.'

'Well, why don't you come and mooch about here? Have a bite to eat with us?'

'Are you sure? Aren't you too busy?'

'Got it in one,' David said. 'You can come and be busy too. Help us organise all this stuff, and then we'll feed you. How about that for a bargain?'

It was a day of pure delight. The mid-winter sun shone into the house, low and steady, illuminating the rooms with extraordinary clarity. Bridget and Merry commandeered the hi-fi system and found music for them to listen to while they worked, making the place resound to Britten's *Ceremony of Carols* and Vaughan Williams' *Fantasia*. Sarah put mince pies and sausage rolls into the oven, David warmed ginger wine, and Laurie rolled his eyes in delight. 'That smell!' he declared. 'Essence of Christmas!' And all the while, under Claire's skilful direction, perched on ladders, balancing on chairs, passing the secateurs from hand to hand, winding garden twine round straying branches, delicately tapping and hammering and snipping and fixing, they managed to conjure up great banks and columns and swags of greenery that filled corners, overflowed along shelves and bookcases and hung down in delicate strands from door-frames and cornices.

'I think we've really finished,' Sarah said at last, gazing wide-eyed at the transformation they had created. Then her face changed. 'The holly wreath! We've forgotten the wreath for the door.'

'Find me a coat hanger and some red ribbon,' Bridget told Merry. 'We can do that. I made a brilliant one for Mum last year.'

At last, with the wreath firmly in place, they all sank exhausted into armchairs. 'Now,' Sarah said, 'we really are all ready for the big day. The only thing I have to work out is where I'm going to put all my visitors.'

'Don't worry about that,' David told her. 'People will just fit in.'

'Have you got a problem?' Claire asked.

'Two extras, all of a sudden,' Sarah said. 'Pam and Zack are coming up from Norwich. I want them to have a good time. Pam thought that her daughter was going to her for Christmas but suddenly Matty changed her plans and decided to go to Austria with her father instead. Pam's in a bit of a state.'

David looked impatient. 'Don't fuss, darling. Pam can have the sofa-bed in my study, and Zack will go in with Will. No problem.'

'There *is* a problem.' Sarah reminded him. 'His name is Chris, remember? Where is Chris going to sleep? I know you think we can squeeze him in with the boys, but it's not fair. Will always seems to draw the short . . .'

'Chris must come to Dolphin House,' Claire stated, smoothing over the disagreement. 'We have plenty of room and we'd enjoy having him. Bridget will take care of him, won't you, darling?'

'Are you sure?' Sarah asked.

'Of course, I'm sure. It'll be a pleasure.'

From then on it all went like clockwork. The party happened exactly as planned, except that it was even better. Pam took it upon herself to organise the games. When Zack and Matty were tiny, Sarah remembered, Pam had run the neighbourhood playgroup. It must have been then that she had learned to cultivate the special tone of voice, low, gentle and determined, that insisted upon being obeyed.

'Now,' she addressed the assembled company of fifty guests, 'in my left hand you will see I am holding several paper kippers. In the laundry basket I have a great number of toilet rolls. And in this smart carrier bag – Harrods, no less! – there are some large and delicious oranges, whistles, sticky labels, two sugar mice, packets of marbles, balloons . . . and so on.' She smiled around with steely radiance, deaf to the chorus of groans. 'So – this is what we're going to do.'

As if hypnotised, they obeyed her every word, formed themselves into lines and circles, crawled over the carpet pushing table tennis balls with their noses, clamped oranges between their knees, wound each other into bandaged mummies.

'I do not believe this,' David murmured as he and Sarah watched Reggie, looking even plummier than usual, perspiring with the effort of keeping a huge, red balloon safely airborne.

'No *hands*, Reggie!' screeched Belle, who, for some complicated reason, had removed her shoes and was wearing wellington boots and three floppy hats. 'You're supposed to blow, sweetie. *Blow*!'

'What I can't believe,' Sarah said, 'is that they all seem to be enjoying it so much. Look at your Dad.'

David shook his head. 'I haven't seen him laugh like that since Ipswich got knocked out of the cup.'

Will came wandering by. In one hand he was carrying a waste paper basket packed with tightly rolled-up newspaper and in the other, a bag of potatoes.

'What are you doing, William?' Sarah asked.

He gave her a bemused grin. 'Search me. But it's more fun

than the French Revolution any day. Zack and Merry are looking for two frying pans, by the way.'

At last, when everybody was gasping for breath and begging for mercy, and the glass baubles suspended above their heads seemed to be quivering and tinkling with the force of their laughter, Pam decided they'd had enough. 'Well done,' she told them. 'You are *all* winners. And good sports, too. Now, if you form an orderly line and process towards Bridget and Chris and the bran tub you will find a little prize waiting for each one of you. Blue-wrapped for the men, pink for the ladies.'

'Come on, Tom,' lisped Wanda, shimmering in a silvery-grey wisp of a dress that made her look like a faery child. 'Blue for a boy, pink for a girl. How sweet!'

Sarah ignored her. She clapped her hands above her head. 'Supper's ready when you are,' she called. 'In the next room.'

After the feasting, and the amazed exclamations of wonder and delight over the delicious food, and all the busy handing-out and gathering-in of plates and dishes, and the filling-up of glasses, and the excited buzz of friendly conversation and laughter, a lull fell upon the crowded rooms. It was as if the guests felt that they'd *had* their party now. As if, lazy and contented and well-fed, they couldn't really believe that Christmas Eve had very much more to offer them, with the Day itself only an hour away.

Sensing the change in mood, David glanced at Laurie and the two of them jumped to their feet, signalled across the room to Jim and Chris, and with the speed of light, it seemed, the furniture was pushed against the walls, the carpets were rolled back, and Will and Zack had put some foot-tapping disco music on the CD player and dragged up Bridget and Merry to start off the dancing. Soon the whole of the ground floor of Peacocks' Acre, even the kitchen, was crammed with dancers, old and young, all swaying and moving to the pounding rhythm.

Chris tugged Sarah's hand as she stood watching. 'Come on, pretty lady,' he said. 'This one with me.'

She danced as if she were in a dream. She was on tip-toe, buoyed up by the wine and music and the sense of the occasion she had created. She felt boneless, light as a leaf. She threw back her head, raised her arms in the air and swung her hips, her body sinuous and lithe. The music possessed her. She changed partners, danced on her own for a while, then beckoned to David and linked her hands round the back of his neck.

'Happy anniversary,' she said. 'Thank you for my lovely present.'

She touched the little ear-rings she was wearing, tiny gold butterflies, wings spread, catching the light. All she wanted was for the music to go on and on. Towards midnight, she found herself dancing with Laurie who had suddenly materialised in front of her.

'Hi!' He grinned. 'Great party!'

'Do you come here often?' she asked him primly.

'Course I do. Best joint in town!'

They laughed, then gave themselves up to the music again, aware only of its insistent beat. When it stopped abruptly there was a murmur of disappointment from the floor until David appeared above them, standing on a chair, holding a small radio in his hand.

'Listen, folks,' he said. 'We're almost there.'

At once the chimes of Big Ben began to sound, and as they listened, thrilled, to the twelve echoing strokes of midnight, David shouted, 'Happy Christmas, everybody.'

Laurie looked down at Sarah. 'Happy Christmas, Sarah,' he said gently, and kissed her on the lips.

She gave a little sigh. A heavy weight of sadness seemed to settle upon her. All the joy of a moment ago drained away, leaving her weak and forlorn. She looked dully around the room. Christmas was exploding on every side. David was holding a tiny sprig of mistletoe above his head and beckoning towards Belle with an evil grin. Reggie, who didn't seem to realise that the music had stopped, was still lumbering about with poor Claire clasped to his paunch. Bridget and

Alison were sitting on the floor with Will and Chris. Chris was talking, animated, gesturing with his hands, and Bridget was watching him with rapt attention. Pam was bending over Jim and Muriel, a bottle in her hand, and Muriel was laughing, covering her glass, shaking her head. And Zack and Merry were turning the bran tub upside down on the floor, scrabbling among the sawdust to see if there were any prizes left.

Sarah saw them all clearly, still and in minute detail, as if frozen in time. She looked yearningly from one face to another. All the people she cared most about in the world. Christmas Day, 1990. She wished that she could stop the clock now. Ten years on, when the millennium arrived, where would they all be? She felt herself sway on her feet and prayed that she would not faint. She was aware, without a shred of doubt, that life would never again be as it was now. It was as if the striking of Big Ben had marked the end of innocence. Because, when Laurie had kissed her, she knew that she loved him, totally and irrevocably. That from now on this was the only significant reality in her life. Compared with this all her other ties and affections seemed, already, as insubstantial as dreams.

She realised that Laurie was still holding her, looking searchingly into her face, puzzled, looming over her like a ghost from her own future. A cold tremble ran down her spine. *That's* what it was. When she had first seen his photograph, months ago, in Belle's copy of the *Bugle*, she'd thought she recognised him as someone from her past. Now, she realised, he was her future.

'Are you all right, Sarah?' His eyes were dark, his voice low, troubled.

'I'm fine!' She gave him a tight, bright little smile. 'Happy Christmas, Laurie. Now, I'm sorry, but I think David needs me. People are beginning to drift off.'

Rapidly she began to move away through her guests. As she passed Muriel she felt her eyes upon her. The blood rushed to her face as she realised that David's mother had seen, and understood, what had happened between her and Laurie. She hesitated, confused and uncertain, then Claire's voice rang out behind her.

'Sarah. Hang on a minute.'

She swung round guiltily, wondering if *she* had been watching as well. But Claire's face was wreathed in smiles.

'It's Christmas Day,' she said. 'So I can give you your present now. I'm longing to know if you like it.'

'There was no need. You shouldn't . . .'

'Don't say that. Come with me. I put it in a drawer in the study to keep it safe.'

Helplessly, Sarah stood holding the shoe box in her hands, feeling its weight, looking from it into Claire's laughing face.

'Do open it,' Claire said. 'It's not a pair of shoes, promise.'

Sarah lifted off the lid, pulling away layers of paper, and gazed down at the carving that lay there. 'Oh! How lovely!' Reverently she lifted it out and turned it over and over, studying it intently, stroking its silky smoothness. The piece of walnut, dark and richly-polished, was carved into the likeness of two hands, life-sized, long-fingered and shapely, joined together in a firm, loving clasp, their thumbs interlocked. Each finger nail was perfect, each knuckle delicately raised, and the grain of the wood formed fine whorls of light and shade on the shining surface. She looked at Claire almost beseechingly, but Claire misunderstood the reluctance in her eyes.

'I wanted you to have them,' she insisted. 'I call them "Hands of Friendship".'

'Thank you.' Sarah sounded brusque, trying to swallow back the tears that were threatening.

'Claire? – Oh, there you both are. We were wondering where you'd vanished off to.' Laurie's voice interrupted the moment. 'Present giving already, is it?' They swung round and saw him framed in the study doorway. He was dressed in his coat and scarf, holding Claire's cape over his arm. 'I think I'd better take you home, lovey. Bridget and Chris have left already. It's been a super party, Sarah. Congratulations.'

'Bridget's gone without us?' Claire asked, surprised.

'I think, perhaps, they wanted a little time on their own. Our daughter has stars in her eyes tonight.' He wrapped the black velvet cloak round Claire's shoulders, carefully lifted the hood over her hair and smoothed it down at either side of her face. Then he gave her a little tap on the end of her nose, as if she were a child. 'Must wrap up,' he said. 'It's freezing out there.'

Sarah trailed behind them to the front door where David was already stationed, ushering out their departing guests into the chilly darkness.

'Thanks, David,' Laurie said, shaking his hand.

David grinned. 'I've said "Happy Christmas" about a hundred times already so with you two I'll change my tune. Happy New Year, folks. Roll on, 'Ninety-one.'

Sarah nodded and stood mutely by his side, watching as Laurie put his arm protectively round Claire and led her out into the starry night.

An hour later the last visitor had left, Will, Zack and Merry had shuffled off to bed and the adults had cleared the littered rooms, stuffed rubbish into black sacks, loaded the dish washer for the second time and got the kitchen into manageable order. The master plan was to turn Christmas Day and Boxing Day back to front, cook the turkey on December 26th and use the 25th for rest and recovery with nothing more arduous to do than exchange their gifts and eat up the party left-overs.

Jim folded up his tea-towel and examined the place with satisfaction. 'There we are,' he said. 'I think we've worked wonders. So, if you can do without me, I'm for my bed now.'

'Thanks, Dad,' said David. 'I can't think of a better idea. Anything that's not done can be done tomorrow.' He looked at the three women. 'Are you lot coming up? Darling, you look like death! What a day you've had.'

'I'll follow you in a minute,' Sarah said. She picked up a tray of clean glasses and carried it to the cupboard.

Pam dried her hands, reached for her rings from the kitchen

window sill and slipped them back on to her fingers. 'I think I'm beyond sleep.'

'Me, too!' Muriel nodded. 'Sarah, why don't we just have a little sit down before we go to bed. My head's buzzing with it all.'

'Do you realise it's two o'clock?'

'I know. But I always find it easier to unwind in an arm-chair than toss and turn in bed. And Jim will be snoring already.'

In the drawing room, Sarah poked the logs in the grate and they spurted into flame again. She sat down by the hearth, staring at the glowing embers.

'Ber-liss,' said Pam, sinking down on to the sofa, kicking off her shoes. She patted the seat beside her. 'Come on, Muriel. Just ten minutes.'

'Didn't it go well?' Muriel said, leaning back against the cushions. 'Real party games!' She burst out laughing. 'Tom's *face*, when you told him to lie on the carpet and pretend he was a porpoise! I don't think Wanda was amused.'

'Everyone joined in, though, didn't they?' Pam said. 'You've met some really nice people, Sarah.'

Muriel nodded. 'Especially the Richleys. I liked them. Their daughter's a beauty, isn't she?'

Pam whistled. 'That little red dress of hers! Will couldn't take his eyes off her.'

'Poor Will,' Sarah said. 'Nothing seems to go right for him these days, does it? He couldn't get a look in, with Chris around.'

'Ah!' Muriel smiled. 'The irresistible attraction of the older man.'

'Don't *tell* me,' Pam groaned.

Muriel looked embarrassed. 'Sorry, Pam! I wasn't thinking. Anyway, your Zack did a great job of keeping Merry amused while Will was languishing at Bridget's feet.'

'Zack's on good form, isn't he?' Pam smiled happily. 'He's been full of the joys for the last few weeks. I don't know what's got into him.'

Suddenly Muriel's eyes settled on Claire's 'Hands' which Sarah had laid on a coffee table to one side of the sofa. She stretched out and picked them up, enjoying their hard smoothness. 'Beautiful, aren't they? "The Hands of Friendship", did you say?'

Sarah nodded.

'You're lucky to have found a friend like Claire,' Muriel told her. 'She and I had a long talk. I often think – well, I'm sixty-four now. Twenty years ago, when I first read *The Female Eunuch* ...'

'Best book ever written,' Pam interrupted her solemnly. 'That's what Jake made me. A eunuch.'

Pam was, Sarah decided, just a little bit the worse for wear.

'I thought it was electrifying,' Muriel said. 'Since then I've watched every twist and turn of the women's movement, everything they've said and done. And now I believe that the best thing that's come out of it, the very best, is the new, special quality of women's friendship. You know, when I was young, you'd make an arrangement to go out with a girlfriend, but if, suddenly, you got a date, then the girl was dropped. It was agreed. Common practice. Dates ... boys ... were more important than female friends.'

Pam gave the matter her careful consideration. 'I don't think that would happen now,' she said.

'No, but it did then. And when you got married, your husband, your family, were paramount. You had to squeeze your friends into the little bits of spaces left over. Nowadays, friendship is considered as important as love, isn't it? More important, perhaps, because often love, sexual love, I mean, doesn't last as long.' She laughed, mildly embarrassed by her long speech. 'Well, I don't know. What do you two think? You're a different generation.'

'I agree entirely,' Pam said. 'Look at me. When that ... that little blonde bit stole my husband away ...'

Sarah looked at her. 'To be fair, Pam, I think it was Jake who stole *her* away. And out of the cradle too.'

'Maybe. But she could have said "No!", couldn't she? She

could have said, "Get back to your wife, you two-timing bastard." All she had to do was say "No." '

Muriel nodded. 'We can all do that. If we really want to.' She kept her face averted from Sarah. 'I'm sorry you lost the battle over that, Pam. A good marriage is worth fighting for. Especially when there are children.'

'You're right,' said Pam. 'Anyway, when Jake buggered off, Sarah was *there*. Every day. Weren't you, Sarah? I was impossible. I got drunk and maudlin. I shouted and raged, and cried myself sick. Literally, I mean. Throwing up.' She looked at Sarah as if wanting her to vouch for her condition, but Sarah was staring into the flames. 'Some days I wouldn't get out of bed,' she told Muriel. 'I hated myself. I thought, if Jake valued that . . . little bit of *nothing* more than me, our marriage and the kids and everything, I must just be rubbish. But Sarah made me think I was worth something, because she just went on *being* there. Do you see what I mean? If it hadn't been for her, I'd have gone under.'

'Of course.' Muriel nodded briskly and stood up. 'I'm sure Sarah would never betray a friend.' Carefully she returned the 'Hands' to their place on the table. 'I think it really is bedtime now,' she said, smiling at them both. 'Now that we've put the world to rights.'

CHAPTER FIFTEEN

Gerald Manley looked appraisingly at the last applicant as she took the seat he indicated, directly in front of him. He'd been interviewing since eleven this morning, four solid hours, and now he was tired. All the applicants had been young women, for some reason, and that was a pity. Gerald would have liked to have been able to consider a man for the post. The girls had fallen into two categories. Either they'd been giggly and flirted with him surreptitiously from the other side of his desk, or they'd given him the haughty drop-dead treatment, as if they'd imagined he were sitting there harbouring lecherous intentions. Boring, boring, boring!

This one, though, was different. To start with, she was older. He glanced again at the brief letter of application in front of him. Thirty-eight. Married. Two children. Also, she seemed strangely remote. He'd have thought she was totally in control of the situation, coolly self-assured, if he hadn't been trained to observe the body language. She was sitting with her legs crossed, and the toe of her right shoe was inscribing tiny circles in the air, four clockwise, four anticlockwise, the same pattern repeated again and again. She was quite a pretty woman, he supposed. Nothing startling, but attractive in a quiet sort of a way. Small, neat figure, good complexion, shiny, black cap of curly hair. Intelligent eyes too. In fact, they were probably her best feature. Appearance was vitally important in this business.

He leaned forward and clasped his hands together in a reassuring way, trying to put her at ease. 'Thank you for coming to see me,' he said. She gave him a slight nod of acknowledgement. 'I do have to tell you though, before we go any further, that you are rather... over-educated for this job. It's not Management, you know.'

'I'm sorry,' she said in a low voice. 'Should I apologise for that?'

'No.' He laughed. 'I don't think apologies are necessary.' He looked at her file again. 'Excellent references! But no actual work experience, I see.'

She shook her head. 'I'm afraid I haven't had any. Except in the voluntary sector.'

'I see. Why is that?'

'Because, since university, I've been a full-time wife and mother. I'm trying to move on now.'

'Mmm.' He fiddled with his gold Parker, playing for time, trying to work her out. There was something at the back of her eyes that he didn't understand, an expression that was at the same time vulnerable and defiant. 'Do you mind telling me what made you apply for the post in the first place?'

She bent towards him. Her tone was fierce. 'Because I need ...' she began, and then her voice drifted off.

Giving her time to marshal her thoughts he scrutinised her details again. She was a married woman, not a desperate divorcee or penniless single mother. Good address too. It couldn't be lack of money that was driving her into the workplace.

'I need occupation,' she told him at length. 'I want to be stretched. Fully employed.'

'I see.' He laid down his pen and gazed at a patch of sunshine on the wall above her head. Dare he take a risk with this one, he wondered. He liked the look of her. Felt he could trust her. She was smart, bright, well-spoken, honest. But she also had the appearance of a woman on the edge.

Suddenly, a smile illuminated her pale face. 'I am good, you know,' she said. 'You only have my word for it, I see that, but I'm very efficient and I actually like hard work. I set myself high standards.'

He looked at her in surprise. 'Do you now? And do you achieve them?'

'Yes. In almost everything I do.'

'Well, I'm glad to hear it.'

Noticing the hint of laughter in his voice, she shook her head, anxious to explain. 'I'm not boasting or anything. It's just how I was brought up, I suppose. My father! But now it's second nature, you see. The way I am.'

He stood up and stretched out his hand across the desk. 'It's been a pleasure meeting you, Mrs Page.'

'You'll let me know?'

'As soon as possible. I have some thinking to do, but I won't keep you on tenterhooks a minute more than necessary. You have my word.'

She smiled again. It was only the second time she'd smiled since she'd walked into the room, he realised. It was like waiting for the sun to shine.

Greenacres Country House Hotel
January 16th, 1991

Dear Mrs Page,
Further to your interview on January 14th, Mr Manley has asked me to let you know that . . .

Sarah was reading her letter for the third time, turning it over and over in her shaking hands, aware that her heart was pounding as if she were a young girl on her first date, when she heard the telephone shrill in the study. She rushed to pick it up. 'Hello! Sarah Page.'

'Darling?' David's voice echoed in her ear. 'Are you all right? You sound a bit strange.'

'I'm fine,' she lied, blushing guiltily. 'Must be a funny line.'

'Listen. Something really exciting! You'll never guess where I am.'

'Not at school?'

'No. I've just had lunch with Laurie, and we . . .'

She closed her eyes and took a deep breath, wanting *not* to think about Laurie, *not* to find herself sucked back into that dark, paralysing coil of her unthinkable obsession.

'Sarah! Are you still there?'

'Yes,' she assured him. 'I'm still here.'

'We're in Drake's Sailing Centre, Laurie and me. And we've just booked – wait for it! – a sailing holiday in the Greek Islands. It's a big boat. We can take the girls. Will, too, if he's keen.' She was silent, listening to his laughter rippling down the line. 'I knew that would take the wind out of your sails – boom! boom!'

'When?' she asked in a small voice.

'What?'

'You say you've booked. When for?'

'Easter hols, darling. March the twenty-eighth till . . . hang on a minute . . .' She heard him confer with Laurie, their relaxed voices murmuring companionably together. '. . . Till April the eleventh. Yeah! Two whole weeks of wine-dark seas and rosy-fingered dawns. We always promised ourselves, didn't we . . .'

'I can't come,' she said. 'I'm sorry.'

'What do you mean? Of course you can.'

'You'll have to count me out. I can't get away then.'

'Can't get away?' he repeated. 'What are you talking about?'

'I've been offered a job. I just heard today. I've been reading through the letter again. I start work on February the first and it says I'm not allowed any leave for the first six months, so . . .'

'Don't be ridiculous!' She flinched at the anger in David's voice. 'Whatever you've been offered, ring them straight away and say you'll have to turn it down. You can't just decide something like this off your own bat. We've never even discussed it. Anyway, the holiday's booked. Laurie paid the deposit with his Barclaycard. So, whatever it is, love, get out of it. Don't hang about.'

'I'm going to take it, David.'

'You can't! It's a ludicrous idea.'

'I will not give it up.'

'I see.' She could imagine the white fury on his face, the pulse beating at his temple, but she was determined not to give in. 'Very well then,' he said. 'We'll talk about it when I come home.' And he rammed down the phone.

When he got back he could hardly bring himself to look at her. She poured him tea and he drank it in silence, rustling the pages of his newspaper. Sarah breathed a sigh of relief that Merry was staying on at school for a choir practice and didn't have to endure their bitterness. 'What is this wonderful job then?' he asked at last.

'Hotel Receptionist at Greenacres Country House Hotel. Just part-time. It's along the valley, in Linfold.'

'And how do you propose to get to Linfold and back?'

'There *is* a reasonable bus service. I've checked. Besides, you don't take the car every day, do you? So I thought we could share it.'

'Hotel receptionist!' He snorted. 'Is that the best you can manage? Your father *would* be proud of you.'

'It's a start.'

'But why?'

'Why not?' she shrugged. 'Every woman I know has a job. Claire. Pam. Wanda, for God's sake. Even Belle helps out in Treasures from time to time.'

'But we agreed you *wouldn't* go out to work.'

'That was eighteen years ago!' she exploded. 'I've done more than your average life sentence.'

'A life sentence. Is that how you think of our marriage?'

Instantly she regretted the remark. 'Oh, darling, of course not. I didn't mean that. But I've never had a career and . . .'

'No. You had a baby instead.'

She stared at him coldly. 'I seem to remember, David, that that was really *your* doing. *Your* idea. "Sarah, let's make love in the rain. Wouldn't it be marvellous?" *Your* lack of care and control. And ever since that day, *I* have had to carry the can.'

'You never complained,' he said.

'Perhaps not. I was always used to doing what other people

wanted. First my father. Then you. But . . . something I never told you. I should have. Things might have been different, you know. My first thought when I discovered I was pregnant was exactly the same as my father's. Not – "Oh, gosh, what will people say? How will I cope?" No. It was just desperate disappointment that I wouldn't be able to take my degree.'

He sighed wearily. 'That's the way it *was*. Why are you dredging all this up now, for God's sake?'

'Because – I must be very stupid or something – but I just realised a few weeks ago that it needn't have been like that. I *could* have done my Finals. I mean, I wasn't in the labour ward then, was I? Will was safely born. And even in the 'seventies there were creches, baby-minders, nurseries. And Muriel standing by, longing to help. But you never suggested anything like that, did you? It was not even discussed.'

'So? What the hell are you saying?' He seemed genuinely baffled.

'What I'm saying, David, is this. I think you were quite glad that I got pregnant. In fact, you might even have planned it that way.'

'Sarah!'

'Because then you could persuade me to forget about a career and be a little home-maker, while you went steadily up the ladder without a care in the world, and broke up the family, dumping Will in Norwich and charging from one end of the country to the other chasing after your own precious ambitions. And to hell with all of us! What I'm saying is . . .'

He was still staring at her, his eyes bulging slightly, when the phone rang again. He turned on his heel and stalked away to answer it.

'More bad news,' he told her, when he came back. 'It's not Friday the thirteenth, is it?'

'What's happened?'

'That was Pam. Apparently Zack has been expelled. Out on his neck completely this time.'

'Not his *hair* again?'

'Oh no! It's drugs now, Sarah. Our son's best mate has

been doing drugs. No doubt it'll be Will's turn to be found out next and, of course, it will be *all my fault*. Because everything always is.'

'I didn't say that.'

'Didn't you?' He gazed at her scornfully. 'It must be really nice to be Sarah Page and know that you're always in the right. Always perfect.'

'Please, David. I'm sorry. Let's stop shouting at each other and try . . .'

But already he was on his way to the door, picking up his coat from the chair where he'd hurled it when he came in. 'I think I'll forgo the delights of dinner *chez nous* tonight and grab a sandwich at the Eagle. Don't wait up, Sarah. I'll be home as late as possible.'

It was past eleven when he got back. He ràn up to their bedroom but it was empty. He glanced in at Merry and saw that she'd fallen asleep, her radio playing, her bedside lamp shining on a copy of *Jane Eyre* still held loosely in her hand. He pursed his lips. Merry's idea of doing her homework, no doubt. Gently he removed the book, covered her with her duvet, switched everything off and tip-toed away. He found Sarah downstairs, stretched out on the hearthrug, her eyes closed. She was wrapped up in the old blue dressing gown she'd had since she was sixteen, her hair was tousled, her cheeks streaked with dried tears. She looked not a day older than Merry and even more defenceless. Tenderly he knelt down beside her and stroked her face.

'Sarah. I'm home,' he whispered.

At once she was awake, struggling up, rubbing her eyes, looking at him anxiously. 'I said some horrible things. I didn't mean . . .'

'No. My fault.' He smiled. 'That rotten temper of mine.'

'I've been thinking. If you really hate the idea . . . really, really hate it, I mean . . . I'll turn the job down.'

'Why should you? It's obviously important to you, and you say it's just part-time.'

'But you don't want me . . .'

'I was upset because we hadn't talked about it. You must have seen it advertised? Had an interview? But you kept it all secret. We used to share everything.'

'I didn't see the point of our even thinking about it. There were fifteen applicants. I thought I'd just do it . . . as a sort of practice run. To see what it was like. I've only had one interview in my whole life, and that was for Durham.'

'Well done you,' he grinned. 'A hundred per cent success rate so far.'

'So you don't mind?'

He shook his head. 'The main thing was being disappointed about the holiday, I suppose. I thought it would be a real treat.'

'But you can still go. Take the children. I'll be all right on my own.'

'Not without you. I saw Laurie in the pub and he understands perfectly. He says he'll take Mark and Lou and Alison in our place.'

She chose her words with care. 'I know it sounded a lovely idea, darling, a shared holiday. But really, I enjoy doing things on our own. Don't you? We can get away in August – Ireland, perhaps, down to the west coast.'

'Yes. That's always been on our list, hasn't it?'

'I mean, the Richleys are great, but we don't have to go around in a group all the time.'

David looked at her seriously. 'I do know how you feel about Laurie, you know. You don't have to pretend.'

'What do you mean?' Her heart began to knock against her ribs so violently that she thought David might feel it, sitting on the rug close beside her.

He laughed. 'You've never really liked him, have you? Not since he gave poor Wanda such a trouncing at our famous dinner party? I've seen the look on your face sometimes when he's around. You're always a bit wary. Suspicious.'

She took a deep breath. 'I suppose you're right,' she said casually. 'I've never really thought about it.'

'But he's a nice guy, you know. When you get to know him. He can be a bit alarming sometimes, but his heart's in the right place.'

'If you say so, David. I'll take your word for it.'

He kissed her gently, then stood up. 'Time for bed, sweetheart.' He reached out his hand to steady her. 'The pair of us are going to be like zombies tomorrow, I know it.'

A few days later, Sarah sat alone at her kitchen table among the remains of their breakfast. Thoughtfully, she read through the newspaper cutting that Pam had sent her.

REBEL ZACK SOWS HIS WILD SEEDS

Norwich schoolboy, Zachary Peters, who hit the headlines last autumn when deputy headmaster, Mr Harold Trent, banned him from school because of his pony tail hair-style, is in hot water yet again. 'This time he has not been excluded, he has been expelled,' Mr Trent told our reporter. 'We must deal with drugs offences with the utmost severity and set an example, for the sake of the other boys in our care.' It seems that Zack, who for the past year has worked in a part-time capacity at Cherry Trees Garden Centre, has been putting his horticultural training to practical application by growing hemp in a derelict greenhouse. It was 'purely experimental' he assured us. 'I am a supporter of the Green Party and we know that hemp is an ecologically invaluable plant. It is a natural, sustainable resource for many products, cloths, cosmetics and paper, for instance. The fact that it also produces cannabis resin is purely coincidental.'

In her letter, Pam seemed very relaxed about the whole affair.

'I can't pretend that this is either a complete disaster,' she wrote, 'or a total surprise. As you know, Zack has hated school for the last two years and he was getting less and less keen about university. Mr Gallagher has offered him a full-time job at Cherry Trees – he seems to think the sort of publicity that Zack generates is good for business! I really believe, if he stuck at it, he could do well for himself there – a growth industry, in more ways than one! But he's restless, full of ideas. Most of them revolutionary and anti-establishment, of course. He might waft into politics eventually. Or even journalism. He's got the contacts already! He's a black cat. He'll land on his feet every time. I just feel sad about poor Will being left at that awful school without him. The first time in their lives they've been separated! And Mr Trent does seem to pick on him sometimes. It's almost as if he can't forgive him for doing a bunk from the Grange . . .'

'Poor Will.' Sarah sighed. It always seemed to be 'poor Will' these days. Yet only last year he'd been their golden boy. It was frightening how fast things could change. But at least he'd got into Cambridge *and* the college of his choice, and that was what it had been about. All he needed now was two As and a B, and she knew he'd take that in his stride. According to Will, his interview had been a piece of cake.

'We talked about football most of the time,' he'd told her on the phone. 'When I informed him I'd scored sixteen goals this season, I was home and dry. "Emmanuel has need of students of your calibre," he said. "And your history seems pretty good too!" '

She must write to him straight away. Send him a book or something to cheer him up. She was in the study, rummaging in the desk for her writing paper, when she heard an insistent knocking on the front door. She looked at her watch, surprised. Not nine o'clock yet. Probably Belle, in need of coffee and a chat. But even Belle didn't usually arrive this early. An eager-beaver salesman, then? She opened the door and found Laurie on the step, his face grey and worried.

'Laurie!' Unconsciously she took a step backwards. 'What's the matter? Is something wrong?'

'May I come in for a minute? I just wanted to talk to you, that's all. David's gone to school?'

She led the way into the kitchen, filled the kettle automatically and set it to boil. 'Sorry about the mess,' she said, lifting buttery plates from the table.

'What? Oh, don't think about it.' She stood looking at him, waiting. 'This is a bit embarrassing,' he began.

'Is it about the holiday?' she asked. 'Greece? Do you want us to pay our share of the deposit or something?'

'Deposit? – No! No, of course not.' He stared about him distractedly.

'It's *not* about the holiday then?'

'No. Well, yes, I suppose. In a way. The thing is . . .' He looked at her uncomfortably. '. . . I saw David in the pub the other night . . .'

'Last Thursday, you mean?'

'That would be it. He said . . . He told me that you didn't want to come sailing with us . . .'

'It's not that I didn't want to,' she interrupted. 'Didn't he explain that I'd got a job? I'd only just heard. That very day.'

Laurie nodded, watching her carefully. 'But David thought that was just an excuse. He said he was sure the hotel would have honoured holiday obligations.'

'Did he?' Sarah's voice was grim.

'He seemed to think it was because of me that you pulled out. Because you didn't like *me* very much. And that was why you wouldn't be on my road safety committee either.' Sarah felt the colour rising to her cheeks. She couldn't trust herself to speak. Laurie's eyes were fixed on her, boring into her. 'What I want to know is, have I done something dreadful? Have I upset you, or insulted you?'

'Of course you haven't.'

'I *do* have a reputation for being tactless, but often I don't even realise it, you see. So if I've said something, cracked some stupid joke . . . I want us to be friends, Sarah. For Claire's sake, I mean.'

Sarah rubbed her hands across her face. 'I don't know what David was thinking about. No, you haven't upset me. Or said anything you shouldn't. You've always been courteous and helpful and kind. Both you and Claire. Ever since we first arrived. Look how you helped us with our party. We'd never have managed it without you two.' She gave a little laugh. 'I can only think . . . David must have had too much to drink when he said that. We'd just had . . . I'm afraid we'd had a row. That's why he went to the pub in the first place, to get away from me.'

Laurie's brow cleared and a look of immense relief and delight spread over his face. 'So perhaps we will persuade you to come sailing after all? Claire would love it.'

'I'm sorry,' she said gently. 'I don't really think I can go cap in hand asking favours before I even start the job.' And then she suddenly remembered what it was all about. What had driven her to apply to Greenacres in the first place. Her tone changed. Her voice became bright and brittle. 'And it is all going to be rather time-consuming, you know. Once I start working. Life's going to have to be different from now on, when I become a career woman.'

'I see.' His eyes became hooded again, narrow and glittering, as though a visor had come down. He stood up abruptly. 'I must be on my way. I'm going to be very late at the office.' As he began to go down the steps that led on to the pavement he turned and looked back at her strangely. 'Thank you for not hating me, anyway.'

The words were lightly spoken, almost ironic, but she knew that somehow she had hurt him. She stood for a while, watching him walk slowly away from her, his shoulders hunched against the chill wind, his bare head bowed. She could hardly bear it. She had to hold, very tight, to the side of the door, feeling its hard edges pressing against her palm. Otherwise she could not have prevented herself from running after him, throwing her arms about him and begging him to stay, pleading with him never to walk away from her so coldly, so unforgivingly, ever again.

She closed the door, moved stiffly to her desk, sat down and began to write.

January 21st, 1991

My Dear Laurie,

I love you. There, it is out at last. And I'm glad. I'm not good at pretence and acting. I think I have loved you since the moment I first saw you. Since before that even. I really believe that I fell in love with your photograph in the *Bugle*. Is such a thing possible, do you imagine?

Please don't think that you have to *do* anything about this free and frank declaration of the sad state of my heart. I know, of course, that you are not in love with me. I understand how deeply you love Claire. But this morning you asked me for my friendship 'for Claire's sake'. For Claire's sake, it is impossible. For Claire's sake there can be no wonderful holidays, no more marvellous parties. For Claire's sake I have taken a job, to keep me stretched and occupied and, for her sake I fully intend to keep my distance from you, now and for ever more.

For David's sake, too, because when I told Wanda that I approved of marriage, thought it the best way to live, I meant what I said. I really do believe in all those old-fashioned virtues, marriage and fidelity, honesty, steadfastness and loyalty. To my husband. To my friend.

So – why am I writing all this to you? Good question!

Because . . . because you looked so hurt just now when you walked away from me that I thought my heart would break . . .

. . . because I want you to understand why I seem so distant . . .

. . . because I can't keep this bottled up inside me for ever without going out of my mind and there is no one else I can tell. In my imagination, you see, and in my dreams (I blush to write it) we are lovers . . .

It seems I am decked out in all my loves. My fingerprints are made of your warm skin, and time is scars and banners, and it seems my bones are bedrock granite sunk so deep
they cannot speak, though they know everything.

. . . and, one final because . . . because I want you to know how deeply, how profoundly, you are loved. It shouldn't, should it? just go to waste. Sometimes, in the years ahead, you may feel lonely or defeated. These things happen. Grief or suffering may touch your life. And if it comes, my dearest dear, I hope the knowledge of this love will be a glow-worm of comfort.

I love you, Laurie. More, a thousand times, than I can say. Probably, I will not dare post this letter. How could I ever look you in the eye afterwards? But if I do, please, read it, destroy it, and take only pleasure from it.

Yours, S

Quickly, she folded the sheets of paper and put them into an envelope. On the front she wrote, very carefully, smoothing out and disguising her spiky handwriting,

> PRIVATE – *For the personal attention of*:
> Mr Laurence Richley,
> Richley, Richley, Burgoyne & Richley, Solicitors,
> Queen's Chambers,
> Drigg Street,
> Newcastle upon Tyne.

Then she laughed. It all felt so unreal, so ludicrously infantile, that she was almost tempted to continue:

> England,
> Great Britain,
> Europe,
> The World,
> THE UNIVERSE!

2

JANUARY, 1991

I've loosed flocks of birds
from my raised hands. They sky-write in a swarm
of rapid hieroglyphics which reveal
my name, my future, everything, except
I can't decipher it quite fast enough
to keep pace with the tempo of their wings
erasing air's white pages, which contain
the poem of myself, which I forgot.

CHAPTER SIXTEEN

When she was old and grey and full of sleep, Sarah thought, she'd remember her sweet, secret time with Laurie as the crown of her life.

The wonderful irony of the situation was that she hadn't really intended to send him the letter. She'd written it, sealed it and pushed it into the pigeon hole of her desk, intending to find a safe hiding place for it later. She'd planned to keep it with her special papers, photographs, cuttings . . . she didn't know why. Some sort of memento of lost love, perhaps. If Will and Merry came across it when she was dribbling and senile, or even when she was dead and they were searching through her boxes, then so be it. It wouldn't hurt them to know that their mother had been capable of passion. And of sacrifice.

But then fate had stepped in. Something had happened to distract her. A woman called, collecting for Oxfam, and they'd got talking. After that she'd completely forgotten about the letter tucked away in her desk, ticking like a time bomb. Until the next morning, as David was hurrying down the street towards the car.

Suddenly he'd lifted his hand and she'd seen that he was holding the envelope, waving it at her. 'Thanks for doing this,' he'd called back over his shoulder. 'I'll pop it into Laurie's office at lunchtime.'

Her legs went weak. She wanted to scream at the top of her voice, 'No! For God's sake, don't do that.' To hurtle after him, even though she was still in her dressing gown, and snatch it back. But how would she be able to explain herself to David? He obviously thought it was a straightforward business letter. He'd been going on about transferring their affairs to Richleys ever since he'd met Laurie.

'Just drop him an official line, would you?' he'd asked her. 'I have had a word, but he needs it in writing.'

Sarah had run and re-run the scene through her head as if she had it on video. Sometimes she'd play it in slow motion. David bumping into Laurie on the steps of his office, calmly handing over her long, creamy envelope.

'Sarah's got round to it at last,' he was saying. 'The thing is, we want to come in and see you about our Wills. Ten years since we did them and we want to make a few alterations.'

And then, the letter changing hands, Laurie slitting it open straight away, impatiently, the way he did everything, talking to David all the while about other inconsequential things, Friday night chess, his Sunday visit to the harbour. Finally, she saw him lowering his eyes, rapidly scanning through the words and phrases that leapt out at him from the page like arrows of flame – 'loved you since the first moment . . . my fingerprints are made of your warm skin . . . how deeply, how profoundly, you are loved . . .'

How had he coped with it all, she wondered. Aware of David's friendly, unsuspecting gaze upon him while her passionate words were beating at his brain. Had he blushed, or turned pale? Had his face betrayed him? Or his voice? Had he lost the thread of the conversation and stood there stammering on his own doorstep, trying to grapple with her declaration of love?

Ever since David had taken the letter she had been in an agony of embarrassment, dreading the thought of what would happen next, Laurie's voice on the phone, or a polite, chilly note through her door, or even worse, coming face to face with him unexpectedly.

But when it happened, it was as natural and easy as birdsong. It was a bright morning, dry and frosty, and she was hanging out her washing, taking her time about it, watching a robin tilt his inquisitive head at her from a low branch of the plum tree. Just another week, she was thinking, and she'd have started her job at Greenacres. Everything would be different.

And then she saw Laurie stepping through the garden towards her, smiling, shining with delight. He ducked his head through the sheets and kissed her swiftly on the cheek.

'Come inside,' he said. 'We've got to talk.'

As if in a dream she followed him into the kitchen. He shut the door, leaned his back against it and pulled her into his arms. For a long while, it seemed, he held her there, not moving, not speaking, laying his cheek down gently on the top of her head. She could hear the steady thumping of his heart, breathe in his male smell of soap and skin and sweat, feel the firm cloth of his jacket lapel rubbing against her face. She felt safe and at peace, as if she'd come home after a long journey. Then he straightened up and held her in front of him, his hands on her shoulders, and looked at her searchingly, his head on one side. Just like the robin! she thought.

'I'm sorry. I didn't mean you to get that letter...' she began, but he laid a finger against her lips to silence her.

'How could you not know that I loved you?' he asked her.

'You love me?'

'Of course I do. I thought you knew.' She shook her head, bewildered. 'Sarah! I saw it in your face. Christmas Eve, when the clock was striking. That's when I realised. And you felt it too, didn't you? I was watching you. You drooped your head. You looked so ... solemn, as if you were over-awed by what was happening to us.'

'You noticed!'

'Of course I did. That's why I couldn't understand your coldness afterwards. I began to think I'd picked up the wrong vibes. Couldn't you guess that I'd organised the Greek trip as a sort of celebration? I knew I was playing with fire but the temptation was too strong. I just longed to live for a while so close to you that I could hear you breathing in the night. I wanted to swim with you, to watch your face when you saw that miraculous landscape. The sea with the moon on it. Didn't you know me well enough to work it out?'

'No.' She smiled. 'I had no idea. You see, I don't really know you at all, do I? And yet, in a spooky sort of way, I feel as if I knew you before I was even born. I can't understand it.'

He kissed her. 'I have to go now. Duty calls. I came here, ostensibly, to ask you to join my road safety committee. Again! Please say yes this time. Then I've got a fool-proof excuse to ring you and see you whenever I want.'

'Of course, I will. But it's just not as simple as that, is it? What about Claire? And David? I don't want anybody to get hurt.'

'Hush! You worry too much.' He bent his head and kissed her again, on the eyelids, on the tip of her nose, then, lingering sweetly, on her lips. 'Nobody is going to get hurt. Promise.'

Sarah moved into a dream world. She was enchanted, bewitched, obsessed. She felt Laurie's presence everywhere, within her, around her. She breathed him in when she fed the birds in the garden, tasted him in her coffee cup, touched him when she folded up the papers and stacked the dishes. He was on her skin when she showered, in her mouth when she yawned. Strangely, it didn't seem to change things between her and David. He was still her husband. Her responsibility. Even when she started at Greenacres, juggling with complicated shifts and bus journeys, working twice as hard as she need so that she could keep the household ticking over with its usual efficiency, she was so happy, so buzzing with life and energy, that she still had time for David whenever he needed her. And for Merry. And, always, for Laurie.

'What are we going to *do*?' she asked him, like a child, the first time they'd met, secretly, and driven along the valley for a stolen hour together. 'You love Claire. And I still love David. I really do. I didn't know that you could love two people at the same time.'

'I have a theory,' he'd told her. 'Love is amorphous.'

'What do you mean?'

'Imagine a cloud. A lovely *summer* cloud. It keeps changing shape and direction. But it can gather up everything within itself, endlessly. Love is like that.'

'Laurie! I'm not talking about clouds. What about Claire?'

'You really want me to tell you about Claire and me, don't you?' She nodded timidly. 'Very well then. I was bowled over when I first saw her. She was sensational, you know. Like Bridget, but even more beautiful, because Bridget's still a girl but Claire was a fully-fledged woman when we met. She was wearing a long green silk dress. Bridesmaid at some ghastly wedding. And that incredible glistening hair of hers! She looked like a mermaid. A mermaid with a fag!' He laughed. 'I didn't even smoke, but I heard myself asking for a cigarette. It was the only thing I could think of as an excuse to sit down beside her.'

'I see.' Sarah's voice was small and polite.

He squeezed her hand reassuringly. 'We had a few wonderful years. The sex was terrific. And we were good friends as well. Always talking, arguing, exploring ideas. We enjoyed all that. But then . . . the miscarriages started, you see. God knows how many. I begged her to give up. "Children only bring you grief," I said. But she was determined. And at last, success! Bridget was born. From that first day, Claire sort of . . . wrapped herself around her. As if that was enough. Mother and child. Sufficient unto themselves. I was still in the frame somewhere, you know. Good old Dad. But they were . . . interlocked.' His voice broke. 'All my life, Sarah, I've been the also-ran. When Mark was run over my mother blamed me. Whenever she looked at me, I knew she was thinking, "If only you'd held on to him *tighter*, Laurie." And then, when Bridget arrived, I'd see Claire's face while she was feeding her – and I'd feel like an intruder.'

Sarah considered his words. Is that what David thought, she wondered. About her and Will. Almost every row they'd ever had, somehow Will had been at the centre of it. Did every man feel himself threatened by his own first-born?

Laurie was looking down at her, his eyes full of wonder. 'That's what is so marvellous about all this, Sarah. I belong to *you*. I felt it myself, on Christmas Eve. And then . . . the things you wrote in that letter . . . It's the first time in my life that I've ever felt that I belonged.'

Later, looking back, Sarah could hardly believe how naive she had been. David had often told her that she thought and felt as a child. And it must be true. The fact was that she had never intended to have a sexual affair with Laurie.

'A loving friendship,' she'd suggested. 'Couldn't we manage that?'

'A flirtation, you mean?'

'No! Of course not. We can be together sometimes. On our own, I mean. And we will always know, inside ourselves, how we feel. Isn't that enough?'

He'd shaken his head doubtfully. But at first, it *had* been enough. Sarah had never known such joy. She felt like a teenager again – except that when she *had* been a teenager it wasn't really fun at all. Too much worrying about exams. Too much worrying about herself, how she looked, how she felt, how she was doing. But now, every day was bliss. Laurie saw to that. Every single day there was something to remind her of him, to bring him close to her even though they could be miles apart. Often it was a phone call. He might decide to call her at work and since she was in charge of the switchboard, that didn't cause any problems. If she was busy, with people at the desk checking out or waiting to be shown to their rooms, she used their code. Their secret message. 'Yes, sir. You do have a reservation.' Sometimes he called her at home, whispering messages of love in her ear even when David was in the same room. And then she'd answer him, 'Still no reply from the council? How infuriating!' Or, 'The Countryside Commission! Gosh, Laurie, that's really good news.' Once David had passed her the phone with a casual, 'It's that boyfriend of yours again,' and she'd looked up at him, wide-eyed with panic. But his face was untroubled. He had no idea he'd stumbled so near the truth. And all she'd felt was relief. Why didn't she feel guilty, she wondered.

The truth was, it all seemed as fresh and funny and harmless as a child's game. Like the letters Laurie sent her. Tiny notes, folded again and again until they were no bigger than a postage stamp. She'd open the Minutes Book at one of their road safety meetings, and find one there, waiting for her. Or she'd put her hand in her coat pocket and feel one pressing against her fingertips. Little unsigned emissaries of love, sometimes no words at all, just minute drawings that made her heart sing. A heart. A flower. A smiling face. She'd discovered his secret. This man, with his reputation for brusqueness and straight talking, was an old fashioned romantic. The steel-grey eyes which had alarmed her so much when she first saw them, the fierce, hawkish face – they were nothing but a mask.

On Valentine's Day he'd even managed to send her a gift. It was waiting for her when she arrived at work, one perfect red rose, in a cellophane box. The card was anonymous. It was simply directed to 'The new receptionist, Greenacres Country House Hotel.'

Mr Manley had handed it over as she'd taken her place behind the desk. He'd looked at her curiously. 'You obviously have an admirer, Mrs Page.'

She'd shrugged, trying to laugh it off. 'A satisfied punter, no doubt. Let's hope he books in again.'

Laurie began to get more and more reckless. One day, when she was checking through some files in the back office, she'd been amazed to hear his voice drift in from the hotel foyer. He was talking to Mr Manley.

'Good afternoon,' he said urbanely. 'Laurence Richley. I'm a neighbour of Mrs Page's. Is she still here?'

'Yes, she is. She finishes at two.'

'Good.' She could feel the smile on Laurie's face. 'I've just been visiting a client in Linfold, so I thought I could give her a lift home. Save her waiting for the bus.'

'How very thoughtful of you,' Mr Manley said. 'Just take a seat and I'll tell her you're here. I'm sure she'll be delighted.'

'What are you *doing*?' she asked him later, when he'd driven her away from Mr Manley's cool scrutiny.

'I really have been visiting a client. She's housebound, and as it happens she lives just around the corner from Green-acres.'

'Really?' She wasn't convinced.

'Really! But I did arrange my timing so that I could pick you up. I thought we might have a little drive before I take you home.'

'Dare we?'

'Why not? David won't be back for hours yet and Claire's not expecting me. Besides, I want to talk to you.'

'What about? Important?' She stifled a flutter of apprehension.

'Not yet. We'll find somewhere good to stop.'

After he'd driven about a couple of miles he pulled the car into a lay-by and helped her out. Taking her hand he hurried her towards a small wooden stile, half hidden in the thick hedgerow. Once they had scrambled over it they found themselves on a narrow path that led them steeply upwards for a few minutes then took them along a high level track winding beneath rugged old oak trees. Their feet crunched through withered leaves, but Laurie made her stop while he pulled down a branch and showed her the clusters of buds that were just beginning to show a glimpse of green.

'Spring is coming,' he told her. 'Our first spring together. This time last year I didn't even know you existed.' He lifted her hand to his lips, then tucked it through his arm and they walked on for a while in silence, enjoying the matching rhythm of their stride.

Suddenly he stopped and tugged her round to face him. 'Sarah, listen,' he said. 'In a fortnight's time I have to spend a night in York. I've thought about it and thought about it and . . .' he studied her face anxiously. '. . . I want you to come with me. Please.' She took a deep breath and turned away, looking down the valley, at the road running towards Deredale, the calm, shining river beyond it. 'Please, Sarah,' he repeated.

'It's not what I intended,' she said. 'Not . . . adultery.'

'But that's only a *word*!' He was impatient. 'What I'm talking about is passion. In my head and heart, oh yes. But in my body too. I'm not made of marble.'

'It would be a betrayal, Laurie. The worst kind.'

His eyelids dropped. She couldn't read his expression. 'What have we been doing then, these past few weeks? O.K. So we haven't jumped into bed together, but all the same . . .'

'I know.' She was trembling. 'It's just . . . the final act though, isn't it? It seems . . . so extreme. A sort of no-going-back.'

'I thought that's what we were about.' His voice sounded strained. 'If this is just a temporary arrangement, you'd better tell me now.'

'Oh, my love. Of course it isn't. That's not what I meant.' But she could see that he was distraught. 'How could I manage it? From a practical point of view, I mean? What would I tell David and Merry?'

He looked at her gravely. 'If you really want to come, you'll find a way. Anything is possible. When it's what you really want.'

She decided to broach the subject at the supper table. 'David,' she said, ladling moussaka on to his plate, passing him the baked potatoes, 'I've just seen an advertisement for a course in Management Skills. At work. It was in the *Caterer and Hotelkeeper*.'

'Uh-huh?' He was reaching for the winter salad, not listening to her.

'A very short course. Just a taster, really. A sort of introduction. Friday afternoon and evening and Saturday morning.'

'Right.'

She took a deep breath. 'I thought I'd rather like to go. If you don't mind.'

At last she had his attention. 'Where?' he asked.

'Near Leeds. I haven't got all the details yet. I just wrote down the phone number.'

'You'd stay overnight, you mean?'

'Well, yes. I'd have to. I'd leave home on the Friday morning and be back early evening, Saturday.'

'Why do you want to go?'

She unfolded her napkin carefully, put the lid back on the vegetable dish. 'I just thought, when I went for my interview, Mr Manley did mention management skills. It seems that if you want to get anywhere in the hotel industry . . .'

'Do you want to get anywhere?'

'I don't know.' She felt herself struggling. She looked at Merry, but she seemed to be ignoring the conversation completely, deep in her own thoughts. 'I do enjoy what I'm doing, but I wouldn't want to be a receptionist for the rest of my life, would I?'

He shook his head. 'I have no idea what you want these days, Sarah. None at all. Is old Manley going to pay for you?'

'No!' she said, in sudden alarm. 'It's got nothing to do with him. It's my long weekend off, anyway. I don't even want him to know.'

'Why ever not? It might do you a bit of good, show him that you are keen.'

'No. He'll think I'm planning to leave, won't he? Using him as a stepping stone and then moving on. I will pay for it myself, though. Out of my own earnings, I mean.'

He smiled at her sadly. 'You seem to have made up your mind already.'

'I would like to go,' she said. 'If you and Merry can cope.'

'Of course we can cope, Mum. What an old fuss you are!' Sarah breathed a sigh of relief. At last Merry had decided to ride to her support. 'We'll have a great time, Dad. Won't we?'

'Will we?' He looked doubtful.

'Course we will. We can have a shimmy down the Metro Centre.'

'Yuk!'

'You'd love it. And *then* . . . you can buy me a Big Mac.'

David looked so appalled that Sarah laughed out loud. 'Don't worry,' she reassured him. 'I'll see to it that the fridge is absolutely groaning with goodies.' She stood up and carried the dirty dishes into the kitchen. She felt almost weak. With relief? With apprehension? She didn't know. She hadn't realised that subterfuge was such an exhausting business.

CHAPTER SEVENTEEN

Laurie had arranged to see her in York Minster at about five o'clock.

'Sorry, lovey,' he'd said. 'I don't think I can get out of my meeting before that. Wait for me beneath the west window. I'll find you there.'

She'd spent most of the afternoon in the cathedral. Now choral evensong had begun and the glorious harmonies of Brahms' 'How beautiful are thy dwellings' surged around her. The light outside had faded. The glowing stained-glass colours of 'the Heart of Yorkshire' had been swallowed up by the encroaching dusk. She'd sat transfixed, gazing up at the reds and ambers of the little windows enclosed in their heart-shaped tracery of stone until the very last moment. Trust Laurie to settle on such a romantic trysting place! She turned her eyes up to the high vaulted ceiling, wonderfully restored after the great fire, pale and perfect with its gleaming gold bosses. She gave an involuntary shiver. Despite the central heating, chilly vapours seemed to creep out at her from the ancient stone of the walls and paving. A priest came striding past her, the skirts of his black cassock swishing against his legs. His face was stern. His eyes were raised and seemed to be looking inward, to be focused on holy matters far removed from the casual tourists who drifted like ghosts around the echoing spaces of the building.

Sarah found herself longing to rush after him, to grab his hand and beg him to talk to her, to spare just a few minutes of his time to listen, to counsel and comfort. She remained motionless, sitting stiff-backed on her upright seat. What

Jennifer Curry

could she be *thinking* about, she wondered. She wasn't even a believer. There might be some universal force, she conceded. Some power beyond mortal understanding. But she was absolutely convinced that there was no friendly, compassionate, man-sized deity, no personal saviour who cared about human behaviour. So why should she have this absurd compulsion to kneel before a haughty, wild-eyed, black-frocked cleric, confess that she was just about to cheat on her husband and beg him to reassure her that it was quite all right really because love like theirs was more important than loyalty.

She sniffed, rummaged in her pocket for her handkerchief, glanced at her watch. Laurie was late. What would she do if he didn't turn up? She didn't even know which hotel they were booked into. What if he'd decided it wasn't a good idea after all? What if Claire had found out? Or David? What if something terrible had happened to him? She began to panic. She felt as if she were losing herself. And then, dead on cue, Laurie was there, hurrying towards her with both arms outstretched.

'Sarah!' he said. 'You're really here!'

'Of course.' She smiled.

'I've been shaking like a leaf all day. I hardly dared come inside.' He gave a strangled laugh. 'I've actually been hanging around out there trying to pluck up courage. I'd convinced myself that you wouldn't come. I almost rang Peacocks' Acre to see if you answered the phone.' He bent and kissed her, caring nothing for the disapproving glare of the verger. 'Sarah,' he said, 'you're a miracle. You will never know how much I love you.'

The hotel he had chosen was a Victorian town house, substantial and dignified, situated in a leafy street about ten minutes' walk away from the Minster. She stood to one side while he signed them in, hardly daring to wonder what their name was supposed to be. She couldn't bear it if he wanted her to pretend to be Mrs Richley, she thought, not when the real Mrs Richley was such a potent presence in her life.

156

When the porter had carried in their overnight bags and whistled off down the corridor, Laurie grinned. 'Mr and Mrs Laurence,' he told her. 'So we won't forget it in the heat of the moment.'

Sarah stared around the room. It was tall-ceilinged, high-windowed, and it *glowed*. The wallpaper was thickly clustered with dense bunches of pink and red roses. The thick carpet and the abundance of cushions were all fuchsia pink. The bedspread was coral pink and magenta. 'It's lovely,' she said, looking around doubtfully. 'Very... very...'

'Very pink!' He laughed. 'Come here.' He sat on the side of the bed and pulled her down on to his lap, but she was anxious and scared. He kissed her gently. 'Don't worry,' he told her. 'I'm not going to leap upon you like a ravening beast. I thought we'd go out for a walk now. Look round the town. Then, I've found a good little trattoria. Highly recommended. You like Italian, don't you? Or would you prefer posh nosh?' She shook her head. 'That's fine then. After that... we'll take it as it comes, lovey. No pressure, eh?'

The evening shimmered with laughter and pent-up excitement. Their *risotto de peoci*, eaten by candlelight, tasted like the food of the gods. Their dark-eyed waiter wafted about his phallic pepper mill and surpassed himself with extravagant compliments about the '*bella signora*', though Laurie was convinced he came from Birmingham. They drank a bottle of good chianti between them, and Sarah felt as if she were flying.

But when they'd got back to their hotel bedroom, when they'd bathed together up to their noses in scented bubbles, and drunk some of the cognac that Laurie produced from his briefcase, when they'd slipped naked between the shell pink sheets... everything went wrong. As he put his arms around her, reaching for her urgently, she felt herself close up against him, become tight and dry, resisting him. He pulled away almost at once, afraid that he might hurt her. He felt between her legs with his fingers, touching her, stroking her gently, then he took his hand away and lay back on his pillows.

'I'm sorry,' she said. 'I don't know...' She began to cry quietly.

'Hey! There's no need for tears.' He smiled at her. 'No need at all.'

'But we were supposed to, we wanted to...'

'The important thing is that we're here. Together. *Really* sleeping together. And we have the whole night.' He kissed her eyelids softly. 'Go to sleep now,' he said. 'That's what you need.' He made her turn on her side and hooked his arm around her waist so that their pale bodies slotted together like two silver spoons.

She woke in the middle of the night, feeling him coiled around her. Instantly, she flared into desire. She felt herself open up for him like a red rose, dewy red petals unfolding in the warmth of the sun, stretching, reaching for him. She knew he was awake, listening to her breathing, waiting for her. She turned on her back and tugged him on top of her, and he clamped his mouth hungrily upon hers. As he slipped inside her she gave a gasp of delight. She wound her legs high around his buttocks, twined her arms about his neck, and they rocked together, gently, at first, wonderingly, and then with a gathering intensity that swept them away like a landslide, casting them about helplessly with a force neither of them recognised. When at last she reached her climax she shouted out in a strange, rough voice.

He covered her mouth with his hand. 'Ssh! We'll wake the people next door.'

'Why not?' She laughed. 'Let them share it. Let them listen to a woman in love.'

They did not sleep again but lay together as if entranced, every sense alert, ideas, images, daydreams floating through their consciousness.

'I feel high,' she said at last. 'Is this what it feels like when you have a good trip? As if you've lost your skin? Turned into an essence?'

He raised himself on one elbow and gazed down at her.

'I'm just so grateful that we *found* each other. Before it was too late.'

She slithered out of bed, showered herself almost reluctantly, not wanting to sluice him out of her, then made some tea and carried it back to him. She drank hers sitting cross-legged on the pillow, feeling as if she didn't even know herself any longer. He smiled up at her lazily, reaching to trace the line of her cheek and jaw with his fingertips.

She took hold of his hand and held it to her mouth. 'When will we see each other again?'

'Thursday night. We're putting leaflets through letter-boxes, remember. Trying to persuade them to turn out for the public meeting.' She pulled a face. '*And,*' he continued, 'I seem to remember that you're all coming round for Sunday lunch next weekend.'

The very thought of it terrified her. 'How will we manage? How will they not know?'

'Ah!' he said. 'Well, to start with, you must not light up like a torch when you look at me, Sarah. You must frown. Or better still, ignore me.'

'Easier said than done.'

'You must remember what I'm like. The real me. Moody and cantankerous. That awkward sod who's always causing trouble.'

'I can't.'

'Yes, you can. Write your own scenario.'

'What do you mean?'

'What about a re-run of that famous supper party of yours? You were furious with me, don't you remember? Because I was rude to Tom Jackson's girlfriend. That glorious smile when you told us the meat was cooked at last.' He laughed. 'I'll never forget it. Your teeth were like daggers.'

'I wasn't furious.' She clapped her hand over her mouth. 'Oh, I was. You're right. But not for the reason you think. David had just told me in the kitchen that you fancied Wanda, and I couldn't bear it.'

'Wanda!' Laurie's face screwed up in distaste. 'Good grief!'

He shook his head. 'We really are going to have to work out what to do though, aren't we?'

She looked bereft. 'I can't see myself getting away like this very often.'

'There is somewhere we could go . . . I don't know what you'll think about this, but . . .'

'Tell me.'

'We have a little hospitality flat. The firm, I mean. Round the corner from the office. It's just a bed-sit really, with a shower and a kitchen cubicle. We use it to put up colleagues, or clients sometimes if a court case is dragging on. We could meet there. Just for the odd hour or so.'

'Wouldn't someone find out?'

'We'd have to be very careful, lovey. From now on, I'm afraid that's the name of the game.'

She nodded. 'I suppose so.'

'Let's make a date now, then. Before we part and the real world swallows us up. A week next Friday? Could you manage that?'

'Yes.' But she was sad. 'I'll get there. Promise.'

He smiled, took a deep breath. 'A patch of sunshine to look forward to,' he said.

Sarah hadn't known that such deep delight was possible. It was as if Laurie peeled off the layers of her respectability and decorum and found a central core of eroticism that she hadn't even suspected. The little anonymous flat was grey, impersonal and sensibly furnished. For them it became a temple of perfumed pleasure.

In the beginning, she had felt not a twinge of guilt. David was happy, engrossed in his work, totally absorbed in Craig-lands, his department, his precious football teams. She was taking nothing from him, she was sure. And Claire seemed as serene and imperturbable as ever, spending long hours carving in her studio. She was working her way through Bridget's A-level syllabus, too, diving into English and French language and literature, even tackling Economics, with the zeal of a convert.

'Why are you doing it?' Sarah asked her one day when she found her in the library, poring over a huge French dictionary. 'Do you think it helps Bridget?'

Claire had laughed. 'No. It helps *me*. I seem to have missed out on this stuff. What the head calls "intellectual rigour". Don't you think that's a wonderful term?'

'I can't say I've ever thought about it.'

'It's all right for you,' Claire said. 'You've done your stint. But when I was at school I did the minimum necessary to get me into Art College.'

'But art is the air you breathe.'

Claire frowned. 'I'm in a bit of a rut. I could go on churning out pretty little things for the rest of my days . . .'

'Pretty little things! Don't put yourself down.'

'But I want to make progress, you see. There's a whole pile of ideas out there, waiting to be tapped. I want to get to grips with them.'

One day, after they'd made love, Sarah said, 'Is it wrong, what we're doing, Laurie?'

He looked at her steadily, his eyes veiled. 'Nothing ever seemed more right to me.'

'But you know, when I was in Norwich I would never have believed . . . it would have seemed quite unthinkable, that I should have an affair.'

'I hope this is more than that.'

'*I* think so,' she persisted. 'Of course I do. But other people wouldn't, would they?'

'It's more common than you think,' he told her. 'A lot of us stray from the marital bed. Over half the adult population, I imagine.'

'But *why*? We all made our vows, didn't we? And meant what we said.'

'Oh, lovey.' He put his arms round her, kissing her troubled brow. 'Who can say why? We have the time and energy, I suppose, and need something to fill the gap when our kids are growing up and don't really need us any more.'

She nodded, thinking of William who had paid them only the briefest of visits at Easter, before taking off with Zack for a holiday in Amsterdam.

'And,' he continued, 'our expectations are higher. We want the excitement of the grand romance, don't we? What we have at home becomes a bit humdrum after all those years of washing up and shopping at the supermarket.'

'But some people manage to grow more deeply in love as the years go on,' she argued. 'Like Jim and Muriel, David's Mum and Dad. They almost seem . . . like one person.'

'They're the lucky ones. They grow together instead of apart. And they've stayed put most of their lives, haven't they? In one place. You've been uprooted. I don't suppose you would have even noticed me if you'd stayed in Norwich . . .'

'How could I not have noticed you! You know how I . . .'

'Yes, lovey. I know you feel you recognised me. All the same, if you'd been in Norfolk, and had Jim and Muriel nearby, and all your old friends around you, holding you firm in *their* pattern of living . . . I think you'd have stayed faithful to David for the rest of your days. But when you left them, you broke the pattern. You were free to find your own. Does that make sense?'

Sarah thought back to the Christmas party, remembering Muriel's watchful, worried eyes, Pam's unbridled fury about Jake's defection. 'Yes, it does,' she said.

He squeezed her hand. 'But it *has* happened. And it's just about the most important thing in my life. I can't bear it if you're beginning to have regrets . . .'

'I'm not. How could I? I just wish . . . I . . .'

'What do you wish?'

'I just wish I'd found you when I was twenty.'

He gave a roar of laughter. 'What a thought! We'd never even have noticed each other. You with your head in your books. Me set upon re-inventing the entire legal system. No. We're like good wine, my darling. We needed time to mature.'

CHAPTER EIGHTEEN

As Bridget strolled through the village to meet the five-twenty train, she felt Chris's letter burning a hole in her pocket, hot against her thigh. She must get her father to herself for a little while. Soften him up with some gentle persuasion. Once he'd talked to Mum they might gang up together and tell her that the whole idea was out of the question. Forbid her, absolutely, to go. But if she could just soft-talk Laurie a bit first . . .

She walked past Rentons and wrinkled up her nose with delight at its tangy smell of fish and salt and sea. Then she stopped and looked in Treasures, noticing that there were two of Claire's pieces quite well displayed in the window, the lovely driftwood 'Goose' and the strange, twisted little figure that looked a bit like a gargoyle. Reluctantly, she hurried on her way. She didn't have time to inspect all the other lovely things, the sea-green pots, the red handblown glassware, the new, exciting collage of a jumping girl. She wanted to make sure that she was at the station before the train got in. Laurie used to say it was one of the best things in life, being met by someone you loved at the end of a journey. He was such an old softy, her Dad, though not many people knew that. A lot of them were a bit scared of him. But Chris understood. He said that Laurie was like a huge, marvellous iceberg. There was the chunk you could see, which could be a bit chilly and glittering. But then there was all the other stuff going on underneath the surface which was a complete mystery. And that's exactly how it *was*.

Anyway, she knew Dad would like it, the two of them walking home together. He was always in a good mood when he came back from work on the train. She grinned to herself. He was a strange character. He got bees in his bonnet, and they buzzed like mad, more busily than anybody else's bees. He was always banging on that the car was 'civilisation's biggest enemy', more so than nuclear power or atomic submarines or germs. 'We've created this monster,' he would say to anyone he could persuade to listen, 'and mark my words, it will devour us, poison us, suffocate us, destroy us.'

He did *have* a car, of course, and he did drive it. He couldn't really manage without one. But whenever possible he left it in the garage and took the train and felt really good about it. He was a bit naive, Bridget decided. Whether he came home in the train or in his car, and whether or not his roads committee managed to ban heavy lorries from the centre of the village, it didn't really make a jot of difference to the environment, or global warming, or anything like that. It just made him *feel* good.

And then Bridget stopped thinking about her father and began to think, instead, about Chris Page. And about the letter in her pocket. She thought about Chris a lot. Most of the time, really. It was just possible that she was in love with him. She didn't really know, because they hadn't had time to find out yet, just those few days at Christmas and New Year and then it was all parties and other people and they'd hardly ever managed to get away on their own. She hadn't seen him since he'd left on January the second. She'd tried to persuade him to stay on for an extra weekend. Most people wouldn't even think about starting work till the Monday after New Year's Day, she said. But he was adamant. He had to get back to Norwich to open up the sports shop because he was manager and he had to set a good example to the staff. Especially since most of them were at least ten years older and longing for him to put a foot wrong so that they could prove that they'd been right in the first place and he was too young for the job. But he'd promised her faithfully that he'd come up for the Easter Bank Holiday so that at least they'd have that to look forward to. *Then*, for some weird reason, her Dad had taken it into his head that they should go sailing round the Greek Islands for a whole fortnight at Easter, all the family together, including Uncle Mark, Auntie Lou and Alison. When she'd protested, and tried to explain, he'd said that Chris could come too, there'd be plenty of room. But that was no good because Chris couldn't get sufficient time off work. Bridget didn't know what had got into Dad to make him do such a thing as organise a sailing holiday, just like that without even discussing it first. Mum didn't even like sailing much, and you'd think *he* got quite enough of it with the Pilgrim Project and everything. Probably, she decided, it was because of Uncle Mark. He'd been a bit depressed after Christmas. Winter weather made his aches and pains twice as bad, and it got him down sometimes. Dad always felt terribly responsible for him. Mark had only been four when the accident happened and it had left him sort of twisted up and lame in his left leg. It was because of that that Dad had started Pilgrims in the first place, to do something for *other* kids who were disabled or disadvantaged, the way his little brother had been. And it must have been because of him that he'd had the idea of the Greek holiday. It had been good fun, too. She'd enjoyed it. But she would rather have been with Chris.

She turned the corner at the end of the High Street and saw the little railway station ahead of her, precise and tidy, with its brightly-painted toytown bridge arching across the line. Automatically she wandered over to the wooden fence opposite the entrance. She could perch there, in the sunshine, while she was waiting. Dad was very sweet, she thought, the way he was always trying to take care of people. Chris was like that, too, gentle and a bit shy. But the best thing about him was the way he made them all laugh. She didn't think they'd ever laughed as much as they had done when Chris was staying with them. It was because he was such a marvellous mimic. He could take anybody off brilliantly. And he noticed such funny little things about him. She felt as if she knew his staff personally.

Prim little Miss Mitchell, with her chanted catalogue of herb teas. 'They're ever so good for you, Mr Page. You should try them, you should, really. You can choose from camomile and comfrey, elderflower and jasmine, blackberry, peppermint, and raspberry leaf *tips*.'

And then there was Yorkshire Roger, the gossip. 'Now as you know, I don't like to speak ill of anyone, not me, but Jenny told me, and *she*'s not one to spread the dirt, but she says she saw him and her, in the park, bold as brass, and they were *not* there to feed the ducks!'

Remembering the way Chris had caught the accent and twisted his face about like a rubber mask, Bridget laughed out loud, sitting on the fence in the sun. She felt for his letter and read it through again, her heart beating with excitement. Only a boyfriend like Chris would have thought up such a treat for her and got it all organised. She just used the word 'boyfriend' in her own thoughts because she was still so shy about it all. To start with, he was twenty-five. And he had quite a high-powered job. The other boys she'd been out with were just her own age, and still at school, so Chris seemed different. It wasn't as if he was very good-looking, or anything like that. He had a sort of squashed nose, because he'd broken it years ago, playing rugby. And he wasn't very tall. Not *quite* as tall as she was actually, though she didn't mind about that, not a bit. He wasn't a patch on his brother David, as far as looks went. But then nobody was, because David looked exactly like Richard Gere, *and* he knew it. Bridget still found it hard to believe that her boyfriend was the brother of her best friend's *father*. It seemed really weird. If she and Chris ever got married – she shivered at the very thought of it – but if they did, she would turn into . . . Merry's auntie! and Merry's grandparents' daughter-in-law. That's who Chris took after, she realised. He was like his father, Jim. Absolutely ordinary to look at, but nice and kind and funny. She closed her eyes, and conjured up Chris so vividly that she could almost feel him, even smell his skin. She longed for him so much that it was like a pain. She was just counting the days till his next visit. Twenty-six days, and he'd be here. Less than a month. But it seemed like a lifetime. She thought, perhaps, she *must* be in love.

Laurie Richley, comfortably settled in his corner seat, watched the countryside slide past as the train ticked along towards Deredale. He'd had an excellent day in the office. Exchanged contracts on two separate house sales that had been hanging fire for months. And helped old Mrs Neep to draw up an equitable Will at last. At his gentle prompting she'd decided not to cut off her black sheep of a son without a penny, though undoubtedly Benny would have been a richer man if he'd treated his mother more kindly. Never mind. He must not take on other people's family problems as if they were his own, as Claire often reminded him.

'It's Bridget who should be your main concern,' she said. 'Not wastrels like Benny Neep.'

And that was true, of course. But Bridget was wonderful. She never gave the slightest glimmer of a cause for concern. So she really didn't need him in the same way as the Benny Neeps of this world, did she? Or some of the poor kids he took sailing every year. That was another source of satisfaction. The Project was going from strength to strength. Only this morning there'd been a cheque in the post for five thousand pounds from a local business man Laurie had taken sailing in the spring, and whom he'd been nursing assiduously ever since.

He stretched contentedly in his seat, feeling the sunshine as warm on his face as a lover's kiss. He had the evening paper open on his lap but he didn't even glance at it. His eyes rejoiced in the familiar scenery, the hedges showing that keen, vivid green that would not last much beyond the end of the month, the cow parsley creaming the edges of the lanes, the sheep tranquil and slow-moving while their lambs straggled, knock-kneed, behind him. May. It was his favourite time of year, so full of promise, with the whole of summer stretched out tantalisingly ahead. 'The year's at the spring.' He smiled to himself. He felt vibrantly alive. 'All's right with the world!'

Quoting poetry, he thought. It was ridiculous. Not his style at all. But he just couldn't help it. It sprang up, unbidden, unexpected, from some secret well deep inside him. It was love that did it. He still had the smell of her body on his own, the feel of her skin on his fingertips. He gave a covert glance at the man in the seat opposite him. They were about the same age, he supposed. He was wearing a suit not unlike his own, striped shirt, plain tie. To the casual observer they might be two peas out of the same pod. Middle-aged, middle-class, middle-of-the-road, middle England. Laurie lifted his paper to conceal the idiot grin that spread itself across his face. So – what did that other guy know about life, he wondered. Were *his* days studded with joy, delight, rapture, discovery, spine-tingling excitement and enchantment?

As if on cue, the man lifted one hand, pale and immaculately-manicured, covered his mouth while he yawned, then looked languidly at his heavy gold watch. Laurie's eyes flashed. It was as he'd imagined. 'There but for the grace of God . . .' He slipped his newspaper back into his briefcase. The train would be pulling into the station any minute now. He might have time to cut the grass before supper. Or perhaps he and Claire would just sit and watch the river for a while. The pair of them were as relaxed and gentle together as Darby and Joan these days. Later in the evening, he'd take a stroll along to the Eagle . . . have a drink with David . . .

The train lurched to a halt and he jumped down on to the platform, bidding a chirpy goodbye to the surprised man who fluttered the beautiful hands that reminded Laurie of Claire's 'Hands of Friendship'. As he strode along towards the ticket office he caught sight of Bridget waiting for him. She was sitting on the railings, her elbows on her knees, her face cupped in her palms. She was wearing faded blue jeans and her bright yellow tee-shirt, the one that had one word, 'WHY?', printed on the front. She was irradiated by the late afternoon sunshine that made her hair glint round her head like a golden aureole.

As soon as Bridget saw him she came rushing across the station forecourt, her face glowing. 'Hi! Dad.' She grinned, and kissed him on the cheek.

'Remind me. Why have you got "Why?" emblazoned on your bosom?' he asked.

She laughed and turned her back. The word, 'BECAUSE!' answered his question.

'I give up,' he said. 'To what do I owe *this* pleasure?'

'I just thought I'd walk you home.' She tucked her arm through his. 'Super day, isn't it?'

'It certainly is. But what's the hidden agenda? You're making me nervous.'

She laughed. 'You've been a solicitor too long, did you know that? It's given you a thoroughly suspicious nature.'

'True! How did school go today?'

'Don't be boring.'

They reached the top of Station Hill and turned into the High Street, waiting on the pavement for a gap to open in the traffic so that they could cross. A huge, articulated lorry roared past them, perilously close to the kerb. Laurie blanched, took a step backwards.

'Don't let it get to you,' Bridget murmured soothingly.

'Sorry!'

She hugged his arm. 'Dad . . .'

'Yes?'

'You've heard about Sting, haven't you? The singer.'

'Of course I've heard about Sting. I'm not in my dotage yet. He's good.'

'He's brilliant! And Bryan Adams?'

'Yes,' said Laurie cagily. 'The name rings a bell.'

'U2?'

'Pass.'

'Oh, Dad! "All I Want Is You".'

'I'm proud to hear it.'

'Number one in the charts! Just last year.'

'What is this? Are we practising for Trivial Pursuit?'

She giggled. 'What about Peter Gabriel?'

'Peter Gabriel. Now you're talking. Genesis – they were the greatest. Your mother and I used to listen to them when you were a tiny baby. They can't be still around, surely?'

'Of course not. Not Genesis. But Peter Gabriel is. All these people, Dad, are coming up here. To Newcastle. A massive great supergig.'

'Why?'

'It's a special. In aid of Amnesty.'

'Are they doing a tour, then?'

'No, that's what I'm trying to tell you. It's a one-off. A once-in-a-lifetime. Sting's organising it. He comes from round here, did you know that? Wallsend, actually.'

Laurie shook his head distractedly. 'Where's it going to be? The . . . supergig.'

'The football stadium. On June the first at St James Park. Don't you think it's amazing?'

'Amazing,' he echoed. At once a cold finger of alarm began tapping at his heart. 'I imagine all the tickets were sold out months ago.'

'They were. *But* . . . I had a letter from Chris this morning.'

'Surprise, surprise!' His tone was bantering, to try to keep his anxiety at bay.

He lengthened his stride but Bridget tightened her grip on his arm and forced him to stop, to turn and look at her. 'Chris has managed to get two tickets, Dad. He's a member of Amnesty International so he got special priority. He's coming up to stay at Peacocks' Acre and he wants me to go to the concert with him.'

'Oh, Bridget. A thing like that!' He felt all the joy drain away from him. 'I don't think so,' he told her. 'You're just sixteen.'

She spluttered with indignation. 'Just sixteen! What's that supposed to mean? It's because I'm just sixteen that I want to go. It's not exactly your sort of music, is it? These days? If I were "just fifty" I'd be happy give it a miss.'

'But it's not . . . it's not . . .'

They'd turned the corner now into Bridge Lane.

'Not what?' she demanded as he surged ahead.

'I don't know, Bridget.' He reached the wrought iron gate of Dolphin House, and stopped for a moment, his hand on the latch, trying not to notice the pleading look in her eyes. 'I'm tired now. I've had a busy day. We'll talk about this after supper, shall we? With Mum.'

'You promise?'

'Promise.'

Then he marched away down the garden path, his back set firmly against her, pushed open the front door and was swallowed up into the cool shade of the hall.

'I think you were a bit hard on her,' Claire said, when Bridget had gone off to her room, tearful and disappointed.

'I haven't said "no".'

'You haven't said "yes" either. She was so excited when she read the letter. She wanted to ring Chris and tell him everything was all right. It's on a Saturday night, you know. It wouldn't affect school or homework or anything like that. And it's for a very good cause.'

'I know! I know! I'll send them money!'

'Laurie! You can't wriggle out of it like that.'

'But these massive pop concerts – they're fraught with danger. They are, Claire. Vast crowds milling about. And half of them on drugs. Out of their minds with the music . . . Anything could happen.'

'The police will be there. They're pretty well supervised.'

'The police can't do a thing with numbers like that. In fact, they make it worse. Look at Hillsborough. It's not very long . . .'

'That was football not pop. And lager probably, not drugs.'

'You think I'm fussing?'

She shrugged. 'We always promised ourselves that we wouldn't wrap her up in cotton wool, didn't we?'

'She's only sixteen,' he said.

'But Chris will take care of her.'

'That's another thing. Chris is a grown man. Why is he so

keen on Bridget? She's just a schoolgirl.'

Claire raised her eyebrows. 'Bridget is going on seventeen *soon* and an extremely attractive young woman. I seem to remember that I'd loved and lost my first serious boyfriend by the time I was her age.'

'So that's what he is, is he? A serious boyfriend.' Laurie's face was grim.

'I don't know, Laurie. She hasn't seen him since Christmas, has she? Just letters.'

'And phone calls. Expensive ones,' he grumbled.

'Don't be such an old skinflint! What I mean is, when they meet up again they'll probably realise it's *not* anything special. I think you're making mountains.'

'Maybe.'

'Anyway, that's not what this is about, is it? You're frightened of letting your little girl go out into the big, wide world.'

'You bet I am. Especially when it's a *super* pop concert. To start with, there's all the business of getting her there and then getting her back at some unearthly hour.'

She pulled a face. 'And worrying about her every single minute she's away. I know. Me too. But Chris has gone out of his way, and spent an arm and a leg getting hold of these tickets, and he's taken a week's holiday especially.'

'So you think we should let her go?'

'Yes, I do. I really think, if we love her, we have to let her go.'

On the last Wednesday in May Laurie telephoned Sarah at Greenacres. He sounded agitated. 'I know I'm not supposed to be seeing you till next week, but can you possibly get away today? Please.'

'Laurie! No, I can't. I'm here till two, and Merry will be home just after four. I won't have time.'

'Please. Please, Sarah.'

A guest wandered up to the desk and began tapping on it with his key, glaring at her, demanding her immediate and undivided attention.

'All right,' she said quickly. 'I've got the car today. I can drop in at home and leave a message.'

'Thank you.'

She lowered her voice. 'Has something happened? You sound terrible. Is it bad news? Claire . . . ?'

'No,' he said. 'Nothing like that. Don't worry. But come as quickly as you can. I need you.'

'Don't ring off, Laurie. I've been meaning to ask you. You haven't found my little butterfly ear-rings, have you? The ones David gave me. They seem to have gone missing.'

She heard his voice change as he smiled. '*One* good thing to report. Yes, I've got them with me. Remind me to give them to you when you come.'

He'd been watching for her from the window of the flat, pacing about, drinking coffee. When she ran along the back lane she always used and rang the bell on the garden door, he opened it at once, and pulled her into his arms. Leading her into the sitting room, clumsily, impatiently, he drew her down on to the bed that he had unfolded and spread with a sheet. He held her so tightly that she felt breathless.

'Wait. Wait a little while,' she begged him, but he seemed beside himself. He tugged off her blouse and buried his head between her breasts. 'What *is* it?' she asked, alarmed.

'I don't know. I just feel so . . . so on edge. It's terrible.'

For the first time, the only time, he was unable to make love to her. He rolled away and lay on his back, staring up at the ceiling. 'I'm sorry,' he mumbled.

She held his hand tightly. 'What you need is talk, not love. If you'd only try to tell me.'

'It's just so stupid,' he said. 'Bridget's going to that awful superconcert thing on Saturday.'

'Don't tell me! Chris gets here the day after tomorrow. I must get some food in.'

'I have such a bad feeling about it, Sarah.'

'Why? There's nothing to feel bad about. They'll have a great time.'

'I'm just . . . scared about the whole thing.'

'You shouldn't let it prey on your mind.'

'I can't help it. It's the first Pilgrims briefing this weekend, so I'll have to leave on Friday morning. I don't know which is worse, hanging around at home or being away while it's happening.'

'What are you so scared *about*?'

'I don't even know. Rioting, perhaps. Some sort of stampede. The stands collapsing . . . crushing them all . . .'

'Laurie. It's not rational.'

'I know. I know. But I just wish she weren't going. I wish I hadn't given in. I should have said no, right at the beginning. But I was so full of *you* – we'd been together that afternoon – I couldn't bring myself to hurt her. I wanted everybody to be as happy as we were.'

'She's seventeen now! You've got to let her grow up. Anyway, she'll be with Chris. He's very level-headed, you know.'

'Yes. Claire says I'm being over-protective.'

'Claire's right.'

'But I have such bad vibes, Sarah. You have no idea. I feel sick in my stomach.'

'Darling!' She put her arms round him, trying to give him some comfort. 'I feel like that sometimes. But it's just nerves. Tiredness. It passes – and then you find nothing terrible has happened at all. Trust me, it's going to be all right.'

He looked at her beseechingly. 'I wish I could believe it.'

'You've got to.' She stood up, bobbed her head in front of the mirror and fixed in the gold ear-rings, enjoying the way they caught the light and shimmered. 'They are pretty, aren't they?' She turned and smiled at him. 'This time next week – my day off – I'll see you then, shall I? We'll be here together, laughing about all this and making magnificent love. Promise.' She gave him a quick hug and made for the door. 'I must go now, sweetheart. Sorry. They'll be wondering. See you soon.'

He stared at her, his face white and frozen.

'You mustn't be such an old worry!' she scolded him lightly.

3
JUNE, 1991

You must excuse me shouting, but my mouth's
a dome of wind. I really don't know who
sent all these dreams, the one about a bowl
of yellow sand, the one about a grave
shaped like a woman's body made of sky.

CHAPTER NINETEEN

Claire never knew whether Laurie had deliberately chosen to go sailing the weekend of the Sting super concert, so that he would have something positive to do, something to occupy his thoughts, or whether he'd been telling her the truth when he said it really was the only possible time he could take the new Pilgrim officers out to sea to let them get the feel of the boats and brief them for the August programme. Before he'd left he'd made one stipulation. Chris and Bridget had to go to the concert by *train*.

Bridget thought it was a ridiculous idea. 'But Chris is coming up from Norwich by car,' she explained. 'And he's a brilliant driver, Sarah says. He travelled hundreds of miles as a rep., you know, before he was promoted.'

'There won't be anywhere to park,' Laurie objected, 'with all that crowd milling about. It's bad enough when there's a football match.'

'Dad! These things are very well organised. They'll have the parking all sorted out, road signs and everything.'

'What about coming home though? People smashed out of their minds. The roads will be a death trap.'

'It's not like that! You're just being paranoid.'

Claire pleaded with him to be more reasonable. 'If you don't trust Chris to drive her and find somewhere to put his car, David says *he*'ll run them in and go back and pick them up when the concert's over. What could be wrong with that?'

Laurie stared at her. 'David offered? Why?'

'Because I told him you were going to be away from home. He was trying to be helpful. Chris is his brother, after all.'

'It's very kind of David, but it doesn't solve the problem, does it?' Laurie's face was set and determined. 'It's not Chris's driving, nor David's, that I'm worried about. It's other drivers. *They're* the dangerous ones.' He looked at Bridget's miserable expression. 'Perhaps I am paranoid. But you know how I feel about traffic, because of Mark. You seem to forget I saw him run over when I was just six years old. I heard him screaming as he went under the wheels. I thought he was going to die.'

'I know, Dad. I know.'

'I'd been holding his hand and I thought it must somehow be my fault because my mother was shouting and shouting my name. Laurie, Laurie, Laurie. Over and over again. If that's paranoia, I'm sorry but I just can't help it.'

'Oh, Dad, I know about that, of course I do, and I do understand. But *please*,' she begged him, 'just this once. The last train home is before ten o'clock. They keep all their best stuff till the end. And all the excitement of the encores and everything. I couldn't bear to miss out on all that.'

He was adamant. He looked at her with that straight, set look, his eyelids lowered, and she knew she was beaten.

'Take it or leave it, Bridget,' he said coldly. 'The choice is yours. You go by train, or you don't go. Chris will have to take Merry instead. And as far as I'm concerned, I'd much rather he did.'

On the Saturday morning Claire woke with a headache. She was surprised. She hardly ever had a headache. And this was no little niggle of discomfort but a bad and persistent pain. At first she tried to conceal it from Bridget who was beside herself with excitement and quite unable to concentrate on anything.

'I can't believe it!' she told Claire as she washed up their breakfast bowls for the third time. 'In just a few hours I'm actually going to *see* them. Bono and 'The Edge'. And all the others. It's like a dream. Pinch me. Pinch me, Mum. I really can't believe it. I mean – Sting! In the flesh!'

Claire smiled and firmly removed the clean dishes before Bridget could start washing them all over again. 'Please don't crow about it too much to Merry, will you? I gather she's a bit peeved with Chris.'

'I know.' A trace of guilt flitted across Bridget's glowing face, then vanished as quickly as it had appeared. 'But, I mean! Merry is his *niece*. You don't take your niece to a gig, do you?'

'Evidently not. When are you meeting Chris?'

'Early. As early as possible. I think we'll get the three o'clock train. There'll be queues miles long to get in, won't there? And all that stuff – the crowd, and buskers and street traders and everything – they're part of the fun, Chris says. I can't wait!'

She gave Claire a hug that made her wince. A pneumatic drill seemed to have switched itself on inside her skull and was boring through her brain.

'Don't you wish you were coming?' Bridget asked. Then, misunderstanding the look on her mother's face, she shook her head. 'Do not answer that question!'

During the afternoon Claire's headache had become unbearable. It was almost like a migraine, she thought, but she'd never had a migraine in her life so she didn't really know. Surely she wasn't going to start having them now. At her age. Or perhaps it was something to do with the change of life? She hadn't thought of that. At last she realised that there was nothing she could do but tell Bridget the truth and take herself off to bed for a while.

Bridget hovered over her as she crept beneath the duvet. 'Is there anything I can get you?'

'No, darling. I've taken a couple of aspirins. Just draw the curtains, will you? It'll wear off soon, I'm sure.'

'Mum?' Bridget's voice was almost a whisper.

'Yes?'

'Perhaps I shouldn't go. To the concert. You're poorly and you'll be all on your own here. Something might happen.'

'Don't be silly. I'll be absolutely fine if I just have a little sleep.'

Bridget sat down on the bed, searching her face anxiously.
'I do mean it, you know. It's not too late. I could give my
ticket to Merry. Dad said he'd like that. And so would she.'

Resolutely Claire lifted her throbbing head and gazed into
Bridget's wide green eyes. 'I will be perfectly all right,' she
told her. 'Nothing would induce me to spoil your night out.
I'm touched that you should make the offer, but I absolutely
insist that you should go. Do you hear? I absolutely insist.'

'You see,' Bridget shifted about miserably, 'it's nearly time
I left *now*.'

'I know, darling. And that's what I want you to do. Just
give me a kiss and go round to Peacocks' Acre straight away.
I'll see you when you come home, sweetheart. By then I shall
be perfectly well again.'

'Will you really?'

'Of course I will.'

'Thanks, Mum.' Bridget bent and dropped a gentle kiss on
Claire's pounding forehead.

'And don't forget, I'll want you to tell me every single thing
about it. Every last detail.'

Bridget flashed her a smile that seemed to light up the
darkened room before she vanished away through the doorway. Five minutes later Claire heard her clear voice calling up
the stair. 'Bye, Mum. See you.' And then the closing of the
door.

Sprawled about in armchairs in the sitting room of Peacocks'
Acre, David and Sarah had spent the evening watching videos
with Merry. At half past ten David firmly pressed the off-
switch.

'O.K., Merry. Enough's enough. Time for bed.'

'Dad!' Merry sounded deeply injured.

'Don't say Dad like that. We've watched your U2 video . . .'

'Twice!' interrupted Sarah.

'. . . And sat through *E.T.* for about the tenth time . . .'

'The third time, that's all,' Merry contradicted him, 'and
I've had it for years.'

Sarah yawned. 'It felt more like the hundredth time to me. I know the dialogue off by heart.'

'It's a great film. Even Barry Norman says so.'

'Bed!' repeated David.

Merry turned tragic eyes towards Sarah. 'You said I could wait up until Chris got back.'

'I said no such thing. They'll just be getting off the train now – *if* they haven't missed it – and then Chris will take Bridget home and no doubt Claire will want to hear all about it. I shouldn't think he'll get back here before half past twelve. At the *earliest*.'

'The very earliest. By which time,' David added, 'all of us will be in bed.'

'It's not fair . . .' Merry began, and Sarah groaned. It was *still* her favourite expression. 'It's not fair,' she repeated, 'that Bridget can stay up till after midnight and I have to go to bed at half past ten.'

'Bridget, you seem to forget, is now seventeen,' Sarah said.

'Just. Just seventeen.'

'And she's been having a very special night out.'

'Why couldn't I have gone? I've known Chris all my life. *And* I'm Bridget's friend. Why couldn't I have gone with them?'

'Two's company,' suggested Sarah.

'But . . .'

'Go to bed, Merry,' David said wearily. 'And I do mean now. Your mother and I will only be half an hour or so . . .'

'*I* think you'll wait up . . .'

'We *won't*,' Sarah said. 'I'm doing an early shift at Green-acres tomorrow. I need a good night's sleep.'

'So there's absolutely no point in hanging around down here, is there?' David added. 'Goodnight, Merry.'

Sarah was woken by the ringing of the telephone. At first it echoed through her dream. She was in an hotel. In a pink hotel bedroom with Laurie. The bed was huge, spread with a rosy red coverlet, and the telephone was ringing and ringing insistently. When she answered it, she heard Claire's voice. Claire knew about her and Laurie. And where they were. She had found the number of the hotel and was telephoning them . . .

Sarah struggled out of her dream, glanced with relief at David's sleeping figure and lifted the receiver. 'Hello,' she said, registering that the clock showed almost one.

'Sarah!' Claire's *real* voice, ragged with fear, tugged her into alertness. She felt chilled. 'Is Bridget still with you? She hasn't come home.'

'What? Bridget?' Sarah's heart began to hammer. 'No. I don't know. Hang on a minute.'

David stirred and looked at her. 'Who is it?'

'Has Chris brought Bridget back here, do you think?'

At once he took the phone from her hand. 'Claire? We've been asleep for hours. They may well be downstairs. Or having a smooch in the garden. I'll ring you back in five minutes. O.K?' He slammed down the phone and hurried out of the bedroom. Sarah heard him shouting, 'Chris. Chris. Are you down there?'

Suddenly Merry was in the doorway, rubbing her knuckles in her eyes. 'What's going on?' she asked sleepily. 'What time is it? Are they back?'

'I don't know. Dad's just gone . . .'

The phone began to ring again and Sarah snatched it up. 'Don't worry, Claire,' she said. 'David's looking . . .'

The voice on the other end of the line was cool, faintly puzzled. 'I'm sorry to disturb you at this time of night, but would it be possible to have a word with Mr David Page please?'

'Who is this?' Sarah struggled to sound calm. 'Go and find Dad,' she hissed at Merry. 'He's probably in the garden.'

Merry's eyes widened but she hurried away to do as she was told.

'I'm ringing about Mr *Chris* Page,' the voice continued. 'Of Swan Lane, Norwich.'

'David's . . . my husband's brother. Yes. He's staying with

us. Why? Where is he? What's happened?' She could hear her voice rising hysterically. 'Has something happened?'

And then David was leaning over her, prising the phone from her rigid fingers. 'David Page here,' he said. 'Where? City Bank Hospital?' Sarah watched as the colour drained away from his face leaving him grey and haggard. 'Yes. That's right,' he continued. 'A crash? No. No, I hadn't heard.' He sat down heavily on the bed. 'I see. Is it bad? No, of course not. We'll be there as soon as we can. Thank you.' He was just about to ring off when another thought struck him. 'Sorry. Are you still there? Just one more thing. Bridget is with him, is she?' There was a pause. Sarah saw that Merry had come back and was standing just inside the door, staring at the phone in disbelief. 'Bridget Richley,' David continued. 'They would have been together. Yes. On the train.' He waited. Then, 'I see,' he said. 'Yes, I see. Thank you.' He replaced the receiver and took Sarah's hand. 'There's been an accident,' he told her. 'The train was derailed. Chris is still unconscious.'

'What about Bridget?' Merry asked urgently. 'What did they say about her?'

David shook his head. 'No news, I'm afraid. They don't seem to know.'

'They must know,' Sarah objected. 'Is she all right or is she hurt? Surely they can tell us that, at least.'

'It all sounds a bit chaotic. A lot of casualties. They haven't got things sorted out yet. Chris just happened to be one of the first to be admitted, and they were able to find us because he'd written our telephone number in his diary.' He ran his hands through his hair. 'I suppose I should ring Mum and Dad, shouldn't I?'

'Darling. No! Not at this time. Poor Jim might have a heart attack. Anyway, we don't know how he is, do we?'

'No. You're right. Better leave it until the morning.'

'One of you is going to have to tell Claire though,' Merry said, her face crumpled with anxiety. 'You can't put that off till the morning.'

'I'll do it now.' David's voice was steady. 'But I'm sure we don't need to worry about Bridget. She's probably sitting in the waiting room . . .'

Sarah shook her head. 'She would have phoned Claire.'

'It's an emergency. They're probably queuing up. Or she might be having a check-up from one of the doctors. Even an X-ray. I'm just sure that if anything very terrible had happened, Claire would have heard by now.'

'What are you going to tell her then?'

He shrugged. 'Just that there's a bit of a flap on. She'll probably want to come to the hospital with us.'

'Me too,' Merry said. 'I'd like to come with you.'

'Sorry,' David said. 'I'm afraid not. I think you should go round to Dolphin House to answer the phone. Just in case there are any messages. Besides, we'll probably be bringing Bridget home with us, so we'll have a car-full.'

Merry nodded, at once practical and sensible. 'O.K. Dad. That's fine.'

David looked at Sarah who was throwing on yesterday's discarded clothes, wriggling into her old gardening trousers, pulling her navy sweatshirt over her head. 'Just nip next door and tell Belle what's going on, will you, darling?' he asked her. 'While I ring Claire. I'm sure she wouldn't mind going along and keeping Merry company for an hour or two.'

The news reader's voice was impersonal and solemn. 'News is just coming in of a serious rail accident on the Newcastle to Carlisle line. A passenger train, which left Newcastle at eleven fifteen this evening, has been involved in a head-on collision with a stationary goods train only ten minutes after leaving the city. Three of the passenger train's carriages have been derailed and an intensive rescue operation is now under way. The number of casualties is not yet known but it is thought that most of them are young people. A British Rail spokesman explained that this was an extra train that had been laid on because of a pop concert in aid of Amnesty which had attracted thousands of fans from across the north of England. It had been decided that normal rail and bus services would not be sufficient to deal with the expected influx. Anyone anxious about the safety of friends or family should contact the emergency enquiry line at . . .'

Without a word, David leaned forward and switched off the car radio.

Claire, sitting beside him in the passenger seat, stared out through the windscreen at the dark road ahead. 'Eleven fifteen,' she said. 'They weren't even on the right train. Laurie told her she had to catch the one before ten.'

'Perhaps they tried and didn't manage to get on,' suggested Sarah. 'There must have been a bit of a scrummage even then. Or perhaps Bridget *did* get the early train and Chris had to follow on behind. They could easily have got separated.'

For a brief moment Claire's taut shoulders seemed to relax. Then she shook her head. 'So where is she? If she'd got that one she'd have been home hours ago.'

Sarah thought through the possibilities. 'Unless she went back to try to find him. No. Of course not. She couldn't have *got* back, could she?'

The two women lapsed into anguished silence again. David cleared his throat.

'Look, there's no point in speculating like this,' he told them firmly. He sounded solid and comforting, Sarah thought, as if she and Claire were sixth-formers agonising over their A-level results. 'I just know we'll find her waiting for us when we get there. Try not to worry, Claire. It's going to be all right.'

As David drove towards the forecourt of the hospital they could see at once that the whole area was in a furore. Cars had been parked haphazardly in the streets nearby and abandoned. Little groups of people were standing around aimlessly in the darkness, not knowing what to do. He saw television crews struggling to reach a good vantage point, and the face of a weeping woman was briefly illuminated by the brutal flash of a press photographer.

As he brought the car to a standstill near the big iron gates, a uniformed porter stepped out into the road in front of him. 'Can I help you, sir?'

'The hospital telephoned. My brother is in a coma.'

'Right.' The man was sympathetic and efficient. 'We need to keep this area clear for ambulances, but there is emergency parking at the back of the building. Straight on, first left. There'll be someone there to direct you.'

Once they'd managed to get inside the hospital, they found that the mood there was one of barely-controlled panic. The reception area was crammed with anxious men and women, all of them urgently demanding the attention of the scurrying staff.

'You two stay here,' David said. He looked at the cramped rows of chairs. 'You might find a bit of wall to lean against, I suppose. I'll go to the desk and see what I can find out.'

The receptionist looked harassed. 'Yes?' she asked.

'I'm David Page. My brother . . .'

'I'm sorry, Mr Page. I'm afraid you'll have to take your turn like everyone else. All these people are asking for information, too. So, if you wouldn't mind joining the end of the queue . . . I promise you, we're getting things sorted out as quickly as we possibly can.'

Grimly, David beckoned to Sarah and Claire and the three of them took their place in the line that straggled half way round the edge of the room. It was more than half an hour before they reached the desk again. The hands of the big clock above the door stood at five to three.

'I'm enquiring about Chris Page,' David said. 'The hospital phoned two hours ago and told me that my brother had been brought in unconscious. Could you please tell us how he is now, and whether we could possibly see him?'

'Page?' The receptionist consulted the long list in her hand. 'Yes. Dr Stevens will be able to tell you how he's doing,' she said. 'Along the corridor, third door on the right. Next please.'

'*And* Mrs Richley here would like news of her daughter, please,' David continued firmly. He looked at Sarah. 'You stay and help Claire,' he murmured. 'She doesn't look too good to me. I'll catch up with you later on. Say . . . beside the drinks machine?'

'Name?' asked the receptionist.

'Bridget Richley,' Claire told her.

The woman put on her glasses again and scanned the lists. 'Richley with an R or with a W?'

'An R.'

'I'm afraid we have no details of anyone of that name. Are you sure she was on the train?'

'I think so.'

'But you don't know?'

'How could we know for sure?' Sarah interrupted. 'But her boyfriend was, so the chances are, she was too.'

'I see. Just one moment, please.'

The woman got up and went into the office that opened off behind the desk. They could see her bending over, talking to a thin, grey-haired man who was sitting in front of a flickering computer screen. When she came back she was carrying a clip-board. 'Not all the casualties have been brought in yet,' she said. 'There are two ambulances still on their way. And as you will appreciate there is a lot of confusion at the site. The rescue teams are having to cope with crowds of spectators, I'm afraid, as well as the fact that it's still very dark.'

'I see,' whispered Claire.

'The other thing is, a lot of the passengers probably weren't hurt at all, so they might not be brought here. It's possible that your daughter has been given a lift home by now. Apparently some people have taken their cars along especially to offer this sort of assistance. I've just had a word with Mr Stringer – he's supervising things. His advice is that first of all you phone home to find out if she's got back. Is your husband there at present?'

'No,' Claire said faintly. 'Two of my neighbours.'

'Fine. If she *isn't* at home, will you fill in this form, please?' She unclipped a piece of paper from her board. 'Every detail will be useful. We'll need to know as much about . . . Bridget, did you say? . . . as you can tell us so that we can find her as quickly as possible. All right?'

'All right.' Claire took the form gratefully. 'Thank you.'

'Next,' the receptionist called out.

It was Belle who answered the phone at Dolphin House. 'Claire!' she said at once. 'What's the news? How's Bridget?'

Claire held tightly to Sarah's hand as the bitter taste of disappointment welled up in her mouth. 'She not with you, then?'

'No. What do you mean? I thought she'd be at the hospital.'

'Apparently not. They thought she might have made her own way home.'

'I'm afraid I've heard nothing,' Belle said. 'Mind you, she might be walking. I wouldn't put it past her.' She forced a laugh.

'She must be somewhere, mustn't she?' Claire asked her, like a child yearning for comfort. 'She can't have vanished into thin air.'

'It'll be light soon. That'll help. Goodness knows how they're managing to do anything at the moment. What about Chris?'

'David's with him now,' Claire said. 'He's still unconscious but the doctors are very hopeful.'

'Thank God for that, anyway! Keep your chin up, Claire. Do you want me to try to get in touch with Laurie? Is there a ship's radio or something?'

'Oh no!' Claire was distraught. 'No. What's the point? She'll be back safe and sound before Laurie gets home. No need to worry him with all this.'

Sitting huddled together in a corner of the cafeteria, pushing away empty coke tins, crisp packets, paper plates greasy from hamburgers and smeared with tomato ketchup that looked like stage blood, Claire and Sarah struggled to fill in the form the receptionist had given them.

Name
Address
Age
Height
Colour of hair
Colour of eyes
Distinguishing characteristics, e.g. mole, birth mark, scars, tattoos . . .
Clothes
Jewellery . . .

Claire studied the list in despair. Her glorious silvery hair had lost its sheen, Sarah noticed. The pallor beneath her tan had given her skin a yellowish tinge. Her hands were shaking. She seemed to have aged twenty years in the course of the night. It was three-thirty now. When would it all end?

'I don't even know, for absolute sure, what she was wearing,' Claire said. 'I had such a headache. I'd asked her to draw the curtains because the light was hurting my eyes. And she might have changed before she went out anyway. I wasn't there to wave her off, the way I usually am.' Her voice broke. 'Oh, God, Sarah, what a bloody mess we're all in.'

Tears were running down her face now, splashing on to the half-completed form, smudging the inked-in answers. Carefully, Sarah took it from her.

'I'll finish it,' she said. 'I saw her.' She began to write. 'Blue denim jeans. Matching bomber jacket. White trainers. Tee-shirt . . . I think it was white.' She looked at Claire. 'Was it the white one with the Mr Smiley logo, do you think?'

'Either that or the yellow one. That one that always makes Laurie laugh, with . . . with 'WHY?' plastered all over the front.' She caught her breath. 'Oh, God! That *is* a laugh, isn't it? – No, I'm sorry. I really can't remember which it was.'

'Never mind,' said Sarah hurriedly. 'I'll just put down "tee-shirt". I'm not sure about jewellery, though. I don't think she wears any, does she?'

'I do know that. A tiny, gold signet ring on her little finger, engraved with her initials. My mother gave it to her on her fifth birthday and she's worn it ever since. To start with it was so big she used to put it on her thumb!' She gave a strangled laugh that turned into a sob. 'But now she can *just* fit it on to her little finger. Sarah! Where in God's name *is* she?'

Sarah stood up, the piece of paper in her hand. 'I'll take this back to the desk, shall I? And see if there's any more news.'

Claire struggled to her feet. 'I'll come with you. A change of scenery . . .'

'And another cup of their revolting coffee?'

'Is it a nightmare, do you think?' Claire asked. 'That headache, perhaps. It might have been a migraine. I've heard that they can trigger off horrific nightmares, you know. Am I going to wake up soon and take Bridget her Sunday morning cup of tea?' Sadly, silently, Sarah put her arm round her shoulders and hugged her. 'Please tell me that's what it is,' Claire begged her. 'It's got to be a nightmare.'

By five o'clock in the morning, with the light of a grey dawn seeping through the high windows, the reception area had almost emptied. One after another those who had watched through the long night had received the news they had been waiting for and wandered away into the darkness. One or two of the crash victims had been allowed to leave too, some of them bandaged and shaky, smiling sheepishly as they made their way slowly towards the swing doors. Sitting bolt upright in a neat row, on uncomfortable, green plastic chairs, Claire remained with David on one side of her and Sarah on the other. They were all gone so far beyond the reach of tiredness that they felt strangely light-headed and unreal.

'This must be what it feels like to be on drugs,' Claire thought. 'As if you're outside, on the edge, looking at life through a glass window. Or a film of water.' She realised that the receptionist was making her way towards them.

'Mrs Richley,' the woman said, her voice gentle now and

comforting. 'I'm sorry you've had such a long night of it. Mr Stringer suggested you might like to go into one of the little waiting rooms. At least you'll have a comfortable chair. And a bit of privacy. He'll be along to speak to you shortly.'

Claire was clutched by a spasm of hope. 'Has he some news?'

'He'll speak to you,' the receptionist repeated. She nodded to Sarah and David. 'If you'd all like to come this way.'

She showed them into a small room, ivory-painted and prettily furnished with a sofa upholstered in a strangely old-fashioned chintzy material, poppies and cornflowers scattered over a cream background. There were matching armchairs and a low coffee table, with a vase of real carnations and a pile of glossy magazines, *Vogue* and *Vanity Fair*.

'This is nice!' Claire stooped to pick one up, but David took it from her hands and led her towards the sofa.

'I think you should stretch out and put your feet up, just for a little while. Have a cat-nap.'

'I *couldn't*. I feel wide awake.'

'You're exhausted, love,' he insisted. 'You must rest.'

She allowed herself to be over-ruled, felt Sarah take her shoes off for her and then stroke her hair with long measured strokes. Instantly, she fell asleep.

And when she woke, Bridget was there. Right beside her. Relief flooded through her. It was like a miracle. Bridget was bending over her, touching her hand. Her face was luminous, her hair gleamed like candlelight. 'Hi Mum!' she said. 'It's all right. I'm here. I'm fine!' She looked radiantly happy.

Claire gazed at her, hardly able to believe that she had her back again, safe and well. Totally unharmed. 'And you're wearing your *yellow* tee-shirt,' she laughed. 'Not the white one. Neither Sarah nor I could remember, could we?' She turned her head to look at Sarah and saw that her face was disfigured by unutterable grief. Startled, she turned back to Bridget. But Bridget wasn't there any longer. The man called Mr Stringer was there instead, where Bridget had been. He was bending over her, touching her hand. He looked very grave. She noticed that he was wearing an incongruous yellow tie with a pattern of little black squiggles that looked a bit like letters. What a strange tie for a medical man to choose, she thought. She'd have imagined that he'd have gone for something a little more . . . sober. Dignified. Then she realised that his mouth was opening and closing. He was trying to speak to her.

'Mrs Richley,' he said at length. 'Are you awake?'

She nodded helplessly.

'A girl has been brought in who answers to the description you gave us of your daughter.'

'Where is she?' At once Claire was bolt upright, struggling to her feet.

'I'm afraid it's very bad news.'

She felt Sarah's arm clamp around her waist. 'She thinks I'm going to faint,' she told herself. 'She knows. Sarah knows that Bridget is dead.' She looked beseechingly into Mr Stringer's face, shaking her head from side to side. 'Tell me it isn't true,' she said. 'Please tell me.'

'I am so very sorry,' he replied. 'Do you feel strong enough to come and identify . . . ?'

At once David interrupted him. 'My wife and I can do that,' he offered. 'We know Bridget very well.'

'Yes. We'll go,' Sarah added.

'No!' Claire was fierce. 'No one else. My child.'

'Where is her husband?' Mr Stringer addressed the question to David as if he imagined Claire was incapable of giving him a rational reply.

'I don't need my husband,' she told him. Gathering every ounce of her strength she drew herself to her full height and stood before him, tall, dignified and beautiful. 'Please take me to Bridget now.'

Bridget was lying on a narrow white bed in a small white room. Her pale hair was flattened out against the white pillow. Her face was pallid, her lips like ashes. 'No colour,'

Claire thought. 'All the colour of my life is taken away.' She groped beneath the sheet and found Bridget's hand. It felt like marble. She lifted it to her mouth, then laid it against her cheek as if trying to warm it into life. The little gold ring gleamed and she touched it gently with her forefinger. She realised that Mr Stringer was standing close behind her. 'This is my daughter,' she told him.

He swallowed. 'She will have died instantly. A blow to the head. No pain.'

'Thank you,' Claire said, her eyes still on Bridget's face.

With infinite tenderness she placed the lifeless hand beneath the sheet again. Then she ran the tips of her fingers across her daughter's broad forehead, down the line of her nose, side to side across her mouth, into the hollows of her cheeks and around the firm edge of her jaw. As if, through touch, she would imprint her in her mind for ever.

CHAPTER TWENTY

The national press had a field day with the accident. Every newspaper carried a disaster photograph on its front page and more inside. Details of suffering, loss and bereavement were graphically described, eye-witnesses' accounts squeezed out like dish cloths, melodramatic soundbites gobbled up, savoured and spewed out in print. Only the *Valley Bugle*, too close to the events to be able to enjoy their entertainment value, attempted to moderate its coverage.

Across the whole of the north of England, shocked families are grieving for the victims of Saturday evening's train crash which occurred just outside Newcastle. Now, at last, the final, terrible toll is known. Three young people were killed; Kelly Anstruther, 18, and her brother, Callum, aged 15, both of Haltwhistle, and Bridget Richley, 17, of Deredale. 42 people were injured. Of these, 23 are still in the City Bank Hospital, some of them suffering from multiple fractures or serious head injuries. Yesterday some of the stars of the pop concert which all the crash victims had attended paid a flying visit to the hospital to speak to their fans. Sting told our reporter that they were all devastated by the tragedy and loss of life but it had been decided that none of them would be attending either of the funerals. Their presence, they felt, and the added publicity it would generate, would only cause further suffering to the families involved. However, they would be sending flowers, and personal messages of condolence to the bereaved parents . . .

Merry had never been to a funeral before and she was finding the whole thing totally amazing. Here they all were at

Dolphin House, out in the garden because the weather was incredible, boiling hot and sunny. And it was just like a party. Lots of people wandering about, admiring the roses. She could hear them twittering on to each other.

'Isn't the herbaceous border superb? Just look at those delphiniums.'

And they were all eating little *vols-au-vents* and things, and knocking back the white wine.

'Wonderful sculpture, isn't it? Yes. It's Bridget, of course. Poor Claire. She's so talented.'

That's exactly what it was like, Merry thought. A posh garden party. Not a real one though. More like something on telly or in a film. And the major players were not very good at playing their parts. Claire looked incredible in a soft, silky dress, a sort of burnt orange colour. But her face was tight and shiny like a mask. She was moving about restlessly, nodding and talking to people, and a lot of them were putting their arms round her and hugging her. She must be getting a bit tired of all that. Laurie looked like a zombie, there was no other word for it. His whole body seemed stiff and mechanical, as if he were having to figure out how to move his arms and legs properly. Her own Mum too! Sarah looked all to pieces somehow. She'd been fond of Bridget, of course, but after all, she'd only known her for a year. Less than that even. If it had been William in that coffin . . . Merry shuddered. If it had happened to Will she would have *expected* Sarah to go spare.

The actual funeral service had been more the sort of thing that Merry had expected. Absolutely heart-breaking. They'd chosen a pure white coffin for Bridget, and on the top of it, instead of wreaths of hot-house roses and lilies, there'd just been a posy of wild flowers. Ordinary stuff that you found growing all over the place. Moon daisies and water forget-me-nots. Comfrey. Even common buttercups. All tied up with ribbon in a froth of creamy meadowsweet. Claire had gone out and gathered them herself, Mum said. She'd been wandering around the river meadows, alone at dawn, looking for flowers for Bridget.

The church had been packed, but the wardens had done a great job turfing out the press photographers and making them stand beyond the lych-gate. They were like horrible flies, swarming all over the place, though Claire said it wasn't their fault, they were just trying to do their job and earn a living wage like everybody else. Bridget's Uncle Mark had been at the front of the church with his wife and Alison. And she'd seen old Mr Renton from the fishmongers, all the staff of Treasures, the doctor and his wife and sister. Even Mr Manley, Mum's boss, had been there, sitting next to Reggie Bray. And there'd been a huge contingent from school. The headmistress and three of the teachers and a whole pile of sixth-formers from Bridget's class, all in their navy uniforms, filling three whole pews and sniffing and blowing into their handkerchiefs. Even the boys had not been ashamed to weep openly. Bridget had been one of the most popular girls in the school. Merry had been glad that the head had allowed her to have the whole day off and go to the funeral with her parents because they were special family friends.

Nobody could stop crying. It was when Claire and Laurie walked down the aisle behind that terrible white coffin, holding each other's hands like two sad little children – that's when the crying began. And after that it seemed as if no one knew how to stop. The vicar didn't preach a sermon or give an address. Claire hadn't wanted that. She said it would be better for all of them to have their *own* thoughts and memories of Bridget. So, instead, one of the girls who'd left school a couple of years ago and was now studying music at the Guildhall in London had played the Adagio from Elgar's Cello Concerto, while they all just sat there and remembered Bridget. Merry had thought about the first time she'd seen her, at Belle's horrendous welcome party, and how Bridget had told her wicked stories about all the guests and made her laugh and realise that Deredale wasn't going to be completely grim after all.

Suddenly, sitting on her own in a green, shady corner of the garden, Merry felt as if she were drowning in a well of loneliness. William hadn't been able to come home for the funeral because he was in the middle of exams. Jim and Muriel had been hoping to come, but then they'd decided they'd better stay and look after Chris. Merry *had* thought that Chris would make the effort to get here. They'd only kept him in hospital for a few days and then Dad had driven him down to Burnham Market to recuperate. Muriel said he was getting on fine, but *he* insisted he was too ill to make the journey. Privately, she thought he was just chickening out. He was too scared to face up to the funeral, to see Claire and Laurie the way they were. She'd heard David and Sarah talking about it one night when they'd thought she wasn't listening. Apparently Chris was convinced that it was *his* fault that Bridget was dead because it had been his idea to take her to the gig in the first place. But that was ridiculous. If anybody was to blame it was someone at British Rail. It was their error – signalling failure, they thought – that had caused the accident in the first place. Besides, Chris had tried to get Bridget to the railway station in time for the early train. He'd told her they'd given Laurie their word and that's what they should do. But Bridget had refused to leave. She'd found out there was another one later, because the whole of the crowd next to them was planning to catch it. She'd insisted Laurie wouldn't mind them getting the special train. Besides, he wouldn't be at home worrying himself sick, would he, because he'd gone sailing. And Claire would understand, of course, because Claire always did. Anyway, she'd had that awful headache so she'd probably be in bed and fast asleep and know nothing about anything until she woke up next morning.

Merry pondered the whole sequence of events in her head. If Bridget had persuaded Chris that they should catch the eleven-fifteen then really it was just as if she had signed her own death certificate. But what difference did it make anyway? The only thing that mattered was that now she was dead and everybody was miserable and everything that had been fun was absolutely horrible and nothing would ever be the same again.

She raised her eyes dully and looked round the garden. Her father was talking to the vicar, who seemed to be about to leave. Yes. They were shaking hands. Dad had been amazing, she thought. Laurie had been in such a state of shock when the coast guard had managed to contact him that he hadn't been able to do *anything*, so David had just taken over. Telephoned the Richleys' friends and family, organised the funeral arrangements, dealt with those terrible reporters who'd door-stepped Dolphin House for days and coped with the endless official enquiries. He'd been a hero. And Belle had been great, too. She'd run the house for Claire and Laurie, done all the cooking and stood over them to see that they actually ate some of it, taken their dirty washing away and brought it back immaculate. Good old Belle. Despite herself, Merry grinned. Bridget used to laugh at her false eyelashes and her skinny figure and spiky high heels, but she'd always had a soft spot for her.

'Don't knock old Belle!' she used to say. 'Belle's all right.'

Suddenly Merry saw that Belle was coming out of the house, carefully balancing a tray of cups in her hands. She watched as she walked slowly across to Claire who was sitting in a basket chair beneath the walnut tree. Belle bent over her and said something and Merry got up and began to move towards the pair of them. She should offer to make herself useful, she thought. But then she realised that Claire was quite beside herself. She had jumped to her feet and was staring at Belle's stricken face. She was shouting at her.

'Tea or coffee, did you ask?' she yelled, as Belle shrank away from her.

Merry looked on, paralysed, as she snatched the tray from Belle's hands and hurled it away into the bushes, sending the cups hurtling through the air, showering hot liquid down upon the grass and all over the front of Belle's little grey suit. Her voice rose higher and higher until she was almost screaming, and everyone stopped chatting politely and waving their glasses around and smelling the flowers, and they all turned their heads and stared at her.

'My daughter is dead,' Claire cried, 'and you stand there asking me whether I'd prefer tea or coffee! For Christ's *sake*!' And she ran fleet-footed across the lawn and disappeared inside the house.

Sarah found her in her darkened bedroom. Claire had taken off her pretty dress and put on a long black skirt and a sweater of fine black wool. She had washed every vestige of make-up from her face and brushed down her hair as flat as it would go. She was sitting perfectly still and upright on a small wooden chair. She turned lifeless eyes towards her.

'I must mourn my daughter,' she said.

'I know.' Sarah pulled up the dressing table stool and sat beside her. 'I know how you feel,' she told her. 'If it were me . . .'

'You *don't* know!' Claire's face was livid. 'No one knows.'

Sarah shook her head humbly. 'But if it were William or Merry, I . . .'

'But it's not. And I am myself, not you.' She looked desolate. 'And I killed her.'

'Claire! How *can* you say that?'

'Because it's true. "I insist that you go," I told her. She was in this room. I can almost feel her here now. Can't you? As if you could reach out and touch her? She wanted to stay with me because I was ill. But no. "I absolutely *insist*!" I said. They were just about the last words I spoke to her. And then I sent her away.'

'Oh, please. Don't. I can't bear to see you like this.'

Claire ignored her. 'All those years I waited for Bridget. I felt as if I'd been waiting for her my whole life. But when she was born, the very moment, I looked into her face and it was as if we *recognised* each other. As if we were part of each other and always had been. That's the way it was. We thought each other's thoughts. Sometimes it didn't even seem necessary to speak. Not in words. We communicated on a different level. She was my own real self, you see. And now my own real self is dead. But my body remains.' She looked down at her black clothes as if she couldn't remember the person they belonged to. 'I am the phoenix, Sarah. Somehow I must rise from the ashes. But not yet. I must have a space for grieving.'

Sarah looked at her mutely and stood up. 'Do you want me to leave you?'

'Yes. Please.' A shadow of a smile crossed Claire's face and she put out her hand and stroked Sarah's arm. 'I want to thank you, though. For the night she died. You were the only one in the world I could bear to have with me that night. You are my best of friends, and always will be.'

Sarah sprang back as if she'd been stung. 'No. Don't say that. I'm not worth it . . . I'm sorry.'

Claire gazed at her. The green eyes, that could have been Bridget's, gleamed steadily as if they were shining right through her. 'There's no need to say sorry. Never any need of apologies between you and me, Sarah. Believe it. We have travelled far beyond that, the two of us.'

Sarah blundered out of the room, closing the door noisily behind her. She ran downstairs and out into the garden, looking wildly to left and right. At last she caught sight of Laurie. He was sitting on a bench, making a point of *not* listening to Reggie who was bumbling on regardless because he didn't know what else to do. Sarah tapped him on the shoulder.

'Have you a minute, Laurie?' she asked him. 'I'm just slipping off home now.' Without a word he got to his feet and followed her to the garden gate. 'I must see you. Briefly,' she said. 'Tomorrow, if possible.'

'In Newcastle, you mean?'

'Of course not.' She was impatient with him. 'Is there somewhere near? I don't think you should leave Claire alone for very long.'

He shook his head, confused. 'I don't know what we're going to do, Sarah,' he said helplessly.

'Come to the Sceptre Book Shop tomorrow morning, will you? Around eleven. There's a little place in the garden where the man brings you coffee if he's not too busy. We can talk there.'

'Do you really have to leave now?'

'Yes. I've said my goodbyes to Claire. Tell David and Merry to stay on as long as they can be useful, will you?' And she kissed him briefly on his cheek, then hurried away along the street.

He had reached the bookshop before she got there. She found him sitting at the rustic table in the little back yard, though the day was cool and overcast with the occasional spatter of raindrops. He didn't seem to notice. She realised with an unbearable pang of tenderness that he looked like an old man, much beyond his fifty years. The skin was drawn so tight over his cheekbones, his eyes sunk so deep into their sockets, that it was as if you could see the skull beneath. He hadn't even bothered to shave properly. He had a copy of *Captain Hornblower* in his hands and was flicking through the pages again and again, not reading a word.

'You know, I used to enjoy this stuff,' he told her casually as she sat down beside him. His face was totally expression-less, his eyelids lowered. She had no idea what he was think-ing or feeling. He had become a complete stranger.

'How is Claire today?' she asked him.

He lifted his shoulders. 'As well as can be expected. Isn't that what they say? Why does nobody ask me how *I* am? She was my daughter too, you know.'

'Laurie. Don't be so bitter. It doesn't help.' She tried to make him look at her but he turned his head away, refusing to meet her eyes. 'We can't see each other again,' she said. 'You know that, don't you? I just wanted to say goodbye to you privately. Gently. Without people watching us.'

'Oh, Christ!' He banged his fist down on the table, again and again. 'I knew it. Oh, Christ! Christ! Christ!'

She felt afraid. Of his separateness. His anger. She didn't recognise him in this mood. She began to plead with him. 'It's impossible. You know it.'

'I do not know it. For God's sake, Sarah. I've just lost my daughter. I can't lose you, too. You're supposed to love me, remember? "More, a thousand times, than you could say." I still know your letter off by heart, you see.'

'I do love you. *Just* like that. I always will.'

'Well, however were you brought up, Mrs Page? Did no one ever tell you that you don't turn your back on the one you love, not when he's just about driven into the ground under his load of loss, and pain, and guilt and misery. It's not kind. Not ladylike.'

She flinched at the bitterness of his jibe. 'There's no other way. Claire has suffered enough. We can't make her suffer more.'

'We won't. We don't, for God's sake. What we have has nothing at all to do with Claire.'

'You know that's not true.'

'But it's been almost six months. We've been everything to each other. You've never talked like this before.'

'I was out of my mind. I must have been. I tried to believe we could have it all ways. But we can't. We must stop seeing each other.'

'Don't be ridiculous. Stop seeing each other!' He groaned. 'We're neighbours, remember? Family friends. All that stuff.'

'Just social occasions. We can manage that. If we make an effort.'

'Can we? So what am I supposed to say to you next time we come to supper? "Please pass me the salt, Sarah. And tell me, do your nipples still taste like honeydew?" "Hi there, David! Does she still swear like a navvy when she comes, or does she have to watch her language with the old man?" ' She began to cry quietly, not even bothering to check the tears. 'I'm only asking,' he said. 'How are we to manage from now on? I need instructions. How will we get through each bloody day for the next thirty bloody years? Tell me that.'

She bent her head. 'I must break away.'

'You can't!' he said savagely, taking her chin in his hand,

tilting her face up towards his. 'I belong to you. You found me. You *claimed* me. Remember? If it was just love on a short lease that you had to offer, you should have left me alone.'

'Two black coming up!' The book shop man emerged through the doorway and thrust thick mugs of coffee in front of them. 'Sorry. I'm right out of milk.'

He had a camp, cockney voice that made him sound absurdly like Kenneth Williams. A fortnight ago they'd have laughed about it, Sarah thought. Shared the joke together.

'It doesn't matter,' she muttered. 'Black is fine.'

'She likes it hot and strong,' Laurie told him.

'Does she?' The man smiled vaguely. 'A good read, Forrester,' he said, eyeing the novel in his hand. 'I always think so. Fixed on that one, have you?'

Laurie shook his head and handed the book back to him. 'I was really looking for Thor Heyerdahl.'

'Sorry! We're right out of Heyerdahl. At this precise moment.'

Laurie grimaced. 'The story of my life,' he said. 'Right out of bloody everything. *At* this precise moment.'

CHAPTER TWENTY-ONE

David was woken by the sound of Sarah's weeping. He lay still, listening, not knowing what to do. He couldn't understand the intensity of her grief, this torrent of misery for another woman's child. It seemed . . . unbalanced, somehow. Over the top. He put out a hand and laid it on her shoulder. The sobs became slightly less convulsive but continued. He sighed. The truth was, after all these years, he'd suddenly realised that he didn't understand *anything* about Sarah. They'd always been so close, but now she seemed like a different woman. A polite, efficient stranger, growing further and further away from him with every day that passed.

It had begun almost as soon as they'd got to Deredale. Then, he'd put it down to Claire's influence. Claire and Laurie arranged their lives differently, enjoyed being separate individuals. That wasn't the way he and Sarah had chosen. They'd made a conscious decision, from the early days of their marriage, to be 'a couple'. But obviously Sarah had been attracted to Claire's free-wheeling style. She'd fallen under her spell. He remembered how, last summer, she'd just turned her back on him and the house and the garden – even though they'd just moved in – and had taken Merry careering all over the county with Claire and Bridget.

And then, after Christmas, she'd changed again. Insisted on getting a job and re-creating herself as a career woman. Though he'd been set against it to start with, he had to admit that it had worked out pretty well. Sarah had seemed very happy. Full of energy. She'd got a new lease of life, and had still managed to keep things ticking over smoothly, so that nobody suffered. She was taking the job very seriously too, nipping off for special classes in Management Skills every now and then. She'd even done a little weekend seminar in Leeds and had come back from it with the adrenalin positively coursing through her veins. She'd been like that ever since she was a schoolgirl, of course. If she took the trouble to do a thing she had to get it right. Otherwise she'd walk away from it. But now, strangely, she seemed to have collapsed. Bridget had been dead for more than a month and Sarah was still weeping in the dark. He switched on his bedside light. Three a.m.

'Sarah,' he said quietly. 'Shall I make you a hot drink?'

She sniffed. 'No, thank you. I don't want anything.'

'What is it, darling? You can't go on crying for ever.'

'No. I know.' She found her handkerchief and blew her nose. But even as he watched, her eyes filled with tears again.

'Is all this about Bridget?'

'Yes, I suppose so. What do you mean? What else?'

'I mean, I know it's terribly sad – awful, really, but . . .'

'It's changed everything, don't you see? Our whole lives.' She was sitting up in bed now, gazing at him with wild eyes.

'No, it hasn't. We're all here, the same as before. You and me and Merry.'

'But not William!'

He stared at her. 'What's William got to do with it?'

She jumped out of bed, ran across to the wash basin and began to splash cold water on her face, holding the drenched flannel against her eyes to try to cool them. Then she filled her tumbler and carried it back to bed. 'Are the aspirins at your side?' He unscrewed the bottle and carefully shook out two into her cupped hand. 'Can I have another one, please? My head is raging.'

He replaced the cap firmly. 'Two are sufficient.'

She gave him a ragged half-smile. 'You always know best, don't you? Even after all this.'

'It's only for your own good.'

'David, I want to talk to you. Please don't get cross. I'm just not up to it.'

'Of course, I won't. Why should I?'

She bent her knees, pulled the duvet up to her chin and sat bolt upright, staring ahead of her. 'I've been doing a lot of thinking since . . . since Bridget . . .'

'Haven't we all?' he groaned.

'. . . and I think this whole business, our leaving Norwich and moving to Deredale, has been a dreadful mistake.'

He gave a light laugh. 'Oh Sarah! What nonsense!'

'It is not nonsense. I really think we should cut our losses, now, and go back to Norwich. They always need good teachers. You'll find another job easily. I've thought about it very carefully. We could have William with us again – for his year out – and Merry could go back to her old school and start her sixth-form work with her friends.'

He looked at her as if she were mad. 'Have you taken leave of your senses?'

'Norwich is our *home*, David. We were brought up there. We should never have left.'

'I do not believe this. You talk like a child. The whole thing is so ludicrous it's hardly worth discussing.'

'Why? Why is it ludicrous, David? These are our lives, I'm talking about. Trying to make things work again.'

'Don't be so melodramatic.'

'Please don't patronise me. I want to talk.'

David shook his head. 'To start with, William will be off to Cambridge next year.'

'But *this* year he's got a job in the garden centre again.'

'You know I don't want him to do that,' David frowned. 'Zack's a bad influence.'

'Nonsense. He and Zack have been best friends since they were four. Anyway, William has made up his mind, whether you like it or not. He's going to stay on in Norwich and he's got to have somewhere to live.'

'He can stay with Pam. That seems to work all right.'

'No, he can't. Pam's done enough. She really needs her

spare room back. We can't go on using her . . .'

'I seem to remember that we are paying Pam for Will's bed and board. Perhaps we're doing her a favour.'

'Don't be so horrible. Of course we pay for his food and expenses. But precious little more. And he misses us, David. He's lost a whole year of his own home and family.'

'So you want us to move back – just to put a roof over William's head until the next whim takes him? Do me a favour.'

'You never listen, do you?'

'I do!' His voice rose. 'I just can't believe the things I hear.'

'You're shouting at me. You promised to keep your temper.'

'I'm sorry.'

'You'll wake Merry if you shout like that.'

'I said I'm sorry.' His voice came out like a hiss. 'So, you'd just throw in your job, would you? After Gerald Manley has been so good to you?'

'It's just a job. He'll find somebody else.'

'But what about *me*, for God's sake? My *real* job? I can hardly chuck it in after one year, can I? It would be a terrible move. The end of my career. Nobody would take me seriously ever again. Anyway, I *am* expected to give at least a term's notice, you know. But what's the point of talking about it? I like it here. I'm doing well. I'd be a fool to throw it all up.'

'What about *us* though? Don't you care? What about Merry? She's going to hate *her* school now, isn't she? With Bridget haunting every classroom. And what about me? I've lost my friend too. Claire . . . she isn't *there* any longer. She's an empty shell. The Claire I knew has gone missing.'

David's voice was icy. 'I'm not just being selfish, you know. It's because of Claire and Laurie, more than anything else, that I wouldn't even contemplate leaving. To start with, I feel responsible.'

'Oh, don't start on that one. *Everybody* feels responsible. Laurie. Claire. Chris. I'm sick of all that.'

'But it was Chris who took Bridget to that bloody concert. My brother. And we introduced them.'

'Quite. And *I* sent Chris to stay with the Richleys, didn't I? Because I didn't want to crowd out William. So you could say I was responsible. We all feel guilty after a death like this but it's pointless. It was an accident.'

David looked at her. 'If you say so. The thing is, Laurie and Claire need us here. We are their main support. We're the ones who've been through it with them, aren't we? Without us they'd be lost.' She turned away from him and began to clamber out of bed again. 'Where are you going now?' he asked her harshly. 'You said you wanted to talk.'

'There's no point, is there?' she said. 'Sometimes, you know, you sound just like my father.'

'Thank you very much!'

'It'll be light soon. I thought I'd make myself a cup of coffee and then go out for a walk. I won't sleep now.'

'I . . . I . . . I!' he sneered. 'That's all you think about. What's more comfortable for *you*. Not for Claire or Laurie. Not for me. Oh no. "I don't like it here. It's not fun any more. So I think I'll just bugger off." '

She was picking up her clothes from the dressing table stool, looking for her hair brush. She turned round and stared at him as if she didn't recognise him. 'You may not believe this, but actually what I would like most is to stay here and let things go on just the way they used to. But I am convinced that it would be better if we left. I can't explain why, but for Claire's sake especially, *and* for Laurie's, it would be the best thing. We should leave them alone. Give them a chance to put their lives together again.'

She walked across to the door and laid her fingers on the handle.

'You would really go?' he asked her. 'You'd really turn your back on Peacocks' Acre? Your "heart-home"?' She stopped in her tracks. His words were like a physical blow. 'Don't you remember the first time you saw it?' She convulsed with pain. 'How can you walk away, Sarah? It was love at first sight.'

At once she was transported back to that spring day – it

seemed a lifetime ago – when Ralph Elliott had shown them round the house. Such a *dull* little man he'd seemed to her. But what was it that he'd said? 'Old age. Death. Divorce. They're all sad, Mrs Page.' She'd been so arrogant then, so armoured against life's catastrophes, that she'd imagined that these things had nothing to do with her and David, not for years and years. Now she knew them all too well. Old age would come, and sooner than she'd realised. She'd seen it already, shadowing Laurie's grief-gouged face. Death had already dealt them an unimaginable blow. And divorce? The unthinkable? Had that been lurking among the seeds of Love-in-a-Mist too, along with its grim companions?

4
SEPTEMBER, 1991

It seems as if my throat's an unknown song.
It seems the tides are levied by my breath.
It seems that I might drown in memory.

CHAPTER TWENTY-TWO

His voice on the phone, ten minutes after I've left him, just when I am missing him most. Knowing that he understands that, and cares.

Lying in his arms, on this warm lovely day, on a bank pale with crowding primroses. Not saying a word. Not needing to. Our first spring together.

A love letter pushed into the palm of my hand while we are sitting on the platform, looking very official and proper, waiting to hear the planning officer's proposals . . .

Sarah snapped the notebook shut and thrust it into her pocket. It had been Laurie's idea that she should write it down. 'Just snippets,' he'd begged her. 'Fragments. I'm terrified of forgetting. When we are old and sad and tired, I want to be able to recall it all. Every single moment. Please give me some memory joggers.'

But now the written words made her angry. She didn't want her memory jogged. What was the point of remembering if it only gave you pain? She was getting on well enough. She glanced around the cramped sitting room with its cheap furniture and blowsy curtains. It wasn't exactly Peacocks' Acre, but it was affordable, and central. The bedrooms were too small, of course. Merry's was little more than a shoe-box and Will's wasn't much better. And it was irritating only having one living room for everything. Still, it would do them well enough till David found another school. Then they could make a new start.

She'd been in Norwich for two months now. David had not liked it, but in the end she'd made him see that there was no choice. She knew she was being unfair, leaving him behind to put the house on the market and sort out things at school all on his own, but it didn't seem to make any difference. In the end he'd given in, convinced that she must be having some sort of nervous breakdown. It was, after all, quite irrational to want to run away from the house and husband you love because your *friends'* child has died.

Poor David. Sarah thought about him now with a sort of tender regret. He'd never had a glimmer of suspicion about her and Laurie, so how was he supposed to understand anything? That she couldn't go on living in the same village, terrified of hearing his voice in the next room, of recognising the square set of his shoulders walking along the street. She couldn't face that, not once she had steeled herself to give him up, totally and irrevocably.

When she'd left Peacocks' Acre, taking Merry with her, she had gone first to Burnham Market, to Jim and Muriel. They had listened calmly to her explanation that the move to Northumberland had been a mistake. That she'd been home-sick and now things were worse because Claire had cut herself off and she just couldn't reach her. They had seemed to believe her when she told them that it would be better for Merry to go back to her old school now that she had lost Bridget. And they had nodded their agreement when she said that Will needed her here because he'd decided to stay on in Norwich for another year. They had watched her face, and heard her over-elaborate explanations, and nodded their heads gently, without comment or criticism of the cavalier way she had abandoned their son. But Sarah was sure that they knew exactly what had happened after Bridget died, had noticed that she couldn't even bring herself to mention Laurie's name. Their only concern now was to do what they could to heal the wounds, to try to keep the marriage intact.

So, it was Jim and Muriel who had helped her to find the little furnished house in Gillan Terrace, just round the corner from Treacle Street. And they'd done their best to make it as comfortable and homely as possible for her. Sarah had assured them that she and the children would manage very well there. David would be coming down whenever he could, for half-terms and holidays, and really the months would simply fly. Soon Peacocks' Acre would be nothing more than a distant dream.

Suddenly aware of the loud ticking of the clock on the tiled mantelpiece, Sarah stood up and stretched. It was getting late. Merry was already asleep. Will was spending the night with Zack because they'd been planning to go to a late night film, then on to Zelda's, the newest nightspot down beside the cathedral. He didn't want to come in late and wake her, he said, because he knew she had to get up early for work. She had taken a job at a travel agency, and had been glad to get it. It meant that what she and Will earned between them could just about pay for the rent and the housekeeping, though they were on a pretty tight budget. She didn't want to ask David for anything more than she absolutely had to. It didn't seem fair to make him foot the bill.

She yawned and looked vaguely at the blank screen of the television set. She'd just switch on the end of the news, she thought. Catch the weather forecast. At this time of year you never knew what sort of clothes you'd need – one day it was a cotton dress, the next a warm pullover. The screen flickered into life. 'Not too promising, I'm afraid,' the man said cheerfully. 'Rain and squally winds. Especially on the east coast. And they're going to get worse through the night. So, make sure you batten down the hatches!' The professional TV smile widened. 'And a very good night to you all.'

Laurie tossed about restlessly, sweating and exhausted in a tangle of sheets. He couldn't sleep, but that was nothing new. He hadn't had one night of natural, undrugged sleep since the coast guard had made radio contact with the *Matadora*.

'I'm very sorry, Mr Richley. I'm afraid there's been an accident.'

The most terrible words in the English language. He looked at Claire. She seemed to be sleeping peacefully, but these days he couldn't be sure. She'd developed the knack of lying very still, breathing deeply and regularly to pretend that she'd drifted off. She insisted she did it to stop him worrying about her, in the hope that he might fall asleep too. But he had his doubts. He thought she did it to escape from his endless re-examinations and post mortems. 'Why didn't I stop her, Claire? Why did I let her go?'

But Claire was right. What was the point of questions now? What they needed to be talking about was answers. The new shape of their lives. Their future. He slipped out of bed. He decided to go downstairs for half an hour or so. Have a whisky. Bore himself to death with the bloody *Times*.

He rummaged in the drinks cupboard, found a fresh bottle of Bells and carried it with the newspaper across to his old leather armchair. An hour later the bottle was half empty and his mood had changed from despair to black anger. He raged, his head bursting with fury against a fate which seemed to have singled him out for special punishment. He stood up and stared around the room as if it were a prison cell. He couldn't stay in this house of pain for a moment longer. He *must* get away.

He found his track suit hanging in the downstairs shower room and tugged it on over his pyjamas. Then he picked up his car keys from his desk, went back into the sitting room to collect the remains of the whisky, opened the front door and let himself out into the night.

The road was empty and he drove fast. It seemed, strangely, that the drink had sharpened his reactions. He took corners with precision, even at sixty miles per hour, judged the incline of each hill to the last degree. It felt as if the car had grown wings. To start with he had no idea of where he was going. The only direction he cared about was *away*. But after a while he realised that he was heading, without even knowing it, towards Lithe Harbour. There was just enough light in the sky to pick out the four great chimneys of the power station, the fleet's marker when they were coming home from sea. The car rumbled over the level crossing, bumped over the endless, irritating procession of sleeping policemen, but he hardly noticed, staring ahead, seeing the stretching belt of trees that had been planted to give protection from the fierce winds. Briefly he pulled up at the security barrier and at once the man in the cabin recognised his face, gave him a friendly nod and lifted the bar to admit him. And then he was on the final stretch that led to the harbour, moving beneath the towering lamps that spilled down their pools of bitter yellow light.

He slid the car to a halt on the inner wall, uncorked the whisky bottle and drank deeply. He gazed up at the clouds scudding across the sky, at the fitful moon, half-obscured. Then he climbed unsteadily out of the driver's seat, straightened his tired body and took a deep breath as he felt the slap of chilly air. He propped his elbows on the iron railing and looked longingly at the boats glimmering indistinctly through the darkness. Lined up in the centre of the harbour he saw the Pilgrim sailing ships, big and beautiful, all flying the white flag with their motif of the pilgrim's staff. There the three of them were, safely home from the August cruise – his own beloved *Matadora*, the *Clara Belle* and the lovely *Lady Betty*. His heart turned over. That was *something* he could be proud of, he told himself. To have rescued those splendid craft from dereliction. To have given all those youngsters the chance to sail, to learn about the winds and waves, the tides and the stars, to be part of a crew, part of a real adventure . . . surely that could be counted in his favour.

But . . . other people's children! Despair began to gnaw at him again. He'd always been great with other people's children. Yet when it came to his own daughter . . . He turned back to the car, opened the boot, gathered together the sailing gear he always kept there, boots, thick sweater, oilskins, rope, torch, and bundled it all into his zipped bag. Then, like a sleep walker, he hurried along the walkway and down the steps beneath the light ship that housed the Yacht Club, making his way round it towards the sailing boats tied up together, stretching out from the middle jetty. Their sloop, *Aurora*, was the fourth one along, at the end of the line. Nominally she belonged to Mark. He and Lou had bought her years ago, so that Alison could learn to sail. And then Mark had taught Bridget too, one long, lovely summer when Laurie was away with Pilgrims. Gradually she'd become a family boat that all of them could use and enjoy. She wasn't really an ocean-going vessel, of course. She was too small for that, only twenty-six feet. But she was fine for exploring the river and coastline.

Laurie felt *desperate* to be on board, consumed by urgent necessity. Slithering and stumbling, he scrambled across *Bright Hope*, then the *Evelyn* and finally *Gentle Zephyr* until at last he reached her and climbed on to the deck, lugging his bag down behind him. It only took him a matter of minutes to unfasten the warp. Then he pulled on the jib sheet and the jib unfurled itself without a hitch. Smoothly, silkily, the *Aurora* began to move across the calm water of the inner harbour. When she had reached the end of the pier he jibed and turned her into the channel, heading for the marker buoy, seeing the lighthouse blinking ahead of him on his right-hand side. Another jibe and he would be away, he thought, heading out to sea, breathing in the salty air, thanking his lucky stars for a falling tide and a good south-wester to fill his sails. He was beginning to feel almost . . . happy.

And then he saw Chesil. Chesil was jumping about on the wall like a mad thing, leaping into the air, waving his arms above his head. His mouth was wide open in a scream that was whipped away and scattered by the gathering wind.

Vividly awake, open-eyed, still as a stone, Claire lay in her bedroom, listening through the darkness. What was Laurie doing, she wondered. It must be two hours or more since he'd left their bed. She'd heard him tip-toeing down the stairs, pretending that he was trying not to wake her. It was a polite game that they played, the two of them – making believe that either of them slept. It appeared that they had buried sleep in their daughter's grave. Now it seemed a mere luxury. Almost an indulgence. One could get by without sleep, Claire had discovered. A tiny cat-nap here and there, a sort of wakeful trance of semi-consciousness in the middle of the night, that was enough. Occasionally Laurie took a pill that knocked him out for six hours or so, but she adamantly refused to submit to chemically induced sleep. She wanted the real thing or nothing. No compromises. She felt the same about alcohol. Laurie had started drinking quite heavily since Bridget had died. He said it helped him relax, numbed the pain. Sometimes in the middle of the night he'd down a few whiskies then stumble back to bed and sleep till dawn. But when he woke, pale and puffy-eyed, she could see that the pain was worse. That's what he would be doing now, she thought. Sitting in his armchair, drinking alone in the darkness, making yet another vain effort to dull the agony that was eating him alive.

She got out of bed, reached for her dressing gown and trailed down the stairs. She knew she couldn't *reach* him, but at least she could go through the motions of comfort and care. The sitting room was empty, but the lamp that was still shining on the table next to his chair illuminated the empty tumbler and the newspaper that lay beside it, unopened, unread. She hurried to the kitchen and found it dark and deserted. She looked in the other rooms, study, dining room, cloakroom. Perhaps he was upstairs. She raised her head.

'Laurie,' she shouted. 'Where are you?'

The house seemed drowned in silence. She unlocked the back door and called again, then realised how stupid she was being. If he'd gone out for a breath of air the door would not be bolted on the inside. Perhaps the front door, though? She retraced her steps, hurrying along the hall, turned the Yale lock, peered out into the shadows. And then she realised that the car had gone. She closed her eyes, gripping the doorpost, needing its sturdy support. Laurie was out in the middle of the night, driving the car as only Laurie drove, like a wild thing. And he'd been drinking. The empty glass was proof of that. How much had he had, she wondered? And had he taken a sleeping pill before that? Why wasn't the bottle on the table? She ran back into the sitting room, snatched open the door of the drinks cupboard and searched frantically along its shelves. He was in his car and *still* drinking, she realised, because he'd taken the whisky with him.

She sank down into his armchair, feeling the shape of him still there against the cushions, picked up the glass imagining his fingers still around it. For a moment she sat in silence, giving herself up to grief and dread. She had never felt so alone, so stripped bare. It was as if some force had pulled away each separate layer of her conscious self so that nothing remained but bleached bone and brain. Purged. Purified. Burned to the bone. 'I am the phoenix.'

Suddenly she was possessed. She leapt to her feet and ran to the old cupboard where all the cleaning stuff was kept. She rummaged frantically on the top shelf, impatiently pushing aside pots of paint, palette knives and scrapers, a box of brushes and rollers. At last, with a flood of relief, she found what she was looking for. She dashed back to the sitting room, clutching the rolls of lining paper in her hands. Feverishly she pushed the sofa into the middle of the floor, lifted down the pictures from the long wall and thrust them into one corner. Then she unrolled the paper and fastened it up with drawing pins. Shivering with excitement she gazed at the expanse of empty whiteness, opened the desk drawer and pulled out a box of charcoal. Her hands felt stiff and strange as if they did not belong to her. Without a moment's hesitation she attacked the blank paper, making a round black shape in the centre of it, scribbling it in ferociously so that it became a winking eye, then an egg, a sphere, a spinning world of blackness. Then, from that black centre, she drew sharp, jagged lines that stretched up and out towards the edges of the paper, spiky and angular, like claws. A crown of thorns, perhaps? A diadem of nails? She didn't know. All she did know was that it was an image of pain. And that some of *her* pain was flowing out of her body, along her arm, through her fingers and into the drawing. Soon, when she had spent herself, she would go back to bed, she thought. And then she would sleep.

Laurie fixed his eyes on the channel buoy. He'd do a dog-leg round it, then head out to sea. That was what he wanted. To give himself up entirely to wind and water and let them do what they would with him. He didn't want to make decisions any longer, to have to be 'sensible' and 'responsible'. He couldn't take any more of that. He wanted to be free at last. As free as the seagulls which were borne up, carried hither and thither on the currents of the air. Yes, if he came back to this life, he'd choose to come back as a seagull. A marauding herring gull perhaps, the boldest of them all. And he didn't want to have to think about Chesil, leaping about on the wall like a creature demented. What the hell was he doing there anyway, at this time of night? Why wasn't he tucked up in his little bed like normal people? He must have heard the car drive up, for God's sake. Stuck his head out of his window and seen him arrive. The best thing, he decided, would be just to ignore him. Then he would give up and go back to his room like a sensible chap. Laurie groaned. Not Chesil! Chesil was not known for being sensible. Nor for giving up. Chesil was yet another cross he had to bear.

Laurie had 'found' Chesil, quite literally, a couple of years back. A chilly October day of bleak skies and fretful, plucking winds. He'd been on his way home from the office, hurrying to catch his train, when he'd seen the boy hanging about at the end of Driggs Alley. A pathetic skinned rabbit of a creature, smudgy black eyes, white face, tousled hair.

'Spare us some change, Mister?' he'd whimpered.

Laurie had felt irritated. He didn't have time to stop. He had enough on his mind without having to worry about yet another lost child. He did more than his share of that, didn't he, through Pilgrims. He lengthened his stride and passed by

without a second glance. Then he came to a grinding halt
and the man following him down the busy street bumped
into him and cursed under his breath.

'Sorry,' Laurie muttered. He turned and retraced his steps.

'Spare us some change, Mister?' The boy repeated his
mantra.

Laurie scrutinised the immature, undernourished body, the
soft baby skin of his face. 'How old are you?' he asked.

The dark eyes looked at him as if they didn't understand
the question.

'Where do you live?'

Again the blank stare, hostile now. Laurie shrugged. No
doubt there was a watchful parent lurking around a corner
somewhere, confident that the child's beauty and vulnerability would conjure up sufficient cash from the rush-hour
crowd to provide the next fix. Wearily he felt in his pocket,
extracted a pound coin and laid it in the upturned palm.

The next evening the boy was begging again, despite the
sluicing rain that had drenched through his thin nylon anorak
and jeans. When he stopped beside him he caught a glimpse
of recognition as the hand shot out. Laurie glanced round to
see if there was anyone with him, and as he peered along the
dank alleyway he caught sight of an old duvet, neatly folded
on top of a pile of newspapers.

'Are you on your own?' he asked. He was met by silence,
the same sulky stare. Laurie checked his watch and decided
he'd catch a later train. He smiled at the boy encouragingly.
'Look, there's a cafe round the corner. Let me buy you a
meal.'

It was as if he'd held a knife at his throat. The boy sprang
back against the wall, shaking his head, his face full of dread.
Laurie's heart sank. Poor kid, he thought. There'd been other
well-dressed men before him, offering food, warmth and
friendship, but demanding bitter rewards for their kindness.

'Don't worry,' he said. 'I'll be back.' And he hurried away
in the direction of Fred's Cafe.

When he returned ten minutes later he was holding a little

carrier bag crammed with cartons of hamburgers and chips, a large polystyrene mug of hot coffee with lots of sugar, packets of crisps, chocolate biscuits, a banana and an apple. He handed it over to the boy and watched as he examined the contents with awed reverence, then set about the food ravenously. It must be the first square meal he'd had in days. Laurie stood with him until he'd eaten every mouthful and had even used the paper napkin to clean his mouth and fingers with scrupulous thoroughness. Then he opened his briefcase and took out his lightweight raincoat.

'You'd better have this,' he said. 'I've got my brolly. It looks as if the rain's set in for the night.'

Before the week was out, Laurie had managed to gain the boy's confidence. He was no longer too scared to go to the cafe with him. He even began to talk to him. His name was Chesil, he said. Just that. Nobody ever called him anything else. He'd been living with his mother in one room in a street not far from the quay. They were O.K. They'd managed all right. But then Stan had moved in. Stan didn't like him. His Mum said he made Stan angry just *being* there and that's why he hit him sometimes. Then last week Stan had said he was old enough to bugger off and look after himself. What did he want hanging around with his Mum at his age, he'd said.

'How old are you?' Laurie asked.

This time the question was answered. 'Sixteen.'

'Are you sure?'

He'd been insistent. 'I'm not very big, but I am sixteen. So probably Stan's right.'

It didn't take Laurie long to check his story. Chesil didn't seem to know his exact address and refused to go back to his mother's room because Stan had said he'd take his belt to him if he found him hanging about there again. But, even though he seemed a bit simple-minded in some ways, the instructions he gave were surprisingly precise and accurate, and so was his account of what passed for his home life. Mrs Chesil was younger than Laurie had expected, not much more than thirty, he guessed, a hard-faced, narrow-lipped woman whose pinched features and mascara-heavy eyes betrayed not the slightest glimmer of human kindness.

'Stan's right,' she whined. 'It's not decent, the three of us living and sleeping in one room. Know what I mean? It gets on Stan's nerves, having him hanging around the place all the time. Well, it would, wouldn't it? Any normal man?'

Jenny Dent listened to Laurie's tale with sympathy. As a social worker, she'd often nominated youngsters for the Pilgrim Project and been delighted at the way they'd come on as a result of their month as crew members under Laurie's supervision. Now she was glad to take responsibility for one of *his* lost sheep. Almost at once she found Chesil a place in a hostel and made sure that he got the Benefit that was his due. And the following summer it was Chesil's turn to sail with the Pilgrims, his fees paid, though he never realised it, from Laurie's own pocket.

From the moment he stepped on board the *Matadora*, the boy was transformed. He was a natural, instinctive sailor, instantly understanding by one look at the set of the sails what the rest of the crew had to have carefully explained to them with diagrams. Watching him pulling on a sheet or taking a turn at the tiller, Laurie found himself wondering about Chesil's unknown father, about the seamen who frequented the Tyne, and about whether the sea ran in his blood.

When the August sail was over Chesil couldn't keep away from Lithe. He began to haunt the harbour like a homesick ghost. Gradually, carefully, he found ways of making himself useful. He ran errands for the boat-owners, stood guard over their craft while they went on shore, fetched and carried with a will. He was always polite, meticulously honest. He worked hard. He was clean and thorough. He was a positive asset to the sailing community, so much so that once the new sailing season had begun, the Yacht Club offered him a live-in summer job as general dogsbody and handyman, with a cabin in the club itself.

Chesil had become an institution. He knew everybody and everything within the harbour walls. Nothing escaped his eyes and ears. Especially, nothing to do with Mr Richley, whom he adored and worshipped as if he were a god.

But on this night of all nights, Laurie did not want Chesil's devotion. He was beyond the reach of any human concern. All he wanted was the great grey power of the sea. So, as he rounded the buoy and saw that Chesil had given up trying to attract his attention and was running away from the pier, he felt profoundly relieved. The wind filled the *Aurora*'s sails, he laid his hand on the solid comforting wood of the tiller, and he was heading north, steering by the North Star. He felt as if he were going home.

It was the thudding, insistent and terrifying, that sounded through Sarah's dreams and tugged her back to consciousness. She lay in the darkness for a while, confused, drowned in sleep, listening to the wind that howled around the chimney pots. She glanced at the radio-alarm clock on her bedside table. Three-thirty a.m. The thudding persisted. Reluctantly she stumbled out from under her duvet and opened the bedroom door. The noise was coming from the bathroom. She padded anxiously along the landing and peered inside, then felt almost weak with relief. It was just the little top window above the hand basin. The wind had blown the latch free and the window was knocking against the frame as if it had a life of its own. She reached up and closed it firmly, tested it to see if it was secure, then wandered back to bed, praying that she would get to sleep. Otherwise she'd feel half dead when she went to work in the morning.

But it was the same old story, the regular pattern of her nights. If once she woke her head took over, her busy thoughts refusing to let her tired body get the rest it needed. Yet again she lay wide awake, listening to the wind and thinking of Laurie.

'How are you, my love?' she whispered into the empty darkness. 'Is the wind keeping you awake, too? Are you thinking of me, longing for me, as I long for you? Sleep well, my darling. Be happy. I love you.'

Then, as she tossed miserably on her pillow and tugged at her crumpled sheet, she was invaded by an unspecific, gnawing anxiety. A strange creeping panic that made her pulse race. She switched on the light and looked at the telephone on her table. She longed to dial his number. She didn't even need to talk to him. Just to hear his voice would be enough. To know that he was there. Her hand touched the smoothness of the receiver and she lifted it tentatively. She knew his number by heart. The whole thing would only take seconds. She would hear him say 'Laurie Richley' in that firm positive voice of his. She would say nothing, but he would know at once that she was there, loving him, thinking of him through the bleak watches of the stormy night.

No. It was impossible. She shook her head and replaced the receiver abruptly. It would be Claire who answered, not Laurie. She remembered now that the phone stayed at Claire's side of the bed. Laurie was unreachable. She stretched out her hand for her book. She'd read until daybreak, she decided, then get up and finish the essay she was working on.

The *Aurora* was going like a bird, scudding before the wind. And Laurie was singing, his head thrown back, giving voice to the *Messiah*.

'For unto us a child is born,
Unto us, a child is given,
Unto us . . .'

When he became dimly aware of the sound of an outboard motor he shook his head in disbelief. He must be hearing things. Nobody, nobody but a desperate man, would be out on the water on a wind-torn night like this. Even the manic fishermen who haunted the end of the pier in all the most appalling conditions the weather could throw at them had been noticeably absent tonight. But *he* was loving it. He began to sing again.

'And His name shall be called

Wonderful, counsellor,
The mighty God
The everlasting Father . . .'

He slapped his thigh in delight. Good old Handel. What
marvellous stuff it was. Then he heard the engine again, the
unmistakable sound of an outboard motor. He turned round,
peering into the darkness, and saw a beam of light flashing at
him. He shook his head, narrowed his eyes and tried to focus
on the waving finger of brightness.

'Mr Richley! Mr Richley!'

Now the harbour tender was visible, tearing along behind
the *Aurora* at full tilt, and he could see Chesil, standing up,
steering with one hand, guiding the torch with the other.

'Mr *Richley*!'

Laurie cursed long and loud. Christ and flaming bloody
damnation! What the hell was the boy up to, following him
out to sea? He must have taken a short cut round the buoy,
forced the throttle full out, to manage to catch up. He'd just
ignore him, he decided. He'd throw him off, and then the
idiot would give up and go home. He cursed again. No he
wouldn't. Not his devoted slave, Chesil. He'd dog him to
death. Oh, Christ! Laurie threw back his head and howled.
That's exactly what would happen. Now that they were clear
of the harbour the waves were huge. The tender would simply
break up after half an hour of these high seas and the boy
would drown.

He rolled in the jib half-furled and held the *Aurora* as best
he could while Chesil brought the tender in towards him.

'What in God's name do you think you're *doing*?' he
screamed at the boy's white, scared face.

'Gale warning, Mr Richley. Force 9 in Sea Area Tyne, it
said. You've got to come back in.'

'I don't want to, you fool. Leave me alone. Get back to the
harbour. You can't survive in these seas.'

'But Mr Richley . . .'

'You'll sink the boat, you damned fool. Clear off.'

The screeching wind carried the boy's voice towards him.

'It's not safe. "Veering north-westerly," imminent, it said.'

'That's fine by me. That's the way I like it. Now leave me alone, do you hear? Bugger off.'

The ghostly face glimmered at him through the deep night. 'I'm not going to leave you, Mr Richley,' he shouted. 'You can't make me.'

Laurie knew that he was beaten. 'Blast you!' he roared. 'Blast you to hell, you little cunt.'

Furious, he furled the jib completely, threw Chesil his stern warp, watched him catch it deftly and secure it to the boat. Then he started the *Aurora*'s engine, turned her head about, and sulkily, not casting Chesil so much as a backward glance, he began to tow the tender back to safety.

The return journey was a long slow haul. At times it seemed as if they were making no progress at all, that the strain of the tender would pull the *Aurora* under. The waves crashed over their decks, the wind buffeted them till it seemed they must overturn. The sea, which had seemed Laurie's friend and saviour, had now become a deadly and implacable enemy. Weak and exhausted, he began to think that he was beaten. His strength had deserted him. He started to pray, shouting aloud into the spray that plumed high in the air all around him.

'Not Chesil too, dear God. For Christ's sake, not another death on my hands.'

At last, a lifetime later, they limped inside the entrance to the South Harbour and made for the shelter of the wall. Laurie switched off his engine, crawled out of the *Aurora* and up the ladder, carrying the warp. With shaking hands he secured it to a bollard, meticulously careful. He knew that Chesil was following the same procedure with the tender but he refused to look at him. Then he walked slowly away, his legs threatening to buckle beneath him, his head bent before the gusting wind that pushed him about, plucking at his hair and clothes.

'Mr Richley!' The boy was at his heels again like a determined young terrier. 'Where are you going, Mr Richley?'

'Piss off, Chesil.'

'It's just . . . I'm sorry, Mr Richley, but I don't think you should drive your car. Not tonight, Mr Richley.'

'What bloody business is it of . . . ?' Laurie began. But then, because he was drunk and worn out, because the euphoria of his flight had crumbled into a mouthful of dust and ashes, he gave in. He allowed himself to be led like a child along the swaying walkway to the Yacht Club and guided down perilous gangways to Chesil's pin-neat cabin.

'You lie down on my bed, Mr Richley,' Chesil insisted, 'and I'll get you something nice and hot to drink.' Then he sat over him and watched while Laurie swallowed down strong sweet coffee, nodding his head anxiously as if he were a worried parent. 'Are you feeling better now, Mr Richley?' he asked, when he'd drained the mug and laid it to one side.

Laurie glared at him. 'Better?' he echoed savagely. 'How am I ever supposed to feel better? I killed my daughter.'

Chesil's dark eyes widened in horror. 'No you didn't, Mr Richley. I heard about it on my radio. It was an accident. A train accident. Have you forgotten? You'll remember in the morning.'

Laurie brought his fist down on the locker with a crash that sent his coffee mug flying to the floor. 'I killed her, I tell you. If she'd gone by car the way she'd wanted to . . . do you know, there wasn't one single road accident in the whole of the county, the night of the rail crash. Did you know that, Chesil?'

Chesil shook his head mutely.

'It's true. I checked. Not one. But I said she had to go by train or not at all. It was my fault. Entirely my fault. I should have . . .'

He realised that Chesil was looking at him with an expression that he had never seen on his face before. He looked almost . . . contemptuous. His devotion and loyalty had evaporated. His eyes seemed to darken, the pallor of his skin intensified.

'Do you know, Mister, you make me sick,' the boy hissed.

229

'What *you* did. What *you* didn't do. Who do you think you are, then? Jesus-fucking-Christ?'

CHAPTER TWENTY-THREE

On Christmas Eve the Page family gathered together in Jim and Muriel's cottage, blank-faced, dry-eyed, consumed by memory. Each of them was separately haunted by a tall smiling girl with a wide grin, shining green eyes and hair like dandelion down. Bridget was everywhere, glimpsed through the branches of the Christmas tree, running across the frost-bleached lawn, vanishing up the stairway ahead of them. This first Christmas after her death was an affair to be got over, to be shuffled through and done with as swiftly as possible. None of them had any appetite for celebrations.

'Why don't you all come to Burnham Market?' Muriel had suggested on the phone to Sarah. 'There'll be the two of us and Chris, and the four of you, so your place would be too small. But it would be better to be together, wouldn't it?'

Sarah had accepted the invitation thankfully. She had had a Christmas card from Claire, plain white with the single word GREETINGS embossed in gold on the front, and signed by both her and Laurie. Inside there was a brief scribbled note. 'We're not sending many of these things, as you can imagine, one or two to old friends. We are surviving – just. I'm working again, on something quite new and different. It keeps me sane. Laurie had a very bad patch in September. I was frightened for him. But now he seems determined to get a grip on things. At least we go through the motions. We think of you all and miss you more than I can say.'

Sarah showed the card to Muriel as they were unpacking the suitcases together in the pretty low-beamed bedroom with its view across the Green to the square church tower, already floodlit in the darkening afternoon. As Muriel read Claire's message her face was a map of pain.

'Just a year ago today, Sarah. Your wonderful Peacocks' Acre party.'

Sarah nodded. 'It doesn't seem possible, does it? I can see Bridget now . . .'

'Me too. In that lovely red dress . . . Chris was bewitched.'

Poor, gentle, lost Chris! He was taking it harder than any of them, Sarah thought. Though his flat wasn't much more than a couple of miles from her little house in Gillan Terrace, she had hardly seen him since they'd moved in. She had rung a few times to try to arrange something but he was always elusive. Too busy. A bit of a cold. Sorry, he'd got something else organised. Now she was shocked by the change in him. He looked ill. He'd lost a lot of weight during the last six months. His skin was pale and puffy, his eyes lifeless, and for hours on end he hardly spoke. He'd always been the joker of the family, with his endless fund of stories, but now she found it difficult to believe that he'd ever smile again. She could see from the way that Merry watched his face that she was anxious too. They'd always been good friends, Chris and Merry. It must be a real body blow, Sarah imagined, to have lost Bridget and then to have to witness Chris so reduced and crushed by grief that he was hardly recognisable. And she was still only sixteen. As she used to say so often – but never did nowadays – it just wasn't *fair*.

As Christmas crawled through its rituals and ceremonies, Merry was rarely far from Chris's side. She stood next to him during the midnight service at St Mary's, holding out the service sheet, coaxing him to join in the hymn singing. At first he was reluctant, shaking his head with a sad smile, but eventually he gave in and Sarah, standing behind him, felt a surge of relief as she heard his baritone voice, strong and tuneful, rising to the rafters.

Next morning, when the breakfast things were cleared away, Merry tugged Chris towards the tree. 'You and I will be "present monitors" this year,' she grinned. 'You hand the parcels to me and I'll pass them round.'

And when, at six o'clock, they sat down to try to do justice to the turkey that Jim had cooked, Merry made sure that she had the seat next to his, pulled his cracker with him, and gently, lovingly, bullied him to wear his purple paper crown and read aloud his terrible old joke.

'I say, I say, I say, my dog has no nose.

Oh dear, oh dear, oh dear, that's terrible. How does he smell?

Absolutely blooming horrible! Boom! Boom!'

David and Sarah had planned to take Will and Merry home after breakfast on the twenty-sixth, but Jim persuaded them to stay on for a little while, at least until the afternoon.

'The world and his wife take a stroll on Holkham Beach on Boxing Day morning,' he told them. 'Tradition. And since we've got the weather for it – let's go.' He looked pleadingly at Sarah. 'We're going to feel a bit flat, Chris especially, when you've gone. Please don't hurry off sooner than you have to.'

Striding out towards the dunes, Sarah felt delighted that they'd agreed to Jim's plans. She'd never seen the bay look more beautiful. The heavy frost had persisted since before Christmas, the trees were stiff and white, the huge sky glittered icy blue. It was low tide and the sea lay calm in the distance, covering the ridged sand with a film of water so shallow that it was impossible to tell where land ended and ocean began in that expanse of glimmering gold. Jim had been right about Holkham being a popular place. The beach was crowded, busier than she had seen it on many an August afternoon. There was an air of vitality, of exuberance, about the holiday crowd that lifted Sarah's spirits. Children splashed among the shallow pools, stamping their little red wellingtons and sending up showers of rainbows. A large Great Dane lolloped along the sands, pursued by a yapping Jack Russell. Three girls on horseback galloped past her at the water's edge, their heads thrown back in laughter. Sarah breathed in deeply. The crisp air smelled of salt and seaweed and pine trees. Perhaps things *were* beginning to get better, she thought. Time, the great healer! The point about clichés was that usually they were *true*. Now that they'd got to the end of Christmas, the family seemed positively cheerful. She looked at Merry, dancing ahead of them. Her long brown hair was loose, blowing out behind her in the breeze from the sea. She was calling to Chris, rushing to show him the piece of driftwood she held in her hand. Then, laughing, she hurled it high in the air and threw her arms around him in a bear hug. She was grown up now, Sarah realised, trying to look at her through the objective eyes of a stranger. An attractive young woman, not overweight any longer but sturdy and pretty. She was hardly recognisable as the sulky fifteen-year-old they'd dragged off to Northumberland only eighteen months ago.

She glanced behind her and saw Jim and Muriel just a few yards back, arm in arm, their heads bent towards each other in earnest conversation. And here, surrounded by their family, she and David walked together, one on either side of William, the three of them silent but apparently content with each other's company. She smiled up at Will's profile. They weren't far from the spot where he had been conceived, aeons ago, during a summer thunderstorm. Was David remembering that day too? Abruptly, William's voice interrupted her train of thought.

'Dad,' he said, frowning a little, 'could we have a bit of a talk some time, do you think?'

David looked at him in surprise. 'Of course, Will. Is it something important?'

'Well, yes. Sort of.'

'Come on then. Out with it.'

'What? Now, d'you mean?'

'Why not? No time like the present.'

Will swallowed and Sarah felt a tingle of apprehension, wondering what was weighing so heavily on his mind. Why hadn't he told her? They used to discuss everything.

'I've been doing a lot of thinking,' he began, 'since . . . since I left school, really, and . . .'

'Yes?' David was patient, gently encouraging.

'So this isn't something I've just dreamed up overnight or anything, and . . .'

'Oh, isn't this just *lovely*! I'm so glad we came.' Sarah turned to look at Muriel's smiling face as she and Jim came hurrying up to join them. 'We were just saying we haven't had a chance to talk properly about Peacocks' Acre yet, and you'll be gone soon.'

Jim fell into step beside David and they walked together, shoulder to shoulder, enjoying the crunch of firm sand beneath their feet. 'Is the offer going ahead?'

David nodded. 'Seems like it.'

Will took a deep breath and withdrew into himself again as he realised that he had missed his moment.

'The sale's on then?' Jim asked.

'We're expecting to exchange in January. Fingers crossed.'

'Oh, but it's sad!' Muriel exclaimed. 'That lovely old house. You'll never find another place like it.'

David shook his head. 'It's not the same without Sarah. Frankly, I can't wait to be out of it.'

'But where will you go?' Muriel asked. 'Do you know yet?'

'One of the staff has a little flat in her house that's going to be available soon. Just two attic rooms. But it'll do me fine until I get a new school.'

'And how's the job-hunting?' Jim wanted to know. 'Anything interesting coming up?'

'Not yet. Craiglands is a hard act to follow. First rate facilities. Nice kids. An inner city comprehensive doesn't have the same appeal.'

'But they need good teachers too,' Will suggested mildly.

'That's very true,' David agreed. 'As far as I'm concerned though, I'm not really interested in being a minder for yobs.'

Muriel was shocked. 'David! They can't all be yobs.'

'It only takes one or two to disrupt a class, you know.'

'Can't you single them out, and try to . . .' Will began.

David gave an exasperated laugh. 'What is this! I'm the only teacher here yet everybody knows the score better than I do.'

'We're just trying to take an interest, that's all,' Sarah said. 'An adult discussion . . .'

'O.K. O.K. Don't go on about it, love.' He turned back to Muriel. 'The other problem is that Sarah doesn't want to leave Norfolk again. Otherwise I might be trying for a head-ship. It's difficult to be a high-flyer with a timid little stay-at-home wife.'

Sarah seethed in silence. It was neither the time nor the place to have this one out, and already she could see that Jim and Muriel were shifting about uneasily. But Will had no such compunction.

'Well, I think Mum's got the right idea.' He thrust his hands deep into his pockets and began to stride ahead to catch up with Merry and Chris. 'I never have understood why the hell you had to leave in the first place.' He glared back at David over his shoulder.

'I have explained that!' David insisted, to his son's sullen back. 'Again and again. It seemed the right career move at the time.'

Will turned up the collar of his coat and broke into a run.

'What's the matter with the lad?' Jim asked, puzzled.

'Search me,' David said. 'He says there's something he wants to talk about. Do you know what it is, Sarah?' She shook her head. 'Ah well.' He smiled. 'Let's enjoy the beach while we can, eh? We'll thrash it out tonight, whatever it is.'

Sarah had cooked a supper that was one of their family favourites, ham simmered in cider and herbs, served with sauteed potatoes, broad beans and onion sauce. And she'd de-frosted some raspberries for their pudding course, to be served up with meringues and icecream. A good way to end Christmas, she thought. They arranged themselves around the square table rather formally, the way they had done when the children were younger, though now meal times were usually more casual affairs. David sat at one side, slicing the ham, exclaiming how tender and moist it was, levering it on to their plates on the end of the outstretched carving knife, while Sarah passed around the vegetables and sauce jug. When the food had been served and the meat dish carried away into the kitchen, he lifted his knife and fork and began to eat with relish.

'Wonderful!' he exclaimed, swallowing a mouthful of ham. 'You know, I really prefer a meal like this to all that endless turkey and trimmings.'

Sarah smiled and nodded. 'So do I.'

'Right,' he said, turning to Will. 'Now. What about that talk we were going to have? What's on your mind? Mmm?'

'David! Please.' Sarah said. 'Not now. We're eating.'

He laughed. 'I had noticed! But some of us can eat and talk too, you know.'

Will looked miserably at Sarah and she raised her eyebrows sympathetically. When David was in his schoolmasterly mood there was no way out.

'If you insist,' said Will, looking fixedly at the tablecloth. 'It's just that . . . I've thought a lot about it . . . and I've decided I might . . . it's possible that I might decide not to go to Cambridge after all.'

'I beg your pardon.' David's tone was icy.

'Don't say that!' Will retorted. 'You heard what I said perfectly well.'

'No. I heard something so puerile and stupid that I must have heard wrong.'

Merry groaned. 'Dad! Don't be so pompous. It's *us*, remember. You're not at school now.'

'Don't speak to me like that, Merry. It's none of your business, anyway.'

'Yes it is!' she protested.

Sarah noticed that the colour was beginning to mount David's cheeks and the little vein was throbbing at the side of his forehead. She turned desperately towards Will.

'Everybody gets cold feet before they go to university,' she told him. 'I know I did. I'd happily have stayed at home . . .'

'It's not cold feet, Mum. It's just not something I want to do any more. It suddenly seems irrelevant.'

'Getting a degree!'

'A degree isn't everything, is it?'

'Isn't it? No, I suppose not.'

She bowed her head, remembering how lost she'd felt, how completely desolate, when she'd realised that graduation was suddenly beyond her grasp. And all because of William. Was that why his education had always seemed so important to her, she wondered. So that *he* could achieve what he'd caused her to lose. If so, it looked as if she was set to lose out a second time. What a cruel joke. How her father would enjoy it. She suddenly realised that David was livid with anger.

'May I remind you that you got straight A's in your exams and a place in the Cambridge college of your choice?' he said.

'No. You may not remind me,' Will retorted. 'I know that very well. I did the work. I got the result. So what!'

'So what? So – a place at Cambridge is *not* a toy to be thrown away. It's something very special, to be valued and used. The key to your whole future.'

'It's the key to a future I don't want,' shouted Will. 'And please don't talk to me like a school teacher all the time.'

'I *am* a school teacher.'

'But not *mine*. You're my father. You should behave like one.'

'What's that supposed to mean?' Abruptly David pushed away his plate and his fork toppled off, spilling sauce and beans on to the clean cloth.

'A father should want his son to have what his son wants, not just push his own ambitions.'

David stared. 'What the hell are you on about now?'

'I'm on about the fact that I'm supposed to be going up to Cambridge to read History and I'm not even very interested in History. You're the historian.'

'What *are* you interested in then?'

Sarah saw that Will was beginning to look distressed, and Merry's face was scarlet with the effort she was making to hold her tongue in case she made things worse for him. She herself longed to intervene, to beg David to let things ride, just for a little while, but she knew from past experience that the very sound of her voice would only infuriate him even more.

'I'm interested in the sort of things I'm doing now,' Will said wearily. 'Plants. Horticulture. And conservation. That sort of thing.'

David sneered. 'Don't be so pathetic. Just because you've got a piffling little job in a second rate garden centre, you suddenly think you're interested in horticulture. You haven't got the right qualifications, for God's sake. You should have gone for sciences.'

'I didn't want to do sciences.'

Suddenly Merry was on her feet, incandescent with fury. 'Stop going on at Will like that,' she fumed. 'You seem to think you can treat him like dirt.'

'Oh, Merry . . .' Sarah tried to pacify her, but Merry refused to be quietened.

'You're what they call a control freak, did you know that, Dad? Sometimes you can be really lovely, kind and patient and all that. But if anybody argues against you, or does something you don't want them to, oh boy, you're not satisfied till you've hammered them into the ground. It makes me sick.'

'Merry!' Sarah repeated. 'This is not helping.'

'I don't care. He doesn't understand *anything*. He doesn't even *try*. Will doesn't want to be like him. Why can't he see that? He's not interested in academic achievement and career structures and all that boring stuff.'

Sarah hesitated. 'He's always been so clever, though. It does seem a bit of a waste.'

'But life's not like that any more,' Will insisted. 'Everything's different now. It's not all about qualifications and going in for a profession.'

'More's the pity!' declared David.

'You would say that,' Merry cried. 'But just look at you. You've done all that stuff – your brilliant career! – and it's caused nothing but misery. Will had to stay here a whole year on his own.'

'He had his precious Zack!'

'But he didn't have *us*. And I'd have been miserable too, when you forced me to go and live in Deredale, if it hadn't been for Bridget. And now Bridget's dead.' And she burst into tears and rushed away.

'Merry!' David shouted after her. 'Stop being a baby and come back here and eat your supper.' But the only answer was the banging of her bedroom door. He turned his attention to William again. 'Well done!' he said. 'You've managed to thoroughly upset everybody in the house. What a way to end Christmas.'

'Strange, isn't it?' Will retorted. 'When you're not here we never have a cross word.' Slowly he stood up. 'Sorry, Mum. I don't seem to be very hungry.' He bent and kissed her cheek gently. 'Goodnight. I'm going round Zack's.'

They heard the front door open and close behind him, and Sarah stared at David across the wreckage of their special meal.

'I give up,' she said bitterly.

'I hold you responsible.'

'You what!'

'You encourage them. *Your* example. You do exactly what you want, so they think they can too.'

'In what way?'

'Will was a fine scholar. Now he piddles about with plants and lets his brain atrophy. I told you I didn't want him spending his year out at that place with Zack.'

'I am not his keeper. He's his own man.'

'He's his mother's son. And now it's Merry.'

'What's wrong with Merry?' she asked him coldly.

'Since you brought her down here she's turned into a typical mindless teenager. Flirting with her own *uncle*, for God's sake.'

'Flirting?'

'Making an exhibition of herself with Chris. You saw her. Holding his hand all the time, hugging him, dogging his footsteps. You'd better warn her off, Sarah. Quite apart from anything else, it's probably against the law.'

Sarah felt sick with misery and disgust. For a moment she hated him, almost wished him dead. 'You're making an absolute fool of yourself, do you know that?'

'Well, it takes one to know one.' He scowled at her. 'By the way, I think I'll drive back north tomorrow.'

'But you've got another week's holiday yet.'

'I have another week before I go back to school, if that's what you mean. But you seem to have forgotten, I have a house to look after on my own. And if the sale goes through – please God! – I have a lot of sorting out to do before the move.'

He stood up and stalked from the room. Sarah heard him climbing the stairs, moving around above her head. She got to her feet slowly. She trailed into the kitchen and came back carrying the waste bin. Propping it open with one foot on the pedal, she picked up each of their plates in turn and scraped the barely touched food into its plastic liner.

'Merry Christmas, Sarah, and a *very* happy New Year!' she said to the empty room.

When she had cleared away and stacked the dish washer, she poured herself a large brandy, collapsed miserably on to the sofa and switched on the television. At once the room was invaded by inane grinning faces, a cackle of canned laughter. Yuletide jollity! She grimaced and turned it off again, then rummaged on the shelves for one of the books that David had brought down and found her favourite anthology.

'I sat down under his shadow with great delight,' she read,
'and his fruit was sweet to my taste.
He brought me to the banqueting house,
and his banner over me was love.

Stay me with flagons, comfort me with apples:
for I am sick of love.'

Her mind was full of Laurie, wondering how *he* had got
through this terrible Christmas. She remembered their first
kiss, a year ago, when she had been suddenly overwhelmed
by a premonition of the pain and loneliness that lay ahead.
She had no idea what he was doing now, how he was coping.
He had written to her often, at least two or three times a
week, when she had first moved to Norwich. She had steeled
herself not to open the envelopes. Day after day she had
picked them up from the doormat, run her fingers over the
name and address written in his dashed-off handwriting, held
them against her cheek as if she held part of Laurie there,
feeling the soft skin of his throat, the palm of his hand. And
then she had crossed out her own name and printed in large
red capitals NOT KNOWN AT THIS ADDRESS. Gradually
the letters became less frequent. Finally they stopped altogether. 'Comfort me with apples.' With a heavy heart, Sarah
closed the book, switched off the light and climbed the stairs
to her room.

David was lying in the dark, his back hunched against her.
As she switched on her reading lamp, she saw that his shoulders were heaving. She walked round the bed and looked
down at him. The sight of his tears appalled her. David never
cried. The one and only time she could remember was when
William was born, and he'd stood at her bedside, holding
their son in his hands, still wet and slippery from the womb.
But on that occasion, the weeping was mingled with wild,
ecstatic laughter. This was different. This was despair. She
fell to her knees, put her arms round him and brought her
face close to his.

'Hush,' she murmured, as if he were a child. 'Please don't
cry.'

At once his arms shot out and he clutched her convulsively,
holding her so tight that she could hardly breathe. 'I'm sorry.
I didn't mean it. All those horrible things I said. I love you.

And the children. I don't know what came over me.'

Sarah closed her eyes. The old pattern. The row. The agony. The apology. The making up. It had happened so often. And almost certainly, whatever promises he made now, it would all happen again. She was silent, listening to the thudding of his heart, feeling his lips moving against her hair.

'I know it was unforgivable, Sarah,' he said. 'Spoiling the evening like that. But things build up inside me so that I just can't seem to keep a hold on myself.'

'Everybody gets tense over Christmas,' she told him. 'We all try too hard. All those pressures . . .'

'It's not that, though.' He sat up, swinging his legs over the edge of the bed, persuading her to sit beside him while he kept a tight grip of her hand. 'I just don't know what's happening any more. I still don't understand why you had to leave Deredale. No matter how I try, it doesn't make sense.'

'I know.' She searched for words that wouldn't sound false and empty. 'I was homesick, David. And worried about Will.'

'But . . .'

'I know I shouldn't have been, but I was. And there was too much pain. Everywhere. Whenever I saw Claire . . . I know it all seems childish and emotional and pointless, but I couldn't help it.'

'I get so lonely, Sarah. That great house, without you and Merry. And every time I come down here and bring you some more of your things . . . it just feels worse and worse. Like a skeleton. I loved Peacocks' Acre too, you know.'

She squeezed his arm. 'What about Laurie and Claire? Why don't you see more of them? Invite them to supper and cook them a David Special?'

'No.' His voice was flat. 'You were right about the Richleys. You said they'd be better off on their own. They don't want me, or anybody. Claire spends every minute of every day at the Barns. I think she even sleeps there sometimes.'

'And Laurie?' She tried to sound casual.

'I hardly ever see him. He's stopped going to the Eagle. In

fact, Reggie says he's given up drinking altogether. Thinks he's been overdoing it or something. So *he* works all the time too.'

'Is he all right, though?'

'I think so. A bit greyer. Older. But well enough, I suppose. As I say, I don't see much of him. It's not the way it was, Sarah.'

'No.'

He turned and looked down at her and she flinched at the pleading look in his eyes. She knew that he longed for her to relent. They hadn't yet exchanged contracts on the house. There was still time for her to change her mind and go back to Peacocks' Acre, to pick up the threads of their old life just where they'd left off. He didn't have to put it into words. They'd been together so long she could read his mind.

Resolutely she shook her head. 'I really am sorry, David.'

He gave a little gasp of pain, and as she put her arms out he pulled her down beside him and began to make love to her like a dying man, with a sort of quiet desperation. At first she pulled away, but he clung to her and she couldn't bear to hurt him further. She willed herself to respond, focused her mind on memories of other times when she had lain in his arms and revelled in the power of his muscular body. But now she was quite unable to conjure up desire. Sensing David's mounting frustration at her lack of response, she decided that the only thing she could do was pretend. Hating herself, she manufactured synthetic passion, faked a shuddering, breathless orgasm. At once, she felt David come, silently, joylessly. Then he rolled away from her, his face to the wall.

'Thank you,' he muttered politely.

She knew that he hadn't been taken in. She felt ashamed. She rubbed his back, trying to comfort him. 'Things *will* get better,' she murmured. 'We'll put all this behind us.'

'Maybe,' he said.

And then he pretended to fall asleep.

CHAPTER TWENTY-FOUR

'Shit!' exploded Zack, rustling the newspaper in his hands, stretching it out in front of him to examine it more carefully. 'Fucking hell!'

'What's up?' Will looked at him dreamily, holding the cigarette loosely between his fingers, enjoying the pattern of its fragrant smoke.

'It's a fucking disgrace!' Zack spread the paper on the concrete floor and knelt down to study it.

They were taking a break from work, relaxing, smoking a bit of dope together in the old greenhouse that Mr Gallagher let them use as their hang-out. There were a pair of beaten-up garden chairs that they'd carted in, and an upturned tea-chest they used as a table. On the last stretch of staging that was still standing they'd stacked their gear, their own special tools and gloves, their sandwich boxes and flasks. Clouds of warmth were gusting out from the old paraffin heater that Zack had bought at a car boot sale, and the green mossy windows were opaque with condensation. A portable radio hung from a big metal hook just inside the door, filling the steamy space with loud rock music.

'Turn that fucking thing off,' Zack snapped. 'I can't concentrate.'

Will tapped the switch then dropped to his knees, curious. The whole centre spread of the *Daily Press* was dominated by a map of the north coast of Norfolk. 'NEW ROAD FOR COUNTY' blared the headline. A red line sliced straight across the area between Holt and Hunstanton. Will's face creased up in disbelief. He passed the cigarette to Zack so that he could trace the route with his fingertip.

'It's a joke,' he declared. 'It must be April Fool's Day.'

'It ain't no joke. That smiling face you're looking at belongs to our revered Minister of Transport. It's "a proud day for Norfolk", he says.' He began to read aloud, his voice plummy and pompous. ' "This marvellous inland road will take the pressure off the overused A149 coast road, allowing it to become a scenic route for visitors to our glorious coast-line, and relieving congestion in the lovely unspoilt coastal villages of Cley, Brancaster, Salthouse and so on. We are reclaiming our natural heritage, saving our incomparable beaches and estuaries from noise and pollution and . . ." '

'Shut up,' said Will. 'It's not funny. It's going to ruin all that marvellous country that the visitors *don't* spoil because it's a few miles from the sea. Ancient fields and hedgerows. Lovely stands of trees. It's perfect.' He examined the map again. 'Christ!'

'Christ, what?'

'They're even threatening to go through part of Holkham Park.'

Zack gave a bitter laugh. 'Nah! The aristocracy are more than able to look after themselves. It's the poor ordinary buggers who get shafted.'

'Surely they can't get away with it?'

Zack was concentrating on a column of print at the far edge of the page. 'Seems like they've done it already. Compul-sory purchase orders have been made and land clearance is expected to begin soon after.'

'How come we haven't heard anything about it till now?'

Zack raised his eyebrows. 'They must have managed to persuade the media not to make a big splash. Don't rock the boat, chaps. Keep it in the small print till we give you the nod.'

Will was appalled. 'It makes me bloody sick. I love it up there, and it's going to be . . . desecrated.'

'The fucking car! Everything is sacrificed to the almighty fucking car!'

'D'you know, Zack, I sometimes think I might emigrate.'

'Yeah! Me too. But *where*?'

Will shrugged. 'They say there's plenty of room in New Zealand.'

'New Zealand's shit.'

'Canada?'

'Shit plus!'

'The north of Scotland's O.K. Trees *and* mountains. Argyll. Up round there.'

Zack considered, dragging thoughtfully on the roll-up. 'Nah!' he said at last. 'Too many fucking Scots in Scotland!'

Will laughed, then looked down at the newspaper again and groaned. 'Seriously, though – this is a national scandal, you know.'

'It's no good just saying things, mate. If it's really getting to you, you should do something.'

'Like what?'

'I dunno. Go on a demo. Make a fucking nuisance of yourself.'

'Fat chance. When does it say they're starting? Spring '93? There you are then.'

'What's wrong with spring '93?'

'I'll be up at Cambridge, remember?'

'Fuck, Will. I thought you'd given up that load of shit. You told your old man.'

'I know I did. But he nearly flipped. Said it was all Mum's fault.'

'How did he make that out?'

'Everything is always her fault these days.'

'Parents! They really fuck you up . . . to coin a phrase.'

'Anyway, now *she's* on about it all the time – "Please don't ruin your chances, at least give yourself a year, etc. etc." So I'll probably have to go in the end, I suppose.'

'I wouldn't take all that crap. What's the point of getting a History degree just to please *them*? What the fuck have they done to please *you*?'

'I know, but . . .'

Suddenly, Zack was shining with excitement. 'Let's go for it, Will. There's bound to be a huge song and dance. Friends of the Earth. Greenpeace. All that. Fuck Cambridge. This is important stuff. I'll get on to the Greens tonight, shall I? They'll know what's going on.'

'Sarah, you're my oldest friend but you can be a bit of a wet blanket sometimes.' Pam looked reproachful.

'Sorry!' Sarah continued stroking Jake, the marmalade cat, who had taken possession of her lap and was purring ecstatically. She gazed round Pam's cluttered sitting room, noticing the piles of documents waiting for her attention, the open drawers, the books stacked on the floor. She was obviously right in the middle of a heavy work load. Sarah felt guilty for taking up her time but such a thought, she knew, would never cross Pam's mind.

'I wish you'd stop concentrating on my wretched cat and talk to *me* for a while. You're killing him with kindness,' Pam complained.

'Oh dear. What a sad little person I am these days, aren't I? Desperate for love. Even from a cat.' Sarah tried to make light of it and failed miserably.

'What *is* the matter?' asked Pam. '*Tell* me, for God's sake.'

Sarah pulled a wry face. 'David rang last night. The sale of the house is going through. They're completing on February the thirteenth.'

'That's just ten days.'

Sarah nodded grimly.

'Merry and Will can come here if that will help. Or will they want to go up with you?'

'I'm not going.'

'Sarah!' Pam was incredulous.

'Apart from anything else, I'm not due for any time off work. And it's our busy period. Holiday bookings coming out of our ears.'

'Just *take* some time off. Tell them you've got backache or something. Flu. Yellow fever. What does it matter?'

'I really can't face going back there, Pam.'

'You've got to. There'll be so much to do. What about sorting out all your personal stuff?'

'I've got that here. David fills the boot every time he comes.'

'All the same, organising all your furniture into store. You're not being fair to David. It's too much, putting everything on his shoulders, poor guy.'

'He says he doesn't mind.'

'You're joking.'

'It's his half-term. That's why he fixed it for that date. And he says Jean Anstruther – she's the teacher whose flat he's got – she's offered to give him a hand. The only thing is, it means he won't be able to get back here before Easter.'

Pam could hardly believe her ears. 'But don't you *want* to see the house again? Just one more time. You were so happy there before . . . before Bridget . . .'

'I couldn't *bear* to see it again,' Sarah blurted out. 'It would break me up. I just want to close the door on all that and walk away. I can't go back.'

Her eyes filled with tears and she jerked her head away angrily. She could see from the look on Pam's face that she thought she was being selfish and unreasonable, and she was right, of course. Claire had written and suggested that she and David should stay with them at Dolphin House for a couple of nights while the removal men were busy, but the thought of sleeping under the same roof as Laurie, of seeing him and Claire together, gentle and loving with each other, was more than she could bear. Maybe that was what Laurie had been trying to tell her in all those letters she'd returned. That he'd fallen in love with Claire all over again. No, the only way she could survive, she thought, was to put the memory of their time together in a bell-jar. To preserve it intact beneath a shining glass dome.

Pam gave her a long look. 'Is this *really* what the blues are about? Selling Peacocks' Acre?'

Sarah tried to meet her eyes and failed. She concentrated

on Jake again, feeling his paws kneading into her thighs, his body vibrating with comfort and pleasure. She had never told Pam about Laurie. Now, it was on the tip of her tongue. She longed to lay her head on her shoulder and pour out her desolation and grief. But she couldn't do it. She had promised herself that she wouldn't tell a soul. That she would carry it with her to the grave. Besides, she knew that Pam would find it difficult to be sympathetic. Claire, after all, was supposed to be Sarah's friend. In Pam's personal rule book you'd find it emblazoned in letters of gold. *Do not mess with the husband of your friend.* No excuses. No buts.

She attempted a wintry smile. 'Is that not enough? I loved the place.'

'You loved it and you left it.' Pam's voice was brisk. 'You made your own bed. It seems a bit weird to have withdrawal symptoms at this stage.'

'But now I feel as if I'm in limbo. I suppose I'm lonely, too. If it weren't for you . . .' She cleared her throat, tried to sound bright and sensible. 'I hardly seem to see the children. Merry's working like mad for her exams and when she has time off she's down at the Maddermarket Theatre, painting scenery. She's even managed to get Chris involved, did you know?'

'Painting scenery?'

'No. Acting. He's good, apparently.'

'I'm not surprised. He always had a brilliant range of voices.' She laughed. 'He could even do Margaret Thatcher.'

'Yes.' Sarah's eyes lit up. 'He even managed to *look* like Margaret Thatcher! . . . Do you think it's all right, Pam? The way Chris and Merry seem to spend all their time together?'

'What do you mean?'

'I don't know. I sometimes get the feeling that perhaps Merry's a bit . . . keen on him.'

'You what!' Pam groaned and shook her head in despair. 'You really are round the bend these days. Merry is gorgeous. *And* smart. All the guys are mad about her, Zack says. So she is not going to waste her time lusting after Chris who is not only nine years older but also her father's brother, for God's sake. She just likes him. And she has a kind heart, like her Mum. She's *looking after him*, Sarah. What the hell are you thinking of?'

'It was just something David said. It . . . worried me.'

'Pooh! Fathers!' exclaimed Pam in disgust. 'What the hell do *they* know?' Wearily she smoothed her forehead with the tips of her fingers. 'Now, what else is bothering that busy little brain of yours?'

Sarah pulled a face. 'You are giving me a hard time.'

'That's what friends are for. Out with it.'

'I just wonder. . . have you any idea what Will is up to? He's being very . . . devious. He used to tell things. Talk to me. But now, if ever I manage to pluck up courage to ask him about his plans – I mean, I am his mother. I'd like to know! – he clams up and finds an urgent job to do elsewhere.'

'Mmm. *And* Zack.' Pam nodded thoughtfully. 'I think they're cooking something up, those two.'

'What sort of something?'

Pam hunched her shoulders. 'Search me. But Zack's got that zealot gleam in his eyes again and it's not a good sign. He's getting an awful lot of weird post too.'

'How – weird?'

'Looks like junk mail at first glance, but it's not. Stuff from the County Council and the Department of the Environment. And the Green Party. I thought he'd given all that up when he got expelled but they're back in the frame again.'

'That sounds pretty harmless. Have you asked him?'

'Asked Zack! You cannot be serious. He's turned non-communication into an art form.'

Sarah pushed the reluctant cat on to the floor and stood up to go. 'Sorry for being such an old misery, Pam.'

'It was your turn.' Pam grinned. 'Hang on a minute though. I've got something for you.' She rummaged in the top drawer of her computer bench, frowned, then flicked through a pile of letters and papers stacked on the window sill. 'Eureka!' she yelled, extracting what looked like a flimsy cutting from a newspaper.

' "A career in hospitality management." ' Sarah read it aloud, puzzled. 'What exactly is hospitality management?'

'Read on,' Pam insisted.

She skimmed through the details. ' "A four-year BA Honours course will prepare you to meet the challenges of an expanding hospitality industry . . . management skills . . . tourism/travel operations . . . opportunities at management level . . ." Gosh. Where is it?'

'That's the thing. It's in Norwich. Anglia Polytech,' Pam said. 'It's just you. You've got your Greenacres experience, and the travel agency . . .'

' "Applications invited now for September . . ." ' Sarah twisted her mouth. 'It might have been an idea, but I don't even know where I'll be in September, do I?'

'David still hasn't got anything definite lined up then?'

Sarah shook her head. 'He went for an interview in Ipswich, but he didn't get it. I don't know why. He's usually brilliant at interviews, and since he can offer Games as well as History . . . Perhaps he didn't really want it.'

'Is there anything else on the horizon?'

'He's applied to a school near Holt and he thinks he's on the short list.'

'That's really good news. Isn't it? Holt would be wonderful.'

'Yes,' said Sarah. But the bleak, hopeless expression was settling itself upon her face again even as she spoke. 'Holt would be wonderful.'

She looked at the advertisement, stooped and thrust it into the top of Pam's overflowing waste paper bin. Then, on an impulse, she pulled it out again, folded it neatly and put it into her pocket.

Belle stood at the open door of Peacocks' Acre, on tip-toe with excitement and pleasure. 'Hello-o-o!' she called. 'Hello there. Sarah – it's me.'

David emerged from the drawing room, carrying three table lamps in his arms. 'Belle! Come on in. What can I do for you?'

'I was just passing and I saw Sarah through the window,' she told him. 'I had no idea she was here.'

'David. This tea-chest is full now.'

Belle's face changed at the sound of the voice that called out from the dining room, her eyes widened as a figure came hurrying into the hallway. She saw a stranger, a woman much the same height and build as Sarah, but older, with hair that was beginning to go grey at the temples.

'Oh, I'm sorry,' the woman apologised. 'I didn't realise . . .'

David smiled. 'This is Jean,' he told Belle. 'A colleague of mine. Jean, come and be introduced. Belle lives next door. She thought you were Sarah.'

Jean came forward tentatively, wiping dusty hands on the seat of her neat green trousers. She had a pleasant open face, with a high forehead and large eyes of an unusual milky blue colour.

'Sarah's not coming,' David explained to Belle, still hugging the lamps to his chest. 'She's got a job, you know. And frankly, she couldn't quite face it.'

'You should have let me know. I'd have been glad to lend a hand.'

'That's kind. But there was no need. Jean offered to help – it's our half-term.'

Belle could hardly conceal her disappointment. 'Does this mean we won't be seeing Sarah again?'

'Perhaps not. But you'll have new neighbours the day after tomorrow. They seem nice enough people.'

'We'll miss you, David.' Belle looked upset. 'Just the way we've been missing Sarah and Merry all these months. Still . . . life goes on, I suppose.' Her gaze settled on Jean again. 'I'm sorry, my dear. I didn't mean to be rude. How do you do.'

The two women shook hands, eyeing each other speculatively.

'Belle was absolutely wonderful when we first arrived,' David told Jean. 'Took us in hand straight away. Introduced us to all the neighbours. Before the week was out we knew everything there was to know about Deredale, all thanks to her.'

'He exaggerates.' Belle smiled. 'So, you're one of David's teachers, are you? I've always wanted to know – is he a *very* hard task master?'

David grinned. 'Quite the reverse, Belle. Jean is deputy head. She's the one who keeps *me* on my toes.'

'I'm sorry.' Belle was embarrassed. 'How very sexist of me.'

'There's nothing to apologise for,' Jean assured her.

'Well, anyway, I think it's very good of you to give up your time like this. I imagined, at that level, you would have to work through most of your holidays.'

'Between you and me, Belle, it's not quite as bad as some of our profession like to make out. I always make sure I have plenty of time off. And it's in my own interest to get David safely moved, isn't it?'

'Is it?'

'Sorry. Didn't he tell you? He's moving in with me.'

'Oh . . .' Belle blanched. 'I didn't realise. David . . .'

He laughed out loud. 'It's not what you think, Belle. Jean has a very large house all to herself . . .'

'And I've turned the top floor into a flat. David's renting it from me till he finds a new post.'

'I see.' Belle's brow cleared but she still watched Jean carefully. Then, 'Is there anything I can do?' she asked. 'Shall I bring you a tray of tea or something? Better still – why don't you come and have supper when you're finished? I could easily rustle up some . . .'

'No. Thank you.' David was firm. 'It's sweet of you, but Wanda's offered to feed us later.'

'Wanda!' Belle's beautifully shaped eyebrows shot up until they practically hit her hairline. 'That'll be a Chinese take-away, no doubt.'

'Now, now, Belle. We can't all cook like you.' David bent and kissed her cheek, the lamps bumping awkwardly between them. 'Thanks for everything. And keep in touch, won't you? It was good while it lasted, eh?'

Belle nodded sadly. 'A pity it couldn't have lasted longer. Poor Claire and Laurie. Have you seen anything of them recently?'

'Not for weeks. They prefer to keep themselves separate these days.'

'Who can blame them?' Belle stepped out on to the street. 'Good bye, David. If you need anything tomorrow, just yell.'

'We will.'

'Nice to meet you, Jean. Take care of David for us, won't you?'

David closed the door on Belle's retreating back then turned and looked at Jean. At once, as if on a given signal, their shared laughter erupted, echoing around the house. 'Poor Belle! She thought the worst,' he said.

'She certainly did.'

'And you egged her on. "He's moving in with me." What got into you?'

'Sorry. I couldn't resist it. I've never seen a woman register so much suspicion in one fleeting glance. Will she tell *all* the neighbours?'

'Of course. She'll be hot-footing it across to old Reggie Bray's place even as we speak.'

'Your reputation will be in ruins.'

'And you are now a scarlet woman.'

'What! Little old me?' Jean pursed her lips. 'Spinster of this parish and fifty years old to boot! Whatever would I be doing with a toy boy in my attic?' And the strange blue eyes gave David a milky smile from beneath lowered lashes.

CHAPTER TWENTY-FIVE

Will leapt to his feet and snapped off the television.

David raised his head enquiringly. 'Weren't we watching that?'

'Sorry!' Will said. 'But it was nothing very special. I'm going out soon and I have things to tell you before then.'

'Can't it wait?'

'I've got to go out too,' Merry chipped in.

'But it's Easter Monday,' David protested. 'I thought we could have at least one day together.'

Will refused to be deflected. 'Last time I tried to talk about things I did my best to be polite and ask your opinion and all that, and we still ended up having a row.'

'Did we?' David was vague.

'We certainly did,' said Sarah. 'I well remember scraping everybody's supper into the bin.'

Will nodded. 'So this time I'm just going to tell you, quite calmly, what my plans are. And then I've got a date.' David sighed heavily. 'I've written to Cambridge and withdrawn from my place at Emmanuel.'

'Oh, Will! What a shame!' Sarah felt the finality of his situation weighing down upon her like lead.

'I'm going to work for Friends of the Earth.'

David was outraged. 'You're what?'

'As a volunteer, of course. It's all arranged.'

'What exactly do you mean?' David demanded. 'What are you going to do? Exactly?'

'You know that horrible road they're planning for the north of the county? They're going to need protesters to live on the route. Man it night and day. I'm going to be one of them.'

'Wow!' exclaimed Merry, thrilled by the drama of it all.

'But it's too early for that,' Sarah said. 'They're not planning to start until next year at the earliest.'

'I know. But we're new to all this. We know the area, and that's useful, local knowledge. But we don't really know the score, you see. So they want us to get some experience. There's a big battle coming up at Twyford Down soon, but first we're doing a demo at a by-pass in Devon.'

'Who's we?' Sarah asked.

'Me and Zack.'

David groaned. 'I *knew* that chap would be in the equation somewhere. Sarah, I always told you he was a bad influence, didn't I?'

'You never learn, do you, Dad!' Merry exploded. 'Zack's not a bad influence. He's great.'

'He was expelled from school for doing drugs.'

'No he wasn't.' She was indignant. 'He was expelled for growing cannabis. A lot of people do, you know. And legally, too. There are hemp farms licensed by the Home Office.'

'Yeah,' Will said. 'One of the things we thought about was getting a Business Enterprise Allowance and opening an organic hemp shop in Newcastle. The Greens are very keen on hemp. For paper and cloth, that sort of stuff. And rope. Cannabis is really good for arthritis too, did you know, and . . .'

'And cancer. And Aids,' Merry butted in. 'And glaucoma. And . . .'

'A hemp shop?' David could not believe his ears.

'In the end we had to give it up though. You know what the police are like. They'd have been leaning on us, night and day.'

'I should jolly well hope so,' David said. 'Have you the slightest idea how dangerous drugs are?'

Merry affected a yawn. 'Oh, p . . . p . . . please!'

'I know all about drugs,' Will told him quietly. 'Have *you* the slightest idea that cannabis is *much* less dangerous, or addictive, than that large glass of whisky in your hand? That's your second since six o'clock and I'm sure it won't be your last.'

'The odd glass of whisky doesn't do anybody any harm.'

'Maybe not. And neither does the odd spliff.'

'Really? So I suppose what you're actually telling me is that you and Zack sit around and . . . and "skin up" or whatever you call it, and drive yourselves out of your skulls . . .'

'No. I'm not, *actually*. We smoke a bit of pot every now and then. That's all. People of our age do. It does us a lot less harm than tobacco. Or alcohol.'

'I don't think!'

'I'll tell you something interesting,' Will continued. 'Alcohol accounts for more than three thousand deaths a year! About three thousand times more than cannabis. And . . .'

'Will you stop going on about drugs, all of you?' Sarah interrupted. 'I'm not interested in all that old stuff. I'm much more interested in what Will is going to *do*.'

'You're not interested?' David was scandalised. 'Your own son admits he's on drugs and you're not interested!'

'For heaven's sake! He smokes a bit of grass. So what? How many of them don't, these days? Just be grateful he's not on the hard stuff.'

'Sarah! Don't be so irresponsible. You can't just wash your hands of it like that. You know very well that soft drugs lead to hard drugs. It's a proven fact.'

'No it isn't,' chorused Will, Merry and Sarah in perfect unison.

'Just the way it isn't a proven fact that whisky leads to alcoholism,' added Will. 'You might be glad to know that, Dad.' He turned and smiled at Sarah gently. 'I'm sorry, Mum. I know how much you wanted me to get a degree. But this is what *I* want, you see. If we don't stand up and protest now there won't be anything left that's worth protesting about.

The whole country will have been trashed.'

'But why *you*, darling? Why now? Couldn't you wait till after Cambridge? There must be other people . . .'

'Mum! That's a cop-out. You know it is.'

'Well,' said David, 'I don't suppose we can stop you if you've set your heart on turning hippy and living in a bender and chaining yourself to bulldozers. But I'm telling you, you haven't got a cat in hell's chance of changing *anything*.'

'I think you should be proud of him,' declared Merry. 'What he's doing is much more important than going to Cambridge and reading smelly old History. What's the point of that? History's just all the mistakes of the past. We know about them. We're still living them. But at least Will's trying to make things better. Even if he doesn't save as much as a blade of grass, at least he's trying to get things right. For the future. So that the world is worth living in. I think it's great. And I bet you anybody of my age would agree with me.'

David glared at her. 'I couldn't care less whether people of your age would agree or not.'

'Well you should,' she shouted. 'You're supposed to be a teacher, for God's sake.'

'Quite. I'm a teacher and you're still a child and don't know *anything* yet. This ridiculous anti-road lobby – it's not worth it. Not for somebody as clever as Will. It's a complete waste of time.'

Sarah stared at him. 'Why do you say that, David? When Laurie Richley asked me to join his road safety campaign you begged me to get involved. You told me it was something really important.'

'That was quite different.'

'Why?'

'What?' He jerked his head, irritated at being questioned.

'Why was that different? That was all about traffic. Safety. Quality of life. All the same things.'

'But for you and Laurie it was just a hobby! Not a career. Anyway, it wasn't a *car* that killed Bridget, was it? Nothing to do with *roads*.'

'Dad!' Merry gasped. 'How can you be so crass?'

David knew at once that he had gone too far. He looked at the three shocked faces that were staring at him in disbelief. 'I'm sorry,' he mumbled.

'So you bloody well should be,' Sarah told him, taking Merry's hand, looking at her anxiously.

'It's just that I'm . . . disappointed. I wanted to be proud of my son. I just wanted him to have a proper job, for goodness sake. Is that too much to ask?'

Scornfully Will threw his arm out towards David. 'Behold the dinosaur!' he exclaimed. 'Proper jobs have gone down the plug-hole, Dad. And all the rest of that career crap. Now we just get on with our lives.'

David turned away from him. 'I used to think that we were a family. Now I see we are just a group of me-me-me's. All determined to do our own thing and to hell with everybody else.'

Will snorted. 'Look who's talking. Who *started* the rot, charging off to the other end of the country and bugger all the rest of us?' David fell silent but Will persisted. 'Aren't you going to try and justify yourself?'

'What's the point? I've said it all before. It seemed the right thing to do, at the time.'

'Quite.' Will grinned. 'Same goes for me. Exactly that. *This* is the right thing for *me*, *now*.' He made for the door. 'O.K., then. I'm off. Don't wait up.'

'Will,' Sarah called after him. 'Where are you going? To Zack's place?'

'No.' He popped his head into the room again. 'I told you, Mum. I've got a date. Going to hug a few trees!' He gave her a radiant smile, and then he was gone.

'Good old Will!' Merry said. 'And I suppose it's time I made a move, too.'

Sarah sighed. 'Where are *you* off to? Am I allowed to ask?'

'I'm going to a party. Chris and the gang.'

Sarah felt David stiffen. 'Oh, darling!' she said weakly. She didn't feel strong enough for another confrontation but the look on David's face made her realise there was no escape.

'What do you mean – "Oh, darling"?' Merry looked genuinely puzzled.

'It's just . . .'

'Just what?'

'You do seem to be seeing an awful lot of Chris these days. Dad and I both think . . .'

'What?'

Sarah looked at David for support but he had temporarily retired from the fray. 'That really, you should be going out with more boys of your own age.'

'I do.'

'But it's usually Chris, isn't it?'

'No. It's lots of people. I went out with Zack last week.' She grinned wickedly. 'Wow! He's *the best*!'

David was not amused. 'I know Chris seems very young, Merry, but he is my brother.'

'Well, goodness me!' she retorted. 'Do you know, I'd never figured that one out.'

'We just think perhaps you should back off a bit and let Chris lead his own life now,' Sarah pleaded. 'He can't go on relying on you to prop him up for ever.'

'Prop him up!' Merry began to laugh. For a while she was quite unable to speak. David and Sarah watched her in amazement. She clutched her sides and rocked helplessly. 'You two are *pathetic*!' she spluttered at last. 'I don't know how we put up with the pair of you.'

'I don't see what's so funny,' Sarah told her. 'I have been trying not to interfere, for months now, but all the time you spend with him at the Maddermarket . . .'

Merry smiled at her, her head on one side. 'Listen, I wasn't supposed to tell you this because it's still a secret. Just until they've been up to Burnham Market to see Jim and Muriel. But the party tonight is being given for Chris, and for Veronica. It's a sort of celebration.'

'Who's Veronica?' Sarah was beginning to feel confused.

'She's one of the actresses. She's fantastic.'

'Is it something to do with the show then?'

'No, you idiot. Veronica's probably going to be your sister-in-law. She's moving in with Chris and they're thinking about getting married next year. He's nuts about her.'

When Merry had gone off to the party, carrying their congratulations and a special bottle of wine and a request that Chris should bring Veronica to Gillan Terrace *soon* and a promise that they would keep the secret, of *course* they would, until she gave them the thumbs up, David and Sarah were left alone together. The emptiness of the room seemed suffocating. They searched for gentle words and could find none.

'Is there anything worth watching?' Sarah asked at last, reaching for the *Radio Times*.

'No. Bank Holiday rubbish.' Listlessly, he picked up his book.

'It's no good being cross with them, David. Things have moved on. They're different than we were.'

'I'm not cross with them. It's you. You've taken them away from me.'

'That's nonsense.'

'It isn't. I've lost them now. I was really looking forward to this holiday, you know.' He seemed so crestfallen that she felt a surge of sympathy. He was still such a *handsome* man, she thought. She'd always been seduced by his film star good looks, ever since she was sixteen.

With an effort, she steeled herself. 'I'm sorry, David. But I don't think you're being fair. To any of us.'

'You see, we never agree about anything these days. If I said the sky was blue you'd tell me it was actually a bluey shade of grey. You used to be on my side.'

'It's not about sides!'

'There you go again! It's incredible.' He laid down his novel, unopened. 'It makes me wonder. What is the *point*? Trying to hold it all together.' She sat quietly, almost humbly, and he talked on as if he were thinking aloud. 'I don't want to leave Craiglands. Not yet. I'm happy there.'

'I know. That's why you didn't get the job at Holt, isn't it?'

'Probably. They knew my heart wasn't in it. So I think I'm going to tell the Head that I'd like to stay on for a while. At least one more year. While I think things out.'

'Will he allow that?'

'He doesn't want me to leave. He hasn't even advertised yet, and he should have done it ages ago.'

'I see.' Without looking at him she said, 'Where does that leave me, then?'

He shrugged, his face a blank. 'I don't know, Sarah. You started all this, didn't you, when you decided to leave Peacocks' Acre? You'll just have to find your own way through.'

5
JUNE, 1993

I keep consulting
oracles: I've been the Empress, the Moon
and the Hanged Man.

CHAPTER TWENTY-SIX

Sarah was cycling home from college. She'd just finished a class in International Hospitality and her head was full of it. She was enjoying being a student again. It had brought her back to life. In fact, she thought, as she left the ring road and began to pedal her way through the maze of quieter streets that was her personal route to Gillan Terrace, she seemed to have reached a plateau of contentment. She could not pretend that she was positively, actively *happy*. She knew she could never achieve that without Laurie. But at least the rest of her life seemed to be settling into place.

Will kept in regular touch and made flying visits home whenever he could, to have a bath and wash his clothes and give her a progress report. She hardly recognised him these days. He was lean, bearded, darkly-sunburned and he talked like a man possessed. He had focused his intelligence and learning skills. He knew all that there was to know about the law relating to transportation, could quote planning policy guidelines by heart, section and paragraph, had memorised the name of every MP and council official and planning officer in north Norfolk, talked to them in their own language and even, occasionally, beat them at their own game. He and Zack had also become experts at media manipulation and public relations, and they were popular with the press and television people because they were so bright and un-stuffy and knew how to make people laugh as well as prod them into anger. It was largely due to their efforts that the building of the new Norfolk road had been put on hold while the authorities retreated to lick their wounds and engage in yet another bout of consultation. Public support was haemor-rhaging away from the County Council as people learned that the proposed plan went hand in hand with projects to develop the land between the new road and the coast road, that expensive new housing was envisaged, a holiday com-plex, an eighteen-hole golf course and even a heritage theme park. It wasn't about conservation at all. It was about attract-ing yet more visitors.

Merry had been right about Will, Sarah thought, as she free-wheeled down Ramsay Lane. He was doing much more useful work as a green activist than he would ever have done as a reluctant historian. He had a passionate conviction that the future health and happiness of society depended on the effective control of the motor car. He was a rebel with a cause and she envied him.

She was also quietly delighted by the way Merry was getting on with her life. She had a place lined up at London University, provided that she got the required A-levels, and this time Sarah knew there would be no disturbing year off, no dropping-out and no giving-up to distress David. Merry was absolutely determined that she was going to be a marine biologist, and when Merry set her heart on something, Merry invariably achieved it. Sarah had no worries about her at all. The only cloud on the horizon was that when her daughter went off to London in October, she would be quite on her own. For the first time in her life. She had always lived with other people. At home. In a university college. With David's parents. And then with David. Now she would have to learn to live alone.

She jumped off her bike and pushed it up the front path, leaned over and padlocked it. The old lady who lived next door, sitting in her usual place at her bedroom window, raised her hand and ventured a shy smile. Sarah waved back ener-getically. The world was full of people living on their own, she thought, as she slipped her key into the lock. She'd survive.

When she opened the door she saw a large pale blue

envelope lying on the mat and recognised Claire's hand writing. She felt surprise, then alarm, course through her. She hadn't heard anything from Claire since Christmas, even though she'd written to her at length after Easter, enclosing lots of snaps of the whole family at Chris and Veronica's wedding. She snatched up the letter, ripped it open.

'My dear Sarah,' she read.
'Thank you so much for your news and wonderful photographs. I can't *tell* you how delighted I am that Chris is happy again. I was so frightened for him when Bridget died. And I have another spring wedding to report. Belle and Reggie Bray have taken the plunge at last.

   Now – to my main point. I have a great favour to ask. I will be alone here this summer when Laurie does the annual sail again with Pilgrims. (He's given it a miss for the last two years.) Would you – *could* you – possibly come up and visit me then? You have no idea how I long to see you again. I feel it's important that you and I should spend some time together. We haven't really talked, have we, since the day of Bridget's funeral? Two years *today*, did you realise? Which is why you are so much in my mind. Still, believe me, my best-of-friends.

                                                        Do come,
                                                             C

Trembling, holding the letter by the corner as if it might explode, Sarah made her way to the kitchen and put the kettle on. Merry wasn't back from school yet and she felt the silence of the house pressing in upon her. She switched on the radio, warmed the pot, poured boiling water on to a tea bag, took milk from the fridge. Then she switched the radio off again and re-read the letter. She couldn't go, she thought. It was quite impossible. She couldn't face Claire. She couldn't stay in Laurie's house, sensing his presence in the air she breathed, seeing his jacket hanging on the next peg to her coat. She couldn't use the towels *he* had used. She couldn't walk past Peacocks' Acre, re-live the Christmas party. She couldn't . . .

'Hi!' The front door opened and Merry's feet came striding along the hall. 'Hi, Mum. Tea! Great! Me too, please.' She saw the letter that Sarah was still clutching. 'Anything nice?' she asked.

'What?' Sarah looked haunted.

'The letter!'

'Oh. That! It's from Claire. She's invited me up there at the end of August.'

'Great.'

'I'm not going.'

'Why ever not? It's brilliant. I'll be doing my summer job in Cornwall then, and you've been moaning on about not having a holiday this year.'

'All the same . . .'

'Look, Mum . . .' Merry's face was suddenly serious and for a moment she looked extraordinarily like David. 'Claire's a special case, isn't she? If she wants you there it's because she *needs* you. Right? So I think you should ring her now and fix the date.'

The note pinned to the door of Dolphin House had asked Sarah to go round to the studio, where Claire was finishing off a project. Sarah stood on the threshold, peering into the barn, and felt the last three years peel away as if they had never been. *Déjà vu*! Claire was working at the far end, totally absorbed, bending over something on her bench. She wore the same dark blue overalls, the same peaked cap. And then, it happened again. She sensed Sarah's presence, turned and saw her, lit up with her radiant smile. In an instant she had bounded across the space between them and wrapped her arms round Sarah in a rib-crunching hug.

'Sarah! Sarah! Sarah!' she exclaimed. 'You've made good time. Was the journey O.K.?'

'Yes. My new car! It goes like a bird.'

'I'm so *glad* you've come. Thank you.'

'Don't thank me,' Sarah protested. 'It's lovely to be here again.' With a tingle of surprise, she realised that she meant it. Though she had been dreading looking into Claire's face, she now met those shrewd green eyes without feeling racked with guilt. 'You look wonderful, Claire,' she said. 'You're well?'

'I am. Amazingly so.' Claire removed her cap and, with that characteristic gesture, ran her fingers through hair that was now silver-white. She was thinner too, Sarah noticed, but her skin glowed. And when she moved, turned, stretched – then she looked like a young girl. Like Bridget. 'It's work,' Claire told her. 'It's the best tonic in the world.'

'I know. I feel ten years younger since I started my degree. I thought all those fresh-faced babes would make me feel like an old wrinkly, but I don't. I can't imagine how I survived all those years without real work.'

'There you are, then!' Claire grinned. 'Come and see what I'm doing. After that I'll take you home and we'll have tea in the garden. I've got it all organised. I even made a cake!'

'You did what? Is this the Claire I know and love?'

'I can hardly believe it myself.'

As she was talking she was holding Sarah by the hand and leading her to the end of the studio. Now Sarah saw that things *had* changed. The wooden carvings had disappeared. The fragrant piles of sawdust had been swept away. The cloths and bottles, the tins of polish and varnish and wood-stain had all been tidied on to the shelves, pushed behind cupboard doors. In their place was an artist's easel and about twenty huge charcoal drawings that had been pinned up all around the walls. Claire's hammer and chisels had vanished and the bench was littered with pieces of twisted wire, metallic mesh, a plastic bag of clay, a clutter of sharp little knives and pliers.

Sarah's eyes widened. 'It's all different.'

'I told you I was getting bored with all that *wood*.'

'But the things you made were so beautiful.'

Claire put her fingers to her mouth. 'They didn't seem to be *saying* anything, though.'

Sarah stared at the drawings, thick and spikey black with jagged edges. She shivered. 'What are these saying? Pain! That's what they spell out to me.'

'I knew you'd understand.' Claire was excited. 'I started them just a few weeks after she died. I don't know where they came from. They seemed to jump out of the paper of their own accord. Then they began to change.' She pointed out a different group of pictures on the opposite wall. 'You see, they're more fluid now. More curves, less thorns and hooks.' She gazed at them speculatively, considering them almost as if they were nothing to do with her. 'Metal, I thought. That will be the medium. I used it when I was at Art School, of course, but I'm going back next month for a refresher.' She hugged Sarah's shoulders. 'Just like you. Two very mature students!'

'I still don't understand what it's going to *be*,' Sarah murmured.

'Of course you don't. Neither do I exactly. Not yet. I'm putting it in for a competition. Art in Public Places. They're looking for a really large work to be erected on the Town Moor in Newcastle. It's a northern prize. You have to live and work in Northumbria. But there'll be hundreds of entries, I imagine. It's being funded by a whole raft of bodies, the Council and Northern Arts, the Tourist Board, the European Regional Development Fund . . .'

'High-powered stuff.'

'Oh yes. We all have to submit a dossier.' She ticked off the requirements on her fingers. 'CV, slides of achieved work, a written description and explanation of the work to be undertaken, a maquette or model *and* ten detailed and annotated sketches.'

'Gosh!' Sarah was stuck for words.

Claire laughed. 'As you say! It's all a bit daunting. But I'm really going for it. I feel . . . intoxicated. You know?' She reminded Sarah of Will and his green crusade. 'I *can't* leave it alone. The ideas sit on my shoulders and ride me day and night.'

'I can see that.'

'But I promise that I'm going to take a few days off now that you've come.'

'Knowing you, you'll be creeping back here in the dead of night while I'm sound asleep.'

Claire shook her head. 'I hope not. I could do with a breathing space. It's just what I needed, though. It's strange, but in a way I feel as if Bridget *gave* it to me. She died – and then I found this great *surge* of creative energy. Her last gift. Something to live for. To get me out of bed in the morning.'

'But what about Laurie?' Sarah asked her sadly. 'Is he not enough?'

Claire was brisk. 'Oh, Laurie's got his Pilgrim Project, hasn't he? He's always had a . . . a "green fuse". How does it go? "The force that through the green fuse drives the flower." '

'He's all right, then?'

But Claire didn't seem to hear her question. 'Come on, now. Enough of *art*. Let's go home, Sarah. Enough for the day. And we have so many other things to talk about.'

It was a real holiday. Claire saw to that. For every day they were together she had some little treat planned. A wonderful wild tramp along the Wall. Visits to Chesters and Housesteads. A trip to Durham, where Sarah re-lived her student days as she rowed Claire erratically from bank to bank of the River Wear. In Deredale they lunched nostalgically in the Eagle and pottered into Treasures where Sarah found a hand-painted silk scarf to take back for Merry and a leather-backed notebook for Will. And then they were invited to supper with a new-look Belle and Reggie. Sarah could not stop grinning when she saw the pair of them together. Reggie seemed to have halved the size of his rolling stomach as *his* concession to married life and Belle, amazingly, had put on about a stone as *hers*. The transformation was extraordinary.

Belle kissed her warmly, and demanded all the latest stop-press news about Will and, especially, about Merry, who'd always been a favourite of hers.

Then, 'And how is David?' she asked casually.

'He's well,' Sarah told her.

'Still at Craiglands, though?'

273

'Yes. He's enjoying it there. He can't find another school he likes enough to tempt him away.'

She saw the guarded look that flashed between Belle and Reggie and sensed that Claire, too, was aware of dangerous undercurrents.

'So what's he up to, poor chap, while you're cavorting with Claire?' Reggie wanted to know. 'You've left him sitting at home on his own-i-o?'

Sarah smiled serenely. 'He's abroad at the moment.'

'Oh-ho? Something to do with the school, is it?'

'Reggie!' Belle protested. 'It's none of your business.'

He looked disgruntled. 'Just like your Laurie, Claire. Gadding about all over the place. Not good enough. We married men ought to have more care and consideration of our wives. Responsibilities, you know. All that stuff.'

'Thank *you*, Reggie,' Belle said acidly. 'Now, for heaven's sake – let's talk about something a bit more interesting than husbands, shall we?'

'Like what?' Reggie grumbled.

'Like our new neighbours. I do wish you and David were still next door, Sarah. The new people are just awful. Absolutely no manners. Do you know, they didn't even turn up for the party we laid on for them. Did they, Reggie?'

Reggie guffawed. 'We had to hold it without them. Like a wedding reception without the happy couple. Bloody fiasco.'

'You two should never have left Peacocks' Acre,' Belle sighed. 'It was a great mistake. Don't you agree, Claire? I always said so. And I always will.'

Back at Dolphin House, Claire waved Sarah towards Laurie's chair, threw off her shoes and collapsed on the sofa with her feet up. She groaned.

'Some things never change,' she said. 'And one of them is dear old Reggie.'

'Why did she have to go and *marry* him?' Sarah asked. 'They always seemed fine the way they were.'

'Why does anybody do *anything*? Perhaps it's economy.

"Two can live as cheaply as one". Or perhaps, who knows
. . . she began to be afraid of being old and lonely.'

'That's a frightening prospect for us all,' Sarah said bleakly.

Claire shot her a look. 'You haven't talked about David,
Sarah. Not once since you came.'

'And you haven't asked me. Thank you for that.'

'Is this a good time?'

'As good as any, I suppose. I should have told you. David
wants a divorce.'

'Oh, my dear!' Claire sprang up from the sofa and came to
sit on the arm of Sarah's chair. 'I'm so sorry.' She reached out
and covered her hand with her own.

'It's all right. Really. I think it's probably for the best.'

'Are you sure?'

'We had a bad patch. I thought . . . if we left here and
made a new start, we might be able to work things out. But
– the best laid plans! He's found someone else. Jean
Anstruther, she's called. He always thought I was a bit naive,
you know. *This* one's a real grown-up lady.'

'The deputy head? Belle met her, I think.'

'Yes.' Sarah laughed. 'David told me about it. He thought
it was a joke, the way Belle looked at the pair of them with
her bedroom eyes.' Then the laughter died on her lips. 'But,
as it turned out, it wasn't a joke after all. And I must say they
seem very happy together.'

'What about Merry and Will? How are they taking it?'

'Oh, you know what it's like. They have too much going
on in their own lives to lose much sleep over ours. In a way
things are better between them and David, now that we've
stopped having family rows.'

Claire wandered across to the drinks cupboard, took out a
bottle of Armagnac and filled two little glasses.

'A night cap,' she said, handing one to Sarah and returning
to the sofa with her own. 'Isn't it strange? We've only known
each other for three years, but we've been through so much
together. When we first met . . . Do you remember? It was at
Belle's, wasn't it . . . ?'

'Yes it was. I'd never known people like you and Bridget before. I was so jealous of the pair of you. Isn't that terrible?'

'No. Not at all. It was the same for me. You and David seemed so "together". And Laurie wasn't even *there*, was he? You didn't even know . . .'

Sarah's face clouded, her eyes filled with tears. She took a hasty gulp from her glass, trying to steady herself. Claire looked at her anxiously.

'I'm sorry, Sarah. You really are grieving about all this, aren't you?'

Sarah shook her head frantically. 'I can't keep it back any longer,' she said. 'I have something to tell you. A confession. And an apology.'

Claire smiled. 'About you and Laurie, you mean?'

'You knew?' Sarah's heart hammered in her breast.

'I think I've always known.'

'How? We tried to be so careful. We didn't want to hurt you. We thought that what you didn't know you wouldn't . . . Stupid! Stupid idiots!' She laid down her glass because her hands were shaking so much she was afraid that it would spill.

'Gerald Manley is a member of Reggie Bray's golf club,' Claire told her. 'I don't suppose you knew that?' Sarah shook her head. 'He is also a drinking buddy. They'd obviously had a few one night and Gerald told Reggie that Laurie had picked you up from work one day and he was almost certain he recognised his voice from several strange phone calls to the hotel. Reggie found it necessary, of course, to pass this on to me.' Sarah buried her face in her hands. 'But I really believe, you know, he did it out of kindness. He didn't spread it around. I don't think he even told Belle.'

'That *was* kind. She'd have told the whole of Deredale.'

'Gerald even told Reggie about a beautiful rose you received on St Valentine's Day. That almost put me off the scent. Laurie's not one for hearts and flowers as a rule.' Sarah looked at her and Claire raised her eyebrows. 'Well, not with me, anyway. Gerald Manley is a good hotel manager. He's trained to notice details. But I did think he might be putting

two and two together and making ninety-nine. Until one day,
I dropped in to Laurie's office to take him out to lunch and
your gold ear-rings – the little butterflies – were sitting on his
secretary's desk. She said one of the clients must have left
them in the hospitality flat. I took them home and put them
in the pocket of Laurie's jacket. He never mentioned them,
but they vanished. So then I knew, you see. I hope you got
them back.'

Sarah nodded. 'I'm sorry,' she said.

'Sarah, listen to me.' Claire's voice was firm. 'I told you,
after Bridget died, that there was no need of apologies between the two of us.'

'I remember. I didn't understand it then. And now, after all
this . . .'

'You made Laurie very happy. Changed his life. When he
fell in love with you he seemed to grow, to get younger. The
old self-confidence came back. And the tenderness. That was
the most important thing. I watched, day by day, as you gave
him back his tenderness.'

'Surely it was always there?'

'I don't know. He always felt like an outsider, you know. A
loner. And when Bridget was born, he was lonely again. He
said I had "side-lined" him. And he was right.'

'All women are wrapped up in their babies. And in a case
like yours . . .'

'With Bridget and me it was more than that. Perhaps I
always knew I had her on short loan.'

'Oh, Claire!' The tears were streaming down Sarah's face
now, but to her astonishment she saw that Claire was exhilar-
ated.

'I believe in Fate, you know,' she told her. 'When we were
trying so hard for a baby, if my fairy godmother had stood
before me then and said, "The choice is yours. Have a perfect
child, love her, rear her, then return her after seventeen years,
or go through life childless" – well, of *course*, I'd have chosen
Bridget. No question. She brought me nothing but joy, for all
that time.'

'But when she was taken from you, you needed Laurie. *All* of him. That's why I went away.'

'I thought that was it,' Claire said. 'Did you explain things to David? He was the one I worried about.'

'No. I'm sure he had no idea. All he knew was that I had changed somehow. He didn't know why. He never asked. He just knew he preferred the old me.'

'Good things *have* to come out of all this, Sarah. And they will. I know it. *Now* I do. When Bridget died it all seemed so . . . pointless. A cruel waste. But now I know that nothing is wasted. Everything that happens has a purpose.' Sarah shook her head, but Claire's hand shot out and gripped her like a vice. 'You must believe it. Listen. When I was young I was going to be a great sculptor. The Barbara Hepworth of my generation. I was convinced. No false modesty. I used to tell people. It didn't happen, of course. But it didn't matter, because I had Bridget. But when she died, after the shock and the grief and the despair, all that, I felt as if I'd come through the fire. I was reborn.'

' "I am the phoenix!" '

'You remember. It's there again now, that driving force. The passion to create something *great*. That's what the competition is all about. And you see, if I could do it, it would make sense of everything.'

Sarah looked at Claire's transfigured face in awe. She knew, without a shadow of doubt, that, regardless of the competition, she was going to distinguish herself as a sculptor. The talent, the imagination, the discipline, had always been there. All that had been needed was the vital spark.

Without realising what she was doing she ran her fingers gently over the high leather back of Laurie's old chair. 'Poor Laurie!' she said softly. 'How *is* Laurie coping?'

At once Claire's face changed. 'Laurie's a dead man.' Her voice was heavy. 'He's just about getting through the mechanics of life. Nothing more. That's the reason I wanted you here, Sarah. You're the only one who can help him.'

'I can't!' cried Sarah. 'Not me. How can I?'

'I know that he loves you in a way I can't begin to understand. It's devouring him. Unstoppable. And it's the same for you, isn't it?' Sarah didn't reply. '*Isn't* it?' Claire repeated, watching her face. Then she nodded, satisfied. 'Please . . . for his sake, and for mine . . . Life is too short to turn your back.'

CHAPTER TWENTY-SEVEN

Claire had given her a clearly marked map and told her that the journey from Deredale to Lithe Harbour would take her about thirty minutes.

'The fleet is anchoring off Lindisfarne for their last night,' she'd explained. 'They'll take their time. Have a pleasant sail back. I shouldn't imagine he'll be on shore before say... two-thirty, three o'clock. So we'll have the whole morning.'

But Sarah couldn't wait. Every minute seemed like an hour. By ten she had stripped the sheets off her bed, stuffed them into Claire's washing machine and tidied her room. Half an hour later her case was packed into the boot of the car and she was ready to leave.

'I'm sorry,' she told Claire. 'I must go. I feel as if I'm shaking into little pieces. If I put it off any longer I won't be able to hold the steering wheel.'

Claire laughed and hugged her. 'Good luck!' she said. 'I'll be thinking of you every minute. Give me a ring when he's safely back in harbour, won't you?'

'Promise. And good luck to you, with the competition. I'll be longing to know how you get on.'

'Don't worry. I'll keep you posted.' She checked that Sarah was settled in the driving seat, swung the door shut, and bent to kiss her through the window.

Sarah looked up, her face solemn. 'I don't know when I'll see you again, Claire.'

'No. But it doesn't matter, does it? I know you're *there*. And that's enough. Some day...'

As Sarah drove up Bridge Lane and slowed to pull out into

the High Street behind the customary procession of heavy lorries, she looked in the mirror and saw that Claire was standing at her garden gate, both arms high in the air, waving her on her way.

And then she turned the car and headed first to the east, then north, in the direction of the coast. It was Friday, a fine day in August, and the dual carriageway was busy. She fumed with irritation, blocked in behind an enormous Dutch jugger-naut pounding up towards the Borders. It didn't matter that she had hours in hand. She wanted to be there, at Lithe, watching for the sails of the *Matadora*. Once she'd reached the harbour she wouldn't mind how long she had to wait, but that's where she must be. At last she found herself at the roundabout which was her exit from the crowded A-road and felt able to breathe more freely. She was on the final lap. She saw the chimneys of the power station rearing into the clear sky, rattled over railway lines, then passed a pretty little bandstand, neglected and deserted. It looked like a child's toy, tossed carelessly to one side. At last she took a right turn into the port, rumbled over traffic calmers and was brought to a halt by a barrier lowered across the road. Claire had thought of everything. The security officer skimmed through the note she had written explaining that Mrs Page had come in her place to meet Mr Richley from the Pilgrim fleet.

The man gave Sarah a friendly nod. 'Yer goin' to hev a long wait, pet,' he said in his Geordie voice. 'We're not expectin' them for a few hours yet, yer know.'

She smiled. 'I've got a good book.'

'Aye.' He looked up at the sky. 'And it's not a bad day neither. Yer might hev a bit sit on the beach. I wouldn't mind that meself like.'

'Thanks. I might do that!' She drove the last few metres, past the boatyard and into the harbour itself. She parked on the wall, opened the car door and at once breathed in the tang of seaweed, of salt and sand. Gulls screamed overhead. She leaned against the rail and gazed down at the boats lying in the harbour. On one of them a man in a stained blue shirt was coiling up rope, whistling as he worked. She walked across to the pier and stared out to sea. There were plenty of sails to catch her attention because the wind conditions were ideal, but they all belonged to small pleasure craft, dinghies and sloops. She could see nothing the size of the Pilgrim boats. It was still just after twelve. Far too early, she knew.

As she was walking back towards the car she paused, looked over an embankment, and saw steps leading down to the beach that the man in the cabin had mentioned. It was tiny and perfect, a fan of pale yellow sand scoured clean by the tide. And it was deserted. She collected the packet of sandwiches that Claire had made for her, found a place out of the sprightly wind, propped her back against the wall that encircled her little beach, and settled down doggedly to wait for time to pass.

After two hours she brushed the sand from the pale sweater that she had knotted around her shoulders, gathered her things together and climbed up the steps, making back towards the car. She found a tin of cleansing pads in her glove compartment and wiped her face and hands. She tugged a brush through her tangled curls, dabbed a trace of lipstick on her mouth. Then, resolutely, she locked the car and walked out along to the farthest end of the south pier where the three anglers huddled over their lines ignored her completely.

At last she saw them on the horizon, sailing home in perfect formation, the *Matadora* out in front, the *Clara Belle* and the *Lady Betty* a little behind, flanking their leader to the right and left. They looked as if they were three parts of one whole. Like a great swan or seabird, white wings spread, catching the sun. Sarah had never seen a sight more beautiful.

They'd had a good sail from Lindisfarne. The last leg of the cruise was always special, a time to relax, to enjoy it all. And now they were running in on a south-wester, close-hauled. Outside the harbour, they dropped sails. It was a poignant moment. The end of summer. The return to normal life.

Laurie began to motor in. As he brought the *Matadora* around the channel buoy he noticed a woman standing at the end of the pier. He caught his breath. For a moment – what was it? Something about the way she stood? The tilt of her head? – something about her, he didn't know what, reminded him of Sarah. He grinned bitterly. *Everything* reminded him of Sarah. He'd hear a light laugh, see a hand reach out, catch a reflection in a window . . . and think of Sarah. He looked up at the woman again. She seemed to have something wrapped around her – a creamy scarf or cardigan perhaps – and the wind made her blue skirt billow out around her legs. She was very close to the fishermen. Must be some poor, long-suffering wife or girlfriend, he thought, watching the Pilgrim boats come in because it made a change from watching the fishing lines.

Then, surprisingly, the woman raised her hand and waved. Confused, Laurie dropped his eyes and concentrated his mind on guiding the *Matadora* towards the harbour mouth. Around him he could feel the excitement of the crew mounting to fever pitch now that they were within minutes of their long journey's end.

When he looked up again he saw that the woman in the blue dress was hurrying along the West Pier in front of them. She seemed to be heading towards the very end of it. There she would be so near him as he brought the *Matadora* round that he would be able to see her face clearly. He didn't want that, he realised. Not today. He couldn't bear the pain of looking into the blank eyes of a stranger.

As the boat turned he kept his head averted, staring at the shuttering against the north quay where they would tie up to unload.

'Laurie!'

He thought he heard a woman's voice call his name. He flinched. Even his ears were playing tricks on him now.

'Laurie!'

He raised his eyes, his face vivid with sudden hope. Above him, on the harbour wall, he saw Sarah. It really was Sarah.

She was waiting for him. Her arms were stretched towards him, and she was smiling.

For a moment Sarah stood as if paralysed. She watched as Laurie saw her and recognised her. Then, rapidly, he turned away and began to manoeuvre the *Matadora* through the harbour traffic. At last it dawned upon her that he was making for the far side of the basin where the steep walls were lined with tyres and iron ladders led up from the water to the quay. Though it was so close to her, across a short stretch of water, there was no quick way to reach it on foot. Breathless, terrified that she might lose him again, she ran like a hare back along the pier, along the side of the embankment and then past all the sheds and warehouses that bordered the quayside, frantically pushing her way through the small crowd that had gathered there. She reached the *Matadora* just as Laurie began to climb up the ladder towards her. Without a word he stepped on shore and into her arms and clung to her like a drowning man. At last he held her away from him and gazed into her face.

'I'm not dreaming?' he asked. She shook her head. 'Then I don't understand.'

'Claire sent me,' she told him. 'She asked me to come.'

'Why? How?'

She laughed shakily, hardly able to believe it herself.

'She knows all about us, Laurie. Always has done. She persuaded me to come up from Norwich especially for this. She *wants* us to be together.'

He looked like a man sleep-walking. Behind him, around him, his crew staggered up and down the ladder from the deck, unloading their gear, dumping bags and boxes on the ground, waving to their friends, waiting for their captain to take charge again.

Laurie noticed none of it. 'I can't think of anything to say,' he said helplessly.

'Don't say anything. When you are finished here I'm going to take you home with me. To Norwich.'

Jennifer Curry

'We can't do that.' He looked alarmed. 'What about David?'

'There's no David any more. No David-and-Sarah, I mean. And Merry's away. We'll have the place to ourselves. Just to be. To talk about the rest of our lives.'

'Is it going to be all right?' he asked, like a child.

'Yes. It is. I know it.'

At last he smiled at her. And then he kissed her. 'Did I ever tell you my definition of perfect happiness?' he asked her.

'Always. Ever since I was a little boy.'

'Tell me now.'

'Simply this. To come home, after a long journey, and to find the one you love waiting for you.'

EPILOGUE. SEPTEMBER, 1997

They drove up the A1, skirting the western edge of New-castle, and then they were directed off it and headed east. This was a big event. Yellow A.A. notices were in place, pointing the way. But they had no need of signs and direc-tions. There, on a hill above them, marked out by a semi-circle of tall flag-poles all flying the colours of the European Union, they could see Claire's sculpture. It was huge, explod-ing forty feet or more into the air. From the distance it looked like some unearthly plant that had taken root there, a seed fallen from space, great curls of metal, twisting petals, stretching outwards and upwards against the sky.

Sarah's whole body shivered with excitement. 'Look!' she cried. 'Just look at that!'

But Laurie was having to keep his eyes on the stream of traffic that was flowing steadily towards the designated parking area in a field adjacent to the Town Moor. He swung off the road and was pointed into a space by a sour-faced man in uniform who waved his arm at them bossily while he spoke into his mobile phone.

'Invitation, sir?' The phone remained clamped to his ear.

Sarah produced the large square card, leaned across Laurie and showed it to him.

He nodded. 'Past the sheep dip. Then follow the bunting. The route is clearly marked.'

They left the car and joined the procession of people who were making their way up to the top of the hill, all of them with their eyes fixed steadfastly upwards. The steep path had been roped off from the rest of the area and jolly, multi-

coloured flags fluttered from the barriers. Beyond the ropes the Town Moor stretched away, rough and wild, miraculously unscathed by the city's girdle of concrete, brick and glass. Cows raised their gentle heads and gazed curiously at the intruders who walked across their pasture. Sheep nibbled the grass, oblivious.

Fleetingly, Sarah was reminded of their excursion to Salisbury Crags. She reached out for Laurie's hand and there it was again, still there, that miraculous, electric tingle that leapt between them.

He smiled down at her. 'All right, lovey?'

As they got nearer to the summit of the hill they realised that their path was turning into an incongruous ribbon of red. Sarah gave an incredulous snort.

'Red carpet on the Town Moor! Whatever next?'

'That's what happens when you get European funding.'

'I hope the sheep appreciate it.'

Around the base of the sculpture, a smartly-dressed crowd had gathered. Bottles of wine were being flourished, plates of food offered by waitresses wearing black dresses with frilly white pinafores. They could see a brace of mayors, both glittering gold, and dark-suited officials and women in hats.

'Are we supposed to join them?' Laurie asked.

'Not yet. I want to take all this in.' She gazed up at the sculpture. 'It's so big I haven't got to grips with it yet. Is it a flower, do you think?'

They stared at the extraordinary whorls of metal. The sheets of steel were beaten out, and smooth, and they mirrored the scene around them. They shimmered and dazzled in the sun but also reflected the distorted shapes of the people who drifted vaguely about, the wind-twisted bushes, the clouds, the seagulls swooping past. So that, in their silver stillness, they captured colour and movement.

But the outside edges of the petals, if that is what they were, were roughened, with hints of bronze and blue in their darkness. Sarah looked at it, wondering.

'I think there's more inside,' she said.

288

They hurried forward and peered through one of the narrow spaces at the base into the mysterious, shadowed centre. There they saw a slender, domed cage formed from criss-crossed metal struts. It encased an elongated shape that seemed to be reaching up as if to break through.

'I think it must be a flower,' Laurie said. 'A great poppy, or peony. That sort of thing. And inside, that's the . . . the pistil, is it? Enclosed by stamens. A flower for the Millennium, growing on the moor.'

But Sarah was straining forward, her face glowing. 'No. No. Look, Laurie. The inner shape is a human figure. See, the arms are raised. Standing on tip-toe. Stretching up. She's reaching through the cage, ready to surge up out of the petals. But they're petals of flame. That's why the edges are burnished like that. It's Claire, don't you see? Rising up through the fire.'

He looked at her, his face a blank.

'That's what she told me,' she explained. 'After Bridget's funeral. "I am the phoenix. I will rise from the ashes."'

Silently Laurie turned and looked at the sculpture again, massive and strong and beautiful, burning like a beacon of hope on the hilltop, for all to see and marvel at. Watching him, loving him, Sarah knew that he was on the edge of tears. She put her arm through his, took his hand and held it tightly. Together they turned, and then, there she was.

Claire was breaking away from the knot of politely smiling official representatives and civic dignitaries who had surrounded her. She was shaking her head at the reporters and photographers, mouthing an apology at the television cameraman who had just arrived. She was running towards them, reaching out for them and her face was luminous with joy.

Their hands touched. Their arms went tightly round each other. And for one breathless moment, moved far beyond words, the three of them clung together. Interlocked. Indivisible.

The Amnesiac's Dream

It seems my face is now a race of clouds:
some of them dragons, some of them galleons,
or birds, or ghosts of words, or brief charades.
You must excuse me shouting, but my mouth's
a dome of wind. I really don't know who
sent all these dreams, the one about a bowl
of yellow sand, the one about a grave
shaped like a woman's body made of sky.
The one about the edge that shapes away
into a blindman's template, and you have
to guess its continent. I keep consulting
oracles: I've been the Empress, the Moon
and the Hanged Man. I have been swords
crossed in a corn field. I've loosed flocks of birds
from my raised hands. They sky-write in a swarm
of rapid hieroglyphics which reveal
my name, my future, everything, except
I can't decipher it quite fast enough
to keep pace with the tempo of their wings
erasing air's white pages, which contain
the poem of myself, which I forgot.

At the same time it seems I am a void
in which impressions darken without trace,
while secretly inside me they remake
this landscape, like the network of a brain
without a wiring diagram. It seems
I am a crazy bank of films
with different plots, but playing all at once;
a shadow play, a child's construction kit
made up with some improbable mistakes.
It seems I am decked out in all my loves. My fingerprints are made
of your warm skin, and time is scars and banners, and it seems
my bones are bedrock granite sunk so deep
they cannot speak, though they know everything.
It seems as if my throat's an unknown song.
It seems the tides are levied by my breath.
It seems that I might drown in memory.